HE[A...]
MORE

A "Gemination" Novel
by
Melsa M. Manton

HEAR NO MORE
Gemination – Book 1
Copyright © 2022 by Melsa M. Manton

FIRST EDITION SOFTCOVER
ISBN: 1622535510
ISBN-13: 978-1-62253-551-4

Senior/Final Editor: Lane Diamond
Assistant Editor: Kimberly Goebel
Cover Artist: Richard Tram
Interior Designer: Lane Diamond

EVOLVED PUBLISHING™
www.EvolvedPub.com
Evolved Publishing LLC
Butler, Wisconsin, USA

Printed in Book Antiqua font.

BOOKS BY MELSA M. MANTON

GEMINATION
Book 1: *Hear No More*
Book 2: *See No More*
Book 3: *Speak No More*
Book 4: *Veil No More*
Book 5: *Sleep No More*

DEDICATION

For Isa, the girl who set me on fire.

GEMINATION

HEAR NO MORE

MELSA M MANTON

PROLOGUE

My name is Leyla Stone. It wasn't before, and it wasn't after, but it was then. It's the only one that matters.

I am but one of almost ten billion people on our planet. We are all, whether conscious of it or not, driven by a deep sense of inner restlessness. This restlessness has a purpose. It's designed to transform us, to open a door that will set us on fire and emerge, renewed or charred, on the other side. We're born to realize who we are.

Most of us manage to bury the restlessness under an accrued mound of bills, overconsumption, and gadgets—endless distractions. We stop believing in possibility, and instead live vicariously through a box in our living room, which lulls us further and further into isolation, complacency, and acquiescence.

The box is a shapeshifter. Live in a box, drive in a box, work staring at a box sitting in a box, entertainment in a box—house, car, computer, cubicle, television... box, box, box, box, box. While all this is happening, a box in every hand demands constant attention—the cell phone. Fritter and waste.

But to turn away from the box? To indulge in the restlessness? To embrace possibility? Well that, my friend, will lead the advocate on an interesting journey. So, who am I? A glamorous spy, perhaps? A beautiful but dangerous maiden? No, I'm just like you, a mere mortal.

As mere mortals, a fragment of our human condition is the notion that *something is coming*. On the macro scale, I'm talking about the end of the world as we know it. This is known as *The Rapture, The Apocalypse, Armageddon, Judgment Day, The End of Days....* Pick your poison. For as long as we've walked the Earth, we've waited for the end of the world, and we've waited for a hero to come and rescue us. It's inherent for civilization to believe that the end is near, inherent to believe that whatever is "coming" will save us, liberate us. Yet what exactly do we seek liberation from? We look to the external environment to make right all that we feel is wrong inside of us. If only it were that simple. If only something or someone could do our work for us.

I'll tell you right now, the only impending event is the dawn, and the only hero that approaches is the person looking back at you in the mirror every morning.

To believe the end is nigh gives us the excuse to do nothing. Why wake up if it's all about to topple down anyway? Don't make waves; just wait for the peaceful new world order to rise. Wait for the unicorns puking rainbows to arrive. Then we can get to work. Until then, continue to stare at the box. *Pathetic.* We've become weak. Evolution has ground to a halt, but it's not entirely our fault.

Organizations of all kinds are usually formed with good intentions. What goes wrong is that we rarely account for the darker side of human nature, our capital vices—pride, anger, envy, greed, gluttony, sloth, and lust. Add fear and deceit to that and the list is complete. However, the argument can be made that only two emotions exist, and all others are but shadows of them.

These emotions are love and fear, which translates into expansion and contraction of the physical body. Each of us lives our lives from a place of love or fear. Which is yours? Do you cower and fall back into your comfort zone? Or do you take a gamble and move forward? Ask yourself this: what is it *you* seek liberation from?

Make no mistake: if you only wait on destiny, it will never come. Conversely, if you desperately seek out destiny, you'll overlook it. You must meet destiny halfway, but also recognize when it approaches, for destiny seldom looks like what we think it will, and it is often unwanted.

My destiny came to me out of a blue abeyance, and I followed him down a path so dark, so deep, that the edges of reality and delusion blurred together and time itself stood still. His name was Devlin Vail. That was always his name. It's true that darkness cannot exist without light, but it's also true that light cannot exist without darkness. They're two sides of the same coin.

Here comes the first of many contradictions. Something *is* coming, something you don't suspect and something you will not prefer. I tell you this for one reason: I've only bought you some time. Perhaps bought isn't the correct word. I've paid a price, certainly, but I've not *bought* anything. *Borrowed* is more like it. I've borrowed time for you, as time was once borrowed for me. There's plenty I don't remember, but the Ether, it seems, has filled that in.

The world is not black and white, but it often comes down to two simple types of people: those who move, and those who do not.

Awake! There is no time.

My name is Leyla Stone. I've realized who I am. This is my story.

CHAPTER 1

The dark alley loomed before him like a gauntlet. He stared into the ill-omened shadows with leveled determination, the deep of the night almost more than he could bear, the sky nothing but a blanket of blacked-out stars. A wave of vertigo swept over him and he quickly turned his eyes to the ground, stopping for a moment to take a few deep breaths to steady himself.

At first, the frigid air had helped him focus to some degree, but now it numbed him, burned his lungs, and almost convinced him this was all just a dream.

Hardening his resolve, he once again gazed ahead into the darkness, the alley walls narrowing into an ominous sliver of obscurities. A moment of claustrophobia seized him, rank with fear, reminding him of his old home, and he immediately felt trapped, like a wild animal. The paralysis of panic crept in subtly, threatening to overtake him, and he struggled against it. If fear took him, there would be no hope.

I'm out, he reminded himself. *I escaped.*

He willed himself forward, and his legs reluctantly obeyed, feeling heavy and leaden, as though walking through water. With each step, the darkness folded in around him like a wet cloak, heavy and oppressive. Yet, like a cloak, it also offered protection. The new moon above his head gave him a chance — a slim chance, but a chance nonetheless. That was all the time ahead amounted to — *a chance* — and he would take whatever he could get.

He walked on clumsily, his heavy footsteps echoing off the alley walls. He'd failed to find a way to tread carefully, and was starting to stumble — never a good sign. *They* would hear him, no doubt, but he was losing the battle to care. His intellect was dimming, and the panicky voice in the back of his mind, screaming at him to stay alert, grew quieter and quieter. Soon the warning bells would fall completely silent, lost in the dim.

He ran his fingers down the side of one wall, and they came away slick from the mist. So, his eyes weren't playing tricks on him. The weird haze wasn't a result of the withdrawal from the drugs that *They* had pumped into him.

Though a young man, he'd aged a lifetime in the last forty-eight hours... or however long it had been — he couldn't say for sure. He'd run blindly for so long, all concept of time had been lost, and his physical condition had deteriorated rapidly. That's where the drug withdrawal hit him the hardest: excruciating cramps spread through his torso like wildfire, every joint screamed, and heat poured off his kneecaps in waves of agony. His breath came in ragged gasps, his lungs on the verge of bursting, and he could feel the muscles beginning to tear loose from the ribs, as though they were strings wound too tightly, which would inevitably break from the strain.

Still, he invited it all in — the cold, the pain, and the delirium of it all. Being out, really *out*, felt so surreal. He inhaled deeply, wincing as the cold drove its icy fingers into his ribs. His muscles spasmed in response, but though the mere act of breathing caused him a great deal of pain, it nevertheless refreshed him. It felt good to breathe free air. In fact, this marked the first time he ever had.

The others had disappeared long ago, dropped off behind him one by one, like prey with no chance of outrunning their predator. He wondered briefly if they were still alive. If so, they'd be feeling much like him at this point—overwhelmed, exhausted, and on the verge of collapse. But one of them had to survive. One of them had to tell the truth—the *actual* truth, not the perceived truth—although he'd grown so weary, and the details were so intricate, he almost wasn't sure which was which anymore.

The thought motivated him.

It has to be me.

Since he didn't know who was alive and who was dead, it had to be him. He mentally slapped himself back to awareness, reinforced his hold on the precipice of consciousness, and clung there.

Focus.

He had to focus; this much he knew. One slip and it would be over, for *They* stalked him, surely just a step behind, and if he didn't keep up his pace, *They* would quickly close the gap. If only he could pass through the alley undetected, he might be able to get lost in the crowds of the city.

It was not to be.

The noise came first, but his senses betrayed him in the moment, and he heard it a fraction of a second too late. The crunch of a bone resounded inside his skull. It must have been something in the inner ear, for his sense of balance went askew.

The shadows shifted and *They* came for him. He tried to stand his ground, to do what he'd been trained to do, but his loss of balance made it virtually impossible to defend himself, and *They* overpowered him quickly.

His grip on lucidity first loosened and then slipped altogether, and the periphery faded as he swayed on his feet. His vision blurred, as if a veil had been pulled over his eyes, and he dropped to his knees, classic execution style. He managed to turn his head as his face hit the ground, the asphalt cool and oddly refreshing under his cheek, and the darkness threatened to swallow him whole. He looked up at his pursuers with one eye, and saw his own death — that is, if he was lucky.

Then, from behind, a new form appeared — not appeared, *descended.* He watched through a thick fog as the form moved and the others fell, one by one. He heard the dull smacks of flesh as their bodies hit the pavement beside him.

The form stood alone and completely still for what seemed an eternity, as though deciding what to do with him. Then it drew closer and bent over him.

Nearly blind, he saw nothing more than a nebulous human shape. The shape spoke to him, but he didn't understand. Somewhere in the fight, he'd also lost the ability to comprehend language. He wondered vaguely which part of his brain had cracked to disable that. He tried to focus once more, but the damage was done.

Suddenly, the cold left him completely, replaced by a warm sensation that spread out from the center of his chest. Euphoria washed over his body and cleared it of all pain. He could see now, and quite clearly. He hung precariously to a rock ledge on a cliff. Below him, the chasm of empty, blissful nothingness beckoned. At last, he surrendered, relinquishing his need for control, and fell into the abyss.

Welcome home, he told himself. *Welcome home.*

CHAPTER 2

The autumn morning dawned crisp and clear, and I wore a pressed, clean uniform to match it. I listened to my little white shoes clicking on the sidewalk — one foot in front of the other, one eye on the horizon, the other on the destination — simple as that; no need to get wrapped up in the details. It was the perfect day for a visit to the hospital. I thought about whistling but that would have been a bit overzealous, not to mention arrogant.

As I pushed the gurney, its wheels creaked over the sidewalk, and I looked down at the cracks flashing under me.

Step on a crack, break your mother's back.

The creepy childhood rhyme played in my head on a reel. There were a lot of creepy childhood rhymes, now that I thought about it.

Pocket full of posies... Jack fell down and broke his crown... Lizzie Borden took an ax....

Maybe that's why I never jumped rope, although, considering the way things had turned out, I should have loved it. One, *chop*, two, *chop*, three, *chop*.... How many swings would it take to kill a person with an ax? I figured one was plenty — one to split the melon in half — but Lizzie Borden had been an amateur, blinded by rage in the moment. She gave her father eleven and her stepmother nineteen. I always thought the old photographs of her to be quite terrifying, namely the eyes, which bore the look of demonic possession.

I glanced up and shut down the unlimited semiosis spiraling around in my mind.

Thought leads to a thought leads to a thought.

No distractions, as the entrance was just ahead and the details were about to get very, very important.

An outdoor security guard motioned to me, a scrawny fellow but barrel-chested, with the telltale sign of a sickness I doubted he knew about. He wore his thin, greasy black hair slicked back over his head, making his receding hairline all the more prominent. Sunken eyes peered out at me from hollow sockets with a mixture of disdain and intrigue, the look of a man chronically unhappy and terminally ill — the former being the cause of the latter. His kind liked to squint and stare, while at the same time managing to avoid eye contact — quite an impressive skill — and their manner of speaking was completely indifferent and monotone.

"Clearance," the security guard droned, revealing a crooked line of teeth stained a dull yellow from years of tobacco use. The smell of some horrid cologne, seeming to emanate directly from his pores, wafted thickly through the air.

I held up the security key around my neck for him to scan. *Seamless.*

"Where are you coming from?" He gave me and the direction I'd come from a cursory glance, and then looked away, bored.

"Lab critical care." *Flawless.*

He peered around me as though the thin man might be hiding behind my back. "Where's your driver?"

I looked back at him haughtily. "I drove. They couldn't spare anyone else, and I wasn't exactly needed in the back."

"Where are you headed?"

"The morgue. Dead man."

He picked up the sheet on the gurney, and the ashen, pale face of a young man stared up at him.

This time the guard looked directly into my eyes and, in an unmistakable tone of disbelief, asked, "How did *he* die?"

Odd, but I didn't miss a beat. "Bled out on the table. Doc said to shove him in a slot before he got moldy." I raised my eyebrows at the guard.

He eyed me back for a moment, though more sizing me up than suspicious, seeing if I had a big enough ass for a roll in the hay. He seemed to be weighing his options in his head, trying to decide if I was worth hitting on or not. In the end, he must have decided I wasn't worth the pursuit. Still, he couldn't resist the opportunity to cop a feel.

I held my arms out to the sides as his grubby paws patted me down, but I was clean. Unlike old Lizzie Borden, I was no amateur.

"Continue on." He waved a hand at me in what could only be annoyance.

He ushered me inside, checked under the gurney, and rolled it around to the other side of the security scanner. I passed through the scanner, cleanly of course, and he looked at me again, as if reconsidering his decision.

Although I didn't look a day over twenty-one, I wasn't his type. My type was of the wallflower variety, part of the background, whereas his type wore permanent cosmetics down in the southeast part of the city at three in the morning, part of the foreground. I knew this because I'd followed him last night, all the way down from Prince George County. After he'd picked out a girl named Lita and paid her five hundred dollars for her services, I paid Lita. Her accent betrayed her as a Belorussian immigrant, and I gave her a grand for everything she knew about him. There wasn't much to tell. I wanted to ask her how it felt to be screwed by a rat-faced, beady-eyed son of a bitch, but that wasn't exactly relevant information, so I gave her another grand instead to forget she'd ever seen me.

Not that she was likely to talk anyway, but hookers can be useful. They see and hear things most others don't, partly because they're always awake in the shady parts of town, but mostly because people aren't careful around those seen as non-threatening objects that can be bought. Thus, they are often valuable sources of information. Reliability can be an issue, so discernment on the part of the interviewer is key.

However, if someone did show up asking about me, I didn't believe for a second that she'd keep her mouth shut. Anyone who would give information for money would give *anyone* information for money. The extra grand implied I might be back, serving as both an incentive to stay quiet and a suggestion of more money to come. Often that's enough to deter someone from talking, but it didn't matter. I wouldn't return to her for information again, for that was one of the rules, one of the *Novem: never tap a source with financial motives twice* — no better way to get in trouble.

I'd learned enough from Lita, though, including that the guard wasn't that smart, which made him the weak link in the hospital's security. He was also a creeper with an Oedipus complex, another fact immaterial for my work, and one I wished I could unlearn.

I resumed pushing the gurney and rolled past the guard into the lobby, which immediately enveloped me in white sterile indifference and harsh light cast by fluorescent tubes. Hospitals never offered any hint of comfort, for if they made it comfortable, people might be inclined to stay longer. In my experience, hospitals wanted patients in and out as quickly as possible, with as much money out of their pockets as they could extort — the destruction of ambience for high turnover.

Churches have a similar story, but for different reasons. Why are church pews so damned uncomfortable? So the worshippers don't fall asleep, so the Lord has their undivided attention. The moral of this story? Have church pews for couches, so guests never overstay their welcome.

I signed in at the front desk and looked down at the bowed head of the little nurse behind the desk.

Her shrewd eyes sat behind narrow spectacles perched precariously on the end of her nose, her graying hair pulled smartly back into a bun. Either intensely busy or pretending to be, she'd go home before she'd acknowledge me.

I headed directly for the morgue, courtesy of a little map I'd memorized the day before. No one so much as glanced at me. I became a chameleon, part of the hospital staff. Today, I was here to work, and hoped to be in and out fast. There was one catch, though: I didn't know exactly what I was here for. Only the cadaver knew that.

CHAPTER 3

Oddly enough, the morgue was not in the basement. Usually, they kept morgues underground, away from prying eyes, but this morgue sat about halfway down the east wing, on ground level. Having never encountered one so close to a hospital entrance, it gave me pause — perhaps an omen, or perhaps nothing at all.

I stopped outside the doors to the morgue, pretended to fish something out of my pocket, and inconspicuously glanced through the glass to find it deserted. After making sure no one else in the hallway looked interested in going to the morgue, I gave the door on the right a shove and it swung inward. I caught it as it swung back again, held it, and pushed the gurney inside, letting the door close slowly behind me. I maneuvered it along the wall and into the one corner of the room I knew the camera didn't reach — another glitch in the hospital's defenses. If I'd wheeled the gurney in normally, through both doors, the camera would have picked it up. Of course, why the hospital had so many defenses to begin with remained a damn good question, but not one I'd allowed myself to indulge in.

The only camera in the morgue sat right above my head, focused on the morgue slots. Thus, it missed the corner and most of the sidewall. One could slip in and out easily by hugging the wall and the doorjamb.

I walked to the side of the gurney, slipped a hand under the sheet, hefted the body ever so slightly, and pulled a tiny, nearly invisible fluid-filled pouch from underneath the cadaver's tailbone. I delicately peeled the white sheet back and stared down at the dead man, marveling for a moment at his perfect representation of death — porcelain skin, full powder-blue lips, icy to the touch, a shock of jet-black hair attached to frozen pores.

Then I poured the contents of the pouch into his mouth, and he came to life with a jerk, gasping for air.

"Welcome back," I congratulated.

"I really hate that, you know," Ember choked out, his wide blue eyes staring up at me, the flush of the living beginning to flood back into his face. He blinked several times, which seemed to take a lot of effort.

"Well, I told you I would do it. It was my turn anyway." I eyed him suspiciously.

"Consider it a favor, Stone." Ember sat up stiffly, and flexed his hands and rolled his wrists a few times, trying to get the circulation back in them.

Six hours ago, he'd taken an adulterated antipsychotic, not because he was psychotic, but because of the drug's ability to influence thermoregulation, resulting in a kind of artificial hibernation. The drug shunted all blood from his extremities into his core, mimicking severe hypothermia, chilling the body and slowing the heart rate. Breathing became infinitesimal. Only a trained eye would be able to tell the difference between that and death, and the guard certainly did not have a trained eye. A high dose of sublingual epinephrine, raw adrenaline, sped everything back up again, but when the body came to, it moved at glacial speed for a while. We used this technique every now and then, but extremely rarely, only if we had no other way. Well, Ember had said this was the only way we would get inside the hospital: one of us needed to be dead on the table.

We wouldn't know about the side effects for another twenty years or so, for we were the test group. In my opinion, the drug seemed excessively harsh on the body. It felt like dying... a little more each time. Perhaps the effect was cumulative and presented a threshold for how many times one could go under. I hoped not to have to find that out personally.

Ember grinned. "And now you owe me a favor." He rolled his neck around. "Clothes?"

"Here you go. Monroe pressed them this morning." I shook out the gurney sheet, and another set of starched white scrubs drifted to the ground.

Ember bent down rigidly to pick them up. "Good ol' Monroe. Whatever would we do without him?" He held the clothes awkwardly. "Little help? I feel like I'm trying to run in water."

"Sorry, forgot." I grabbed the undershirt, watching with fascination as his chest muscles twitched as though ants ran beneath them. He raised his arms to pull the shirt on, and I noticed a small white bandage above his left hip as I pushed the shirt down his arms. "What happened there?"

He pushed his head through the shirt and looked down. "Oh, that's nothing, just a flesh wound." He pulled the shirt down over the bandage and smoothed it. "If I can't see it, it doesn't exist." He flashed another smile.

"How did you get it?" I pressed, and helped him with his pants.

"Sparring with Avery. The boy plays hard, you know."

He didn't seem concerned in the slightest, so I let it be. "Oh, I know." Avery had given me a black eye a time or two, and I swear I had a permanent dent in my left temporal bone.

Ember rose from the gurney and pulled on the collared shirt, clearly starting to loosen up a bit. "How did we do on the cameras?"

A chattering pair of nurses, the most action I'd see in this place yet, passed the morgue doors, and I waited until they moved out of range. "The ones outside will pick us up, but I've mostly evaded this one." I jerked my head at the black orb above us. "It will catch the corner of the gurney as it comes through the door. Just stay close to the wall."

"Better finish the job, but bring my chariot back here," he directed.

I arranged the white sheet back on the gurney, fluffed it up a bit, then pushed it back to the doors and across the room to the slots. I checked the log attached to a clipboard hanging from the morgue vault, opened an unoccupied slot, and slid the tray inside. I then wheeled the gurney back over to the corner.

I turned back to Ember. "We better hope no one looks closely at the track anytime soon. There will be a big chunk of time missing from me coming in the door to putting the tray away." I pulled a hospital security key out of the left side of my padded bra — the boys back home called it the *wonder bra*, but for obvious different reasons. *'What else you got in there for me?'* Colvin would always ask when I came back after a *grant*.

Ember gave a sheepish smile as I handed the card over. "And here's your ID."

He put the key around his neck and finished buttoning his shirt. "And my name is—" He looked down at the name on the tag. "—A. Johnson. What is the "A" for?"

"Abraham, of course." I rolled my eyes.

"Abraham?" He raised an eyebrow at me. "Feeling biblical, were we?"

I giggled and looked up at him. "How do you know I didn't name you after a president?"

"Getting sentimental about our great leaders? I doubt it. Come on. Do I even look like an Abraham?" He held his arms out to either side.

I made a mock sweep from head to toe with my eyes. "Well, you're tall."

"Yeah, just call me fucking Honest Abe." He snorted cynically. A good head taller than me, and about three times as big, Ember had an amiable face and bright blue eyes—kind of like an overgrown cherub, minus the chub. He could come across as innocent and boyish, but was actually quite sharp, with a lot of brawn *and* a lot of brain—a rare combination.

I nonchalantly leaned against the gurney, then turned to him and crossed my arms. "Now, do you want to tell me what we're doing here?" I lowered my voice and kept it steady, even though the cameras didn't have audio capability and we were alone. If I'd learned one thing, it was that it paid to be cautious. "What kind of hospital is this, anyway? There's about as much security here as there is back at the homestead—more, even. You know how many times I've been frisked and have had to show this damn card?" I grabbed at the key around my neck and waved it at him. "And the guard practically ignored me until he saw your face. It almost seemed like he recognized you."

Ember sighed a bit and turned to me, locked me in with those piercing blue eyes of his, as if bewitching me. The eyes gave him away, revealed a powerful force to be reckoned with. "Leyla, do you trust me?"

I stared at him and narrowed my eyes. "You know I do, *John*," I said derisively. We rarely called each other by our first names.

He scowled. "Then trust me on this. I will explain everything... when we have time, and right now, we don't."

"That's what you said last night," I reminded him. The vagueness of the instructions at his spur-of-the-moment meeting had been infuriating. *'Turn us into these people. Memorize these schematics. Follow this guy. Meet me at dawn.'* He'd thrust the two security keys and a set of blueprints into my hands and sped away.

The rascal that he so often acted like now winked at me, pulled a pair of white latex gloves out of his coat pocket, put them on with a snap, and reached under the gurney. A clicking noise rose, and then the bottom ripped out and the metal sheet clattered to the floor.

"Ember, what the hell? Be quiet," I began in a hushed voice, throwing a hasty look at the morgue doors. "What are you—" I stopped dead as he pulled two small handguns from underneath the gurney. I could feel the blood drain from my face.

"Beretta, .30 caliber... one for you, one for me," he said seriously, his face deadpan, handing me one of the guns and two extra clips. "Already loaded. Ankle," he commanded as he bent down and began fastening his gun to the inside of his left leg.

I stood shocked for a moment, gingerly holding the gun between my thumb and forefinger. "What are you doing with these?"

"A precaution," he said, his tone completely carefree.

"*A precaution.*" I mimicked his lackadaisical attitude. "Where did you get them?"

He looked up at me with genuine surprise. "Come on, like you don't have a private store," he said knowingly, tapping the side of his nose with one finger.

Private store? What the hell is he talking about? And why did he tap the side of his nose?

I furrowed my brow. "I don't. Why would I?"

He rolled his eyes. "Whatever."

I examined the cold chunk of metal hanging from my fingertips, feeling nothing good could come of it. *'Never begin with excessive force.'*

"Am I going to need this?" An image bloomed in my mind of the last time I'd held a gun in my hands in the field, and I suppressed a shudder. It hadn't been pretty.

"Let's hope not," he replied absentmindedly, and set about reattaching the metal sheet under the gurney.

"God damn it, why the hell didn't you tell me?" I raised a hand to my forehead and covered my eyes.

He straightened up and crossed his arms as he towered over me. "If I had told you, you would have been nervous with the guard. I needed you cocky."

"You're a bastard." I shook my head at him, but he only grinned in response. Beyond annoyed, I pulled myself up to my full height, all five-foot-four of me, barely coming level with his chin. "Ember, you have to tell me what we're up against. I don't want to go into this blind. It's too dangerous."

"Listen to me, Stone. Time is of the essence, so I need you to follow me on this one," he said evenly. "We're already in. The hard part is over." He shrugged his shoulders, acting like a frat boy that had just talked one of his brothers into stealing a keg.

I sighed. "Okay... I'll take that... for now. You're just lucky you have me as an accomplice." I bent down to conceal the gun on my ankle.

"Partners in crime," he said, and I felt his eyes settle on me. "And I'm not the only one that's lucky."

"Fair enough," I conceded, blushing slightly, glad I was looking down at the floor. I straightened up and smoothed my shirt, avoiding his gaze. "What do we do?"

"Well, as you can probably tell, we are hospital staff." He moved towards the morgue doors. "And we need to search the database for records of a patient that was here, or perhaps is still here," he said cryptically.

"Name?" He could at least give me that much.

Apparently, he couldn't, as he just turned and stared me down in answer.

"Okay, okay, never mind," I huffed. "I'm with you. Let's just go and be done with it. There's something off about this place."

I followed him through the halls of the hospital. He walked casually, even made a point to greet other staff members, while I kept my head down and pretended I had somewhere to be, trying to ignore the gun burning a hole in my leg. As before, everyone was so engrossed in their own work that they hardly paid attention to us.

When we reached the data lab, Ember swiped his key to get in.

It worked, to our relief. The two workers I had methodically inserted our personal information over either hadn't noticed, or were too afraid to admit they'd lost their security keys, or worse, had them stolen. Ember deliberately picked two people he knew weren't going to work today, in hopes of minimizing the risk of detection, but there was always a chance a worker would immediately notice their key was gone, and call in to shut it down. Both of ours were still good, which made me feel a *little* better, but not much.

I kept watch while sitting at a desk by the door, pretending to go over some random statistical findings, as Ember sat down at a computer and got to work, doing what he did best: hacking. Not my specialty, as I was rather technologically un-inclined, comparatively speaking. Lucky for me, my partner was a genius when it came to the cyber world.

"Will they know we're doing this?" I asked without looking up.

"Not until we're well on our way," he replied, typing furiously. "It's just going to take a little time."

I glanced at the clock as the seconds ticked by ominously. *'Never stay more than seven minutes.'*

"Do we have that much time? You know, if you told me what you were looking for, I could probably help, and we'd be out of here sooner."

"You?" he mocked, not taking his eyes off the computer. "*You* would somehow manage to set the damn thing on fire. No, no, no... you stand there, keep a sharp eye, and look pretty."

"Thanks a lot. I feel real important," I grumbled, rolling my eyes, though I couldn't keep the grin off my face. "And like I said before, that last one was a freak accident." *Christ, that was a disaster. I nearly burned the building down.* "Freak accident," I reiterated. "You saw the spontaneous combustion."

"Yeah, yeah, I saw," he said. "You're just unlucky that way, but damned lucky in everything else. That's why the Sedition kept you."

My grin faded. "Thanks for reminding me." The beginning of my time at the Sedition had been questionable, as in I'd almost been dropped from training. In this world, being dropped from training could mean going to sleep with the fishes. I knew Ember had intervened, although I didn't know how, and stopped that from happening. "Seriously, what do you want me to do? I can multitask, you know."

He pointed to the door. "Seduce that fool guard if he comes our way."

"Worst job ever," I groaned, half in jest. "And we both know I'm not his type. I made it that way, remember?"

I could see him trying not to smile. "Well, I have a feeling that if it really came down to it, he wouldn't be so picky."

CHAPTER 4

The man in the black suit walked briskly from the parking lot to the hospital entrance, which he thought of as *his* entrance. A smug smile appeared on his face, but quickly faded when he saw who was at the door, certainly the most annoying person he'd ever hired. All the women working at the hospital complained about the man, who'd apparently tried to bed half of them.

He rolled his eyes at the thought; as if that man stood a chance with any one of his girls. No one here held anything under a Ph.D. in general medicine, even the receptionists and orderlies. He doubted the guard had even bothered with a GED. He'd been hired purely for his ruthless reputation.

As he walked up to the entrance, the guard stepped in front of him. "Clearance." He used the same dead drawl every day.

"You know who I am," Black Suit hissed.

"And you know the rules," the guard countered.

"I sure do." He pulled his key from the breast pocket of his suit. "I made them." He cast an icy stare at the guard.

"And that's why you hired me," the guard said, obviously pleased with himself and clearly oblivious to his superior's displeasure. "To follow the rules. No one is exempt."

"Quite right, my boy." Black Suit knew it to be true, but was still annoyed deep down, infuriated even. He sensed the guard still didn't completely recognize who he was. Oh, the man knew his name all right, but not *who* he was. If the guard ever had to find out, it would be one hell of a day.

The guard's handheld device flashed green in affirmation. "All is in order, sir. Proceed." He opened the door and followed Black Suit inside, watching intently as he passed through the scanner. Satisfied that Black Suit wasn't somehow carrying a small arsenal under his clothes, the guard nodded.

Black Suit grudgingly nodded back and continued on his way.

Mere paces away, the guard yet again interrupted his day. "I see you finally got the one you were after."

"What are you talking about?" Black Suit asked almost absently, continuing to walk away.

"The boy on the bulletin. Congratulations."

Black Suit froze for a moment, and then turned around and stalked back to the guard. "What boy?" he asked, now within inches of the guard's face.

The guard, nervous now, swallowed. "The man you've been looking for. He was on the bulletin this morning. The *Striker*."

"The *Striker*?" he repeated in a half-mocking tone. *How does the guard know that term?* "You've seen him?"

"He came through here not half an hour ago on a gurney, dead as a doornail. Hope you got what you wanted from him first." He offered a nervous smile and began to shift his weight back and forth.

"And where is he?"

"The morgue, of course." The guard now looked thoroughly confused. "The woman—"

"What woman?" Black Suit enunciated the words very quietly, edging ever closer to the guard's face.

"Uh... the nurse!" the guard said quickly. "She was pushing the gurney. She cleared security."

Black Suit paused for a moment and stared down the long white hallway, listening.

"The highest level, in fact. Sir—"

He cut the annoying guard off with a raised hand and moved toward the reception desk, where they'd been watching the exchange in enraptured silence. He tapped the desk with his index finger as though communicating in Morse code. "Lock the place down," he said quietly to the front desk staff. "No one leaves the complex. And call head of security. Quietly."

The nurse at the desk picked up the phone immediately and shot a menacing glance at the guard.

As if following her gaze, Black Suit turned around, a black fire burning within.

The guard stood, unable to move for a moment, as if hypnotized by the despair.

"And you, come with me."

"W-what for?" the guard asked timidly.

"To identify what you think is a dead body."

Black Suit lingered long enough at the front desk to find the last entry to the morgue, a scribble of a signature, completely illegible, with a false time entered. "We'll have to move fast." He strode off down the hall, the guard at his heels.

He burst through the doors to the morgue, nearly knocking over a doctor, whom he seized by the collar of his lab coat. "Have you seen anyone in here?"

The doctor, for his part, maintained his composure, though he clearly did not fancy being grabbed by his lapels. He looked down his glasses, or actually up his glasses, at the black suit. "I just got here, sir. It was empty. Perhaps if you tell me who you're looking for, I can be of assistance."

Black Suit ignored the request, released the doctor, and wheeled back around to the doors, where a handful of other staff now milled about. "Did anyone see an unfamiliar nurse pushing a gurney?"

The crowd murmured a variety of negative responses.

He began to jerk open the different compartments in the morgue. "Tell me when you see him," he said, giving the guard an odd look.

"See him?" the guard asked.

Black Suit then began to casually and roughly pull out trays, so that dead bodies, some well on their way to decomposition, clattered to the floor. A few of them had died in less than graceful ways. Some actually broke apart when they hit the floor. One unfortunate soul seemed to have died with two broken collarbones, which tore through his skin as he hit the ground. Another had died with fractures all along the suture lines of the cranium, and the swollen skull split open like a watermelon upon impact, shooting bits of brain in all directions. Yet another had a dislocated shoulder with the arm positioned unnaturally far away from the torso, as though someone or something had tried to wrench it off.

The guard watched in obvious horror as the entire limb snapped off from the shoulder. Someone else vomited, and some of it splattered on the guard's shoes. He stared slack-jawed at his boss.

Black suit asked calmly, "Where is he? Do you see him?"

"No!" the guard finally screamed.

Black Suit pivoted towards him, a threat in his posture, and the room fell silent.

The guard shrank away, but then composed himself and straightened up. "No, he's not here," he said quietly. "How is that possible?"

"This one is empty," said the doctor, smugly holding a door open. "Though there is a tray here that a body would normally be on."

At this point, the head of security appeared. A hulk of a man, he lingered at the morgue doors, his smoky gray eyes watching.

Black Suit thought for a moment, and then his eyes fell on the empty gurney against the wall under the camera. *Oh, they're good.*

He became still, and when he addressed the crowd again, he did so calmly. "Slowly head for the break rooms, and be quiet. Have all the fucking muffins you want. We have an intruder in the hospital, and it's not a dead body. It's very much alive." He stormed out of the morgue.

The head of security fell into place beside him. They kept up a brisk pace away from the gawking hospital staff. Black Suit rarely lost his temper, and had reigned it back in considerably. There wasn't much that pushed him over that edge, but one of those things had just come in right through his front doors.

"Morning," he offered casually, jaw still clenched.

"How many?" the head of security asked, skipping the formalities.

"Two: one male, one female, both white. Male is known, one of the Sedition Strikers — our special friend as of late."

"Well, that's handy. He came right to us. The girl?"

He shook his head. "Female is unknown, but we'll have her soon enough. She'll be on the surveillance tracks."

"I got a brief description from the guard," the head of security said almost hesitantly.

Black Suit raised an eyebrow. "And?"

Head of Security ran a hand through his cropped, dark hair. "He described her as unremarkable, couldn't remember anything distinguishing. She had two legs and two eyes, that kind of thing."

"Of course. He would only remember if she was a stone cold fox. Who knows, she might be, but she made sure to be unremarkable just for him."

"He did say she was young, though — twenties, he thought."

"Who knows... she may have come in with a different look and changed appearance already, or vice versa."

"All bets are off then. Alarm?"

Black Suit shook his head. "No, these people feed off panic. As our unauthorized visitors operate best in high levels of pandemonium, they would use it to their advantage. We sound the alarm and they'll slip through the cracks even faster. That's all they need is a tip-off, and the ensuing chaos to calmly walk away. They cannot escape, do you understand?"

Head of Security nodded. "How many people do we need?"

"Whoever is in the immediate vicinity, but call the others."

"Do you think it's the ghost?" Head of Security's gray eyes lit up as if the prospect appealed to him.

Black Suit understood. Damn thing had been taunting all of them for far too long. "I don't know. Could be."

He wasn't concerned with the identity so much as the capture. Priorities... it was important to have priorities. First, apprehend. The identity would follow.

"Oh yeah," he said. "And dust the damned guard. They chose him specifically because he was the weak one."

Apparently, *this* was the day the guard would find out *who* he was.

CHAPTER 5

"Honestly, I don't know even why you brought me along." I flipped through a stack of papers, berating Ember in an amiable way. Then I noticed an odd sound, or lack thereof. "Do you hear that?" I immediately thought of the Beretta strapped to my ankle.

Not yet, Stone, not yet.

The hospital had fallen quiet—too quiet. The sounds of the staff milling about had ceased.

Ember cocked his head to one side, and a grim smile settled on his face. "Yeah, nothing." He jumped up and grabbed me by the arm. "I've got what I need, just in time. Now let's go."

We exited out the other side of the lab and into the west wing of the hospital. *'Never exit at the origin.'*

A few people still walked the halls, but certainly not as many as before. We'd planned on making our exodus through the underground parking garage, via a set of stairs in between data and medical. Unfortunately, security was already coming from the other end of the hall.

"Change of plans," Ember said, turning in the opposite direction. We fell into stride behind a handful of employees.

"What is this, a fire drill?" asked a young man wearing a white lab coat.

"If it was a fire drill, don't you think you'd be hearing an alarm?" an older man wearing a suit shot back with condescension. Clearly, he was the more seasoned of the two.

"Why have we all been ordered to the staff room?" asked a woman clad in clerical garb.

"There's obviously been a breach," the one with the condescending voice said.

I raised my eyebrows at Ember, but he merely smiled back.

At the next intersection, they all turned right, and we continued straight ahead.

"Next hallway to the right," Ember whispered. We walked quickly, but not so fast as to draw attention.

Suddenly, he stopped dead in his tracks, put a hand on my shoulder, and listened intently. We lingered at the corner.

"What are you doing? Let's keep moving." I threw his hand off.

"They know exactly where we are. They're watching us," he said, as if more to himself. He glanced up at the black orbs in the hallway. "And they're coming from both directions, planning to trap us." He looked down the hall and sighed in resignation. "We've got to separate."

"No. Are you crazy? That's how we die. We stay together," I countered. *'Never separate.'*

He didn't answer, only pulled me in the opposite direction, away from our exit. He opened a door that looked like it led into a walk-in refrigerator, and pushed me through it. "I'll stay here and handle this. You can't get caught. Take this. Go for the alley." He thrust a small plastic bag with whatever he'd gathered from the lab into my hands.

I stared at it for a moment, confused. *Didn't the information already make its way to the Sedition? What do we need the physical copy for?*

Confusion gave way to alarm, and the façade I'd carried into the hospital disintegrated. "We're a team, Ember!" I nearly shouted, and then lowered my voice. "That's how we work. We break the team, we break the grant."

"This is more important. Consider this that favor you owe me." He looked over his shoulder. "Find your way. I'll find you," he whispered, then pushed me back hard and shut the door, bolting me inside.

"Damn it, Ember, open this door!" I screamed, banging on the stainless steel. *What the hell is he talking about, I couldn't get caught?*

Ember had never broken code before. We never separated. It was the golden rule, the most important of the *Novem*. *'Strength in numbers.'* We'd crossed a dangerous line.

Before long, sporadic gunfire came from beyond the door, sending a cold wave of fear up my spine. I beat the fear back and stopped it dead, shoving the plastic bag down my shirt into my bra. Ember and I usually executed *grants* with great ease; it had been too long since we'd run into a snag, and it had made me soft. We were good at what we did—a little too good. Even if I could get the door open, I didn't want to walk into the path of an oncoming bullet. I had to find another way out—quietly.

The room I was in, surprisingly, wasn't a giant icebox. It looked like an examination room in a doctor's office. Why that warranted a secure, nearly indestructible door, I had no idea.

Experiments on lions? Tigers? Bears? Oh my, what the fuck is this place?

Rows of cabinets, all padlocked, lined the walls, and a medical examiner's table sat in the middle. A door on the adjacent wall led to another examination room, nearly identical to the first, except a dentist's chair took the place of the examination table. This room, too, had one door to the hall and one door to the next room.

I worked my way toward the back entrance through the dark examination rooms, all identical except for the piece of equipment the patient would have sat in or lain on. I passed by an optometrist's chair, and then an operating table. *Very bizarre.* I changed direction at the fourth room, the corner room. When I reached the sixth room, the X-ray lab, I peeked into the hallway and found it completely empty. An exit sign gleamed like a beacon at the end of the hall.

I walked towards the exit, doing what I was supposed to do, following Ember's orders. He must have been making a good diversion, as I hadn't encountered anyone at all yet. I stopped at the next junction; not just stopped, *hesitated.* Why was I hesitating? I never hesitated.

Go back.

I looked both ways in the hall, one leading to the exit and other back to where Ember surely must be — back at the fight.

Go back.

"Hell yeah," I muttered. "I'm going back."

As if on cue, shots rang out again. I turned and ran flat out toward the gunfire. If Ember was in a gunfight, which I suspected, he would need me. I flew past medical and then data, both completely empty. As the gunfire grew louder, I slowed my pace. It had been a while since I'd used a gun outside of a shooting range, and from the sound of it, we were greatly outnumbered. To say that erring on the side of caution was called for was an understatement.

Rounding the next corner, I nearly collided with Ember. He'd been running hard and sank to his knees as he stumbled into me. I caught him under the arms and looked down at him, his white uniform splattered with blood.

"Leyla," he sputtered, his eyes wide with horror.

"Motherfuckers," I whispered.

I spun him around to the other side of the corner and set him down on the floor against the wall. Something in his pocket clattered against the floor—the gun. I pulled it out and checked the clip. Empty. I ejected it and reloaded with another from his pocket, then pulled my own gun from its ankle holster and stood up, rage coursing through my veins. The world became tinged with red. It crept into my periphery, and then it was all I could see.

"Stone, no!" Ember screamed.

I ignored him, took a deep breath and brought the Berettas up to either side of my head, next to my ears, and squeezed my eyes shut to concentrate. Though fairly ambidextrous, I hadn't practiced much lately. *'Keep your hands still. Anticipate the recoil. Don't overreact.'*

No easy feat.

I exhaled and brought the guns down, level with my hips, as though I were a gunslinger getting ready to draw. Eyes still closed, I listened intently to the sounds around me. The gunfire had stopped and footsteps now drew near, echoing off the walls, following Ember's crimson trail.

Then, what always happened... happened.

Time slowed, almost stood still as sounds isolated, then magnified. I could feel the blood rushing through my system, my heartbeat a deafening roar in my chest. The wave-like motion of cerebrospinal fluid washed over me, leaving only silence in its aftermath. Breath came to a place of stillness, and in that stillness, a freedom arose that I'd never felt before — not in real life, anyway. I waited... patiently.

Then I saw it, a flash of light — *the path* — the golden eye of the storm, where redemption existed. It shone slightly to the right, in the space between space, where the physical and metaphysical merged. In a moment of brilliant clarity, I swung around the corner and slid right, not quite to the wall, and faced them directly. Only now did I lift my eyes and hands to meet my oncoming enemies. Rounds fired from chambers, but no bullets hit me, and then they were all lying on the floor, dead.

I'd emptied both clips. Total retaliation.

I reloaded quickly and turned back to Ember. Supporting him as best I could, I pulled him toward the west wing exit, conveniently not too far away; he must have been headed for it when he ran into trouble. I kicked open the door to the stairwell.

"I told you we shouldn't separate!" I reprimanded him, furious, then set him down on the landing against the wall. "Let's get some bots in you real quick so we can get out of here."

I pulled another tiny fluid-filled pouch from my bra, much like the one I'd pulled from underneath his lifeless body half an hour ago, and drew its clear contents out with a syringe I'd pocketed along the way. Sedition training: we picked up weapons in the field as we saw them, and an empty syringe... injecting someone's blood with an air bubble was as effective a death sentence as any. In this case, however, it would get the *bots* into his bloodstream with lightning speed. I planned to inject them directly into one of the holes on his chest.

I then went to rip his shirt open, but Ember's two big hands came up on mine very gently. "Don't, Stone," he said calmly.

My eyes widened.

"It's bad. It's *too* bad."

"Yeah, that's what the *bots* are for," I reminded him, as if he needed it.

I again tried to tear his shirt open, but he held my hands fast.

"Ember!" I pleaded, the panic again rising in my voice. "We don't have much time!" If I couldn't get the *bots* into him in the next few minutes, there wasn't much Hamlin would be able to do. As his blood poured out freely and pooled all around us, I tried to wrench my hands from him, but he was stronger, even with the bullet holes, and my effort was futile.

"Why did you come back, Striker?"

The question stopped me dead in my tracks. "What?"

"Why did you come back?" he repeated.

"What the hell kind of question is that?"

Ember sighed. "Obstinate until the end," he said, a twitch of a smile on his face.

"What the hell is wrong with you?"

He didn't answer, only blinked his baby blues in response.

"Help me get your shirt off." I pulled away from him with all my strength, but he clamped down harder.

"Leyla," he said again, and I winced. "No *bots*. I'm staying here. Take the stairwell out."

I stared at him incredulously and enunciated my next words slowly. "I am not leaving you."

"I'm dying, Stone."

I curled my hands into his collar and pulled him towards me. "Then I will carry your dead body out of here... hell or high water. Now cooperate!"

A sibling-like fight ensued. "This is my choice. I'm staying here."

"The hell you are."

"I'm a dead man."

"No, you're not."

"Yes, Stone, I am." So calm.

I stopped resisting for a moment and looked straight into his eyes, as involuntary tears seeped from them. "Why are you giving up?" I asked quietly.

"Unfortunately, the time is right, but we have no time." He chuckled to himself with bitterness. "I've been living on borrowed time, but now I have to pay up. You will understand this later, I promise, but one of us has to get out of here, and I'm in no shape for that. It has to be you. I will only slow you down, and they will catch us."

"So what? I can take them," I argued. "And if we get *bots* in your bloodstream, they'll come pick us up." Aside from being magnificent surgeons, *bots* also threw out a Mayday.

"Damn it!" Not so calm anymore. "You don't have much time! Stop being so stubborn!" He grabbed me by the collar with surprising strength and looked into my eyes. "I need you to listen very carefully and do exactly what I say. No *bots*! Do you understand?" He held my gaze.

An urgency behind his eyes, unlike any I'd ever seen before, compelled me to listen. "Okay, Ember."

Although I complied, I had absolutely no intention of leaving him. With my hands now free, I pressed them with all my strength onto the two wounds on his chest I deemed most critical. I glanced at the syringe now lying on the floor, trying to gauge if I could get it in him before he blocked me.

He heaved a sigh, the tension flowing out with his blood. "No one knows we're here. This is not a Sedition grant. No *bots* because there's no one on the other end. They'd be dead in the water, and we certainly can't have them send up a distress signal."

I looked at him, stunned. "Not a Sedition grant? What grant then?"

"Mine," he admitted heavily.

Yours? The secretiveness of it all started to click into place. "What are we doing here?"

"Where is that bag I gave you?"

I released one hand from his chest and pulled the plastic bag out of my bra. He took it, smeared blood all over the bag, and I returned my hand to the wound.

He started fishing around in it. "Even if I was to make it out of here, I'd never survive the Sedition."

"What are you talking about?"

He laughed. "I have something to admit. Today was my last day. I quit."

"Are you mad? You can't quit." Only the Sedition Heads or death itself could release us.

"Well, I did, and you know as well as I do, with the way I chose to quit, my days are now numbered. I'll be on the Sedition hit list, and I'm in no shape to be on the run from them." He looked down at himself and his eyes widened, as though just realizing he'd been shot. "I never intended to go back. In fact, Leyla, I never intended for either of us to go back. I've become unpopular at the Sedition, and let's face it, you've never been popular—powerful, yes, but not popular. They wouldn't have known for a few days. I could have gotten a good head start and covered our tracks pretty well, but I won't have to work out those details anymore. It's on you now."

"Why?" I asked to his entire statement.

He pulled a single drive out of the bag in answer. With a deep breath, he held the tiny square in front of me as if it were some rare golden artifact. "Take this. There was no relay to the Sedition, and that's good. Show no one, tell no one, trust no one. The world is changing, Stone. The Sedition is no longer safe."

I stared at him in disbelief and put my head close to his. "The Sedition... Spade?" I whispered.

"Spade is trustworthy, but even he cannot keep the Heads at bay. He can offer no salvation or protection, try as he might. Do you understand that?"

I nodded, as words wouldn't seem to come right now.

He pried one of my hands loose, pushed the drive into my palm, closed my hand around it, and then pulled it to his chest. The warmth coming from his fingers seemed impossible given the amount of blood he'd lost. He closed his eyes, took a deep breath, squeezed my hand once, and then let both my hand and his breath go.

"This is more important," he said, for the second time that day. "Consider this your second 'Indigo 11' grant. Take this and run."

"My second 'Indigo 11'?" The thought terrified me.

"There is one last thing I need you to do."

"Okay." I swallowed. "If I can."

His eyes found the depths of my soul. "I need you to put a bullet in my head."

"What?" I gasped. The shock rippled through me like a sledgehammer to the chest.

He put both hands on my shoulders and squeezed gently in an attempt to soothe. "Kill me, Stone. Calm down and kill me, before they do."

The tears nearly came now. *About time.* "I can't, Ember. I can't do that."

"Kill me, or I will be trouble for you later on... Stone...." He began to fade, his words becoming jumbled, incoherent. His eyes closed.

"Ember!" I shook him.

His eyelids fluttered back open, and he looked at me as though he'd just woken up from a nap and realized I was in front of him.

"Ember... Ember, you can't leave me here." It was the only thing I could think of to say.

"I'm not leaving you alone...." He faded away again.

Before I had a chance to react, the door burst open and security reinforcements were on us. I sat there in shock.

Ember's reptilian core fluttered back to life and snatched up the gun sitting beside me on the floor. He lurched up and took another bullet before killing the four men that had come through the door. He turned to me and threw the gun, which I caught clumsily, numbly.

"You cannot get caught, Stone! Don't let me die for nothing! Now run!" He collapsed for the last time.

I spun on my heels and ran, taking no time to descend the stairs. I jumped and was out the door before anyone would have had time to do so much as glance over the railing.

CHAPTER 6

I ran until I could run no more.

I didn't go back that afternoon or that night. In fact, I almost didn't go back at all. I wrestled with the decision on whether or not to carry out Ember's plan and hit the road, but in the end, I didn't have enough information to proceed. It sounded like madness after what Ember said on his deathbed, but I had to talk to Spade.

That meant I had to go back to the Sedition.

The Sedition Underground was an ethical council of sorts founded during the latter half of the Cold War — around the late 1970s. While some of the "meliorists" were concerned with passing the acid test, others were concerned with humanity passing the extinction test. Seven influential individuals, known as the Heads, formed the Sedition in response to what they saw as government's increasing inability to lead its people. For them, the fifty-year stalemate symbolized a widespread lack of cellular intelligence. Humanity had lost the ability to discern, and it seemed integrity, the one thing we couldn't live without, was the first thing we sacrificed. The world was in trouble, and the Sedition

Underground subtly entered the world's subconscious as a kind of International 911 — loyal to no nation, no government, no system... only their own.

Nearly fifty-years later, I went to work for them at age twenty-two, fresh out of undergrad with a degree in international affairs from the political realm of Washington D.C. in the United States. Go international? Have some affairs? Sure, that sounded accurate. I spent that last blissful summer of ignorance interning on Capitol Hill, as was common with D.C. students. I should have left instead, and gone backpacking around the world with the rest of my disillusioned generation, but the Sedition had other plans for me.

The Sedition Underground ran worldwide, on every continent, in every country, in every major city, but its home base was in the United States. The "Heads" decided that since Washington called most of the global shots, they'd better stick around for damage control, especially when we started electing reality TV stars as officials. Employees of the Sedition heard no more than they needed to hear, saw no more than they needed to see, and spoke no more than they needed to speak. Nothing was constant: names and faces changed frequently, even voices changed, and things seen might not actually be real. Anonymity allowed us to thrive.

Essentially, we might have been called human rights activists — twisted human rights activists, freelancers with one employer. We worked in the public sector, though always under the guise of another organization — an establishment that normally appeared before being called, although a few in the highest echelons of society had our number. In return for keeping our existence to an inaudible whisper, we could be called upon in the direst of circumstances. In all likelihood, the Sedition employed a number of their defectives, something they were more than willing to keep quiet. The defectives gave us leverage.

In truth, we were all defectives, but while some defectives hailed from other organizations, the rest of us defectives came from general society. Our lazy half-brothers were the ex-patriots, those who became disillusioned with society and dropped out entirely. In joining the Sedition, we did the opposite. We believed the disillusionment could be corrected, and sought to stop humanity from its own self-destructive course.

Society had become aware of its impending devastation, but always failed to react quickly enough. We were there to help it along... or block it, if it devolved.

It all sounded so romantic: loyal only to our morals, our own ethics; filling the world with truth and justice, with intrinsic goodness; free at last of corruption.

Yeah, sure.

In truth, this place was no fairy tale, and, as always, generations changed.

CHAPTER 7

It wasn't until the next morning that I dragged myself back to the Sedition. I'd missed an evening briefing with Spade, and so had Ember. I didn't know how well I'd be received, but at this point, I honestly didn't care.

"The Sedition is no longer safe." A death wish, perhaps, but I needed to find out why. I never left a stone unturned — hence, my name.

I pulled up to the security booth at the paper mill, put my hand on the biometrics scanner, and drove on. I sat in the dusty parking lot for a moment watching the employees trudge to work.

Poor bastards.

The disgusting place smelled horrible, but that guaranteed no one came sniffing around. Literally. Both massive and fully operational, nobody would notice an extra hundred employees or so. Plus, we controlled the administrative side of things.

After a few minutes, I fell in line behind part of the crew and followed them inside, inconspicuously ducking into the chronically out-of-order women's bathroom. Sometimes I found workers smoking or screwing inside, and for that reason I always dressed as the janitor. That whole "no one looks at the driver in the get-a-way car" applied to the maid too. People caught in the act were always highly embarrassed, and I took great pleasure in their distress. They'd spend the next seventy-two nerve-racking hours wondering if their boss, and, by extension, their spouse, would find out.

With the bathroom clear today, I shut myself in the supply closet, pressed my hand into an invisible biometrics scanner mounted on the back wall, and looked directly into a chip in the wall. I wondered who might be keeping watch today.

What day is it anyway? Tuesday. Wicus... that's who'll be down there.

I smiled extra wide for him, though I didn't feel like smiling at all. Dean Wicus and I were generally friendly with each other, as we'd been in the same Striker class, but I didn't want to tip him off that something was wrong.

After a moment, the wall slid open and allowed me passage down a set of stairs to the Underground. The wall closed behind me and, as darkness took me, Ember filled my mind.

We'd both been brought on as emissaries at the Sedition, the equivalent of field agents, meaning we did the grunt work. They casually referred to an emissary as a *striker* for reasons unknown to me. There were a number of teams, each with five strikers — two pairs and a leader, called a subordinate, all initially hired between the ages of twenty-two and twenty-five. Charlie Spade, the head of our striker team, had about five years on the rest of us. Ember and I were — *had* been — one-half of the ensemble, with me five years deep into my career, and Ember twice that.

I reached the bottom of the stairs and again repeated the entry process, but didn't smile this time.

The door slid open, and Wicus sat at the desk to the right in his usual black, hooded sweatshirt and pants. He had this idea that if you were black and dressed in all black, the face was harder to distinguish.

He raised an eyebrow curiously. "Where have you been, girl?"

"Why, did you miss me?" False cheer.

He suddenly became very dashing, flashing his million-dollar smile. "Always. Seriously, though, seems like you and Ember have been gone a while. Where is he anyway?"

"Right behind me," I lied, and then dropped it, as another dagger firmly planted itself in my heart. "Spade is in his office?"

"As far as I know. Have a good day, babe."

"Later."

Luckily, only Spade would know we had missed the meeting, and as he wasn't a hasty fellow, wouldn't have raised any sort of alarm yet. Spade infamously let situations play out, sometimes a little too long. I imagined him sitting there behind his desk, watching the clock, shifting around in his chair a few times as he ran his hands repeatedly through his dark brown hair. After about fifteen minutes, he'd rise from his desk and say something like, "Well, isn't that unusual?" Then he'd put on his coat and hat and go home, scanning the Sedition on his way out, but he wouldn't find us, our desks empty. He'd call both of us on his way home, but neither of us would answer. He'd call again in the morning, and still, no response. Upon arriving at the Sedition and still seeing our desks empty, he'd say, "Well, that's odd." Then he'd go back to his desk to wait.

That was exactly how I found him: waiting.

I didn't bother knocking. His office door was cracked, expecting at least one of us, so I just pushed it open. His dark eyes looked up from his laptop, but he said nothing as I closed the door slowly and took a seat in front of him. He eyed me for a moment, no doubt extracting whatever information he could from my appearance, but I tried to remain neutral.

"Where have you been, Stone?" he asked evenly.

"Ember is dead," I said bluntly, never one for formalities. I avoided his gaze.

He tensed for a moment, and then his facial muscles relaxed. "Tell me what happened."

I told him the story, starting from two nights before, where Ember laid out the plan for me, to the next night, where I followed the guard, through the following day at the hospital, and to our final conversation in the stairwell. I did, however, leave out a few minor details. I didn't tell him that Ember also intended for me to leave the Sedition, or that he'd said the Sedition was no longer safe. I also neglected to tell him about the drive Ember had singled out. I kept that one to myself — self-preservation at its finest.

"Ember told you he quit?" Spade asked in disbelief after I stopped talking. He sat rigid and wide-eyed, his arms tense and hands splayed across his desk, as though attempting to keep the world steady.

"That's right." I shrugged, feeling absurdly casual.

"Why would he say such a thing? Why would he think he could *do* such a thing?" He dropped his head into his hands and grabbed two fistfuls of coarse hair.

And that's not the half of it, pal. What Ember had said about Spade offering no protection from the impending fallout left me uneasy. "I suppose because he could. He seemed pretty resigned to die."

He sighed. "I'm sorry, Stone."

"Yeah," I snorted cynically.

"Leyla...." His tone was one of surprise, in reaction to what surely had sounded like an accusation. "I mean it." He stared at me from across his desk, and given the peculiar look on his face, I knew I wasn't doing a good job of controlling myself.

I looked up into his hazel eyes, finding sincerity and concern there, and forced myself to relax. "I know, Spade. I'm sorry too."

"He was a good man," he said, as though attempting some kind of eulogy.

"He certainly was," I said shallowly. "My other half...." I stared down at the floor sullenly, trying to think of something else to say.

"But we move on, right?" He raised an eyebrow at me.

"Of course," I said without hesitation, my responses now apparently on autopilot. *Perfect.*

Satisfied, he returned to an earlier train of thought. "You have no idea what the two of you were doing inside that hospital?"

I shook my head. "No clue. He wouldn't give any kind of information, just asked me to trust him."

"And you did?"

I gave him a hard look, slightly irritated. "Of course I did. The man saved my life a hundred times over," I said more harshly than I'd meant.

"Okay, okay, relax." He sighed and sat back in his chair.

I threw my hands in the air. "I assumed it was a Sedition-approved grant. We might have been a team, Ember and I, but we both knew who was really in charge. He'd never deviated before."

"Fair enough, and he was looking for information on a patient?" he asked rhetorically.

"Yeah." I tossed a drive on the desk in front of him. I had to give him something. "And he found it, though no bots were released to relay the information."

He picked up the drive and examined it, running his thumb over its surface as though he could extract the information that way. He held it out towards me. "Do you know what's on this?"

I nodded. "Patient files, as in plural. Ten of them. I've flipped through them and they don't mean anything to me. I don't know the faces, and they don't have names, just numbers." I looked past Spade and off to the side, as though out a window, but only a blank wall sat in front of me. The Underground contained no windows, and my circadian rhythm had often malfunctioned because of it. "He kept breaking the Novem. We separated, stayed longer than seven minutes in the data lab, and it was surely more complicated than necessary. I kept trying to figure out why he was breaking protocol, and it was because we were going by *his* protocol, not the Sedition's." I huffed. "And, Spade, I don't even know what kind of hospital this was... or if it even *was* a hospital. Too much security, morgue practically next to the front doors, weird examination rooms... nothing about the place made sense."

He seemed to ignore the last part of my statement and continued to stare at the drive, hypnotized. "Is this everything?" he finally asked.

"Yes." I nodded. *Minus one*, I thought. I'd never lied to Spade before, but something was off. The look on his face suggested... *something*, but I couldn't quite catch it. *Maybe he knows something.* "Do you know what Ember was doing in there?"

In response, he stood up and leaned into me from across the desk, hackles raised. "What kind of question is that?"

"Just a question," I answered evenly.

"Well, forget it," he said harshly.

"As you wish."

He sat back down and pressed his fingertips together thoughtfully. "You mentioned the Novem, said that you and Ember separated. That *is* highly unusual."

"I'm aware. I fought him on it, told him it would get us killed, but he wouldn't listen, kept saying something about it being more important."

Spade took on the tone of Sedition Head. Actually, I'd never heard a Sedition Head speak, but I could guess what it sounded like: imperial and judicious. "Don't you find all this strange, Stone? Unapproved Sedition grant, veiled in secrecy, broken Novem?"

What exactly is he getting at? "Yes, I do find it all rather peculiar," I said, a hard edge to my voice. "But there is more to this than Ember simply defecting. He certainly quit for some reason, but he didn't defect."

"I didn't say Ember defected."

Full on the defensive again, I let him have it. "Well, it's what you're thinking. So stop it. I never want to hear you think that again."

He slammed his hands down on the desk. "How can you hear me think?"

"It's my job, remember?"

He took a depth breath and held up his hands. "Hang on, Stone, let's back up. We're not enemies. We're a team." He ticked us off on his fingers. "Me, you, Ember, Hamlin, and Colvin... we're a unit, and we're down one now, which makes us vulnerable. We don't need to turn on each other."

I wanted to stay angry — angry for Ember, angry for Ben — but I couldn't take it out on Spade. I didn't have many allies left, so I forced myself to back off... again. "You're right, Spade. Sorry."

"We're going to reorganize and regroup," he furthered. "I know *Ember didn't defect*...." His voice carried the slightest inflection, the slightest pause. I raised my eyebrows, but he continued. "I'm only trying to gather as much information on the situation as possible. I'm confused by his decision to take on something outside of Sedition approval, and to involve you in it. Maybe he told you he quit because he was trying to give you incentive to leave him."

I looked him right in the eye. "He wanted me to kill him. Why did he want me to kill him?" My voice pleaded for an answer. I hated the sound of it.

Spade merely looked at me. "I don't know."

But there is knowing in not knowing.

A long pause ensued, and I'd put this off long enough. I had to tell him. "There's something else."

"Yes?" he asked, almost hesitantly.

I sighed heavily. This was not going to go well. "Another Novem we broke." I ran a hand over my face. "We had guns."

"You what?" he asked in a bare whisper, so stunned he could hardly speak. Pallor crept into his face.

I spoke quickly and quietly. "I didn't know about them until we were already inside. Ember hid them under the gurney, a false bottom. The gurney didn't go through the scanner."

"Stone...." He was barely breathing. "Did you use them?"

I only nodded.

"Oh my god." At last, he gave up and put his head in his hands.

'*Never begin with excessive force.*' The Novem most likely to get you killed.

Nothing was more suspicious than a gun, especially if you left it behind with your prints, so at Sedition, we didn't carry them. We were well versed on their use, of course, but there were better ways to get things done. Guns remained a weapon of last resort, another golden rule of the Sedition, the golden rules collectively referred to as the Novem, Latin for nine—nine things one didn't do in the field. The rest of that rule was: *Be subtle. Go low profile until there is no choice.*

The hospital had been anything but subtle.

I continued. "Ember had emptied a clip when I found him, and someone had put several holes in him. I had no choice—the only way I could get out." This was a half-truth, as I could have run, but I'd chosen to stay and fight. This had "forest fire" written all over it.

"Okay, okay." Spade hyperventilated, recoiling and recovering at the same time. "We'll figure this out." He tried to sound reassuring, but totally failed.

"I just can't quite wrap my head around it. I don't understand," I said more to myself.

"I know," Spade placated. "That's all right. Take some time."

A warning bell went off in my head and I looked up sharply. Spade had never ever told me to take some time. That kind of behavior was unacceptable at the Sedition. People died every day, and those close to them moved on from it—moved on immediately and never looked back. This day was no different, *or was it*?

He stood, came around the desk, and put a hand on my shoulder. His touch felt ominous.

I glanced down at his hand, at the faux wedding band on his fourth finger—a thick, single band of white gold. *Lies*, I reminded myself. We all lived in a web of lies — our pasts, the names we were born with, all of it. I didn't know the man with the hand on my shoulder. I thought I did, but I didn't really — no more than he knew me.

He broke my reverie. "In fact, Stone, take *a lot* of time. I want you to forget about all of this, okay? Forget about the hospital, and put Ember in a good place in your memory, but do not dwell on the past. That's dangerous. I'll handle it."

I nodded, which seemed the easiest thing to do. "Okay, I'm going home." I tried to be convincing, as though having a good rest at home would clear this mess and my head. I stood, and stole a glance at Spade's computer before I walked away. Ember's file lit up the screen, tinged in gray, denoting nullification, deactivation.

Deactivated. Ember was deactivated. The emotional cauldron within me boiled over, but I remained calm, cool, and collected on the surface. I started for the door. One foot in front of the other...it's as simple as that.

"Hey, Stone," Spade called to me right as I reached the door. I turned back to see him looking at me rather oddly. "Did you sleep last night?"

An innocent question. "Not much."

"And how was it when you *did* sleep?" His voice sounded strange, unsettled.

Not such an innocent question. I chose my next words — word — carefully. "Restless."

"What *were* you doing last night?"

I paused, trying to find the hidden meaning in the seemingly mundane dialogue. "Thinking," I finally said, and slipped out the doorframe before he could venture another inquiry.

CHAPTER 8

Spade sighed and sat back in his chair. He pressed his fingertips together and thought for a moment, then picked up the phone and dialed.

The other side picked up on the first ring.

"She escaped." He breathed into the phone.

He crossed his legs and listened for a moment, toying with a small paperweight on his desk.

"I sent her home."

Another pause.

"No, I don't believe we should do anything—yet. Let's see how this plays out."

Pause.

"Yes, I'll be there tonight." He dropped the phone into the cradle and pressed his fingertips together again. This game of five-card draw had just gotten interesting. He'd risked everything for an Ace and drawn a Joker. Now he had to bluff his way out of it.

CHAPTER 9

As I walked out of Spade's office, Hamlin and Colvin, Ember's and my better half, eyed me from the bullpen—as above, so below. The Sedition was not a fancy place. They crammed us all into a room roughly the size of a small warehouse. The subordinate offices rimmed the striker desks, so they could watch us like hawks. A handful of boardrooms, as well as a kitchen and an infirmary, lay in the halls beyond, but I'd yet to encounter where The Heads lay in wait.

Probably behind another invisible biometrics scanner.

Colvin and Hamlin backed Ember and I up in the field and vice versa. Normally, Colvin would have received the intelligence Ember extracted out of the hospital database via *cyber bot*, and Hamlin would have been on the other end of the *med bot*, patching Ember up from the inside out. Nature is a good healer, but a poor surgeon. Nanotechnology had revolutionized intensive care.

This time, though, we'd really been flying solo, no one to receive information on the other end, and no one to call in case of emergency. A *med bot* entering the bloodstream usually sent out a signal for emergency evacuation. If this had been a by-the-book grant, Hamlin and Colvin would have been pulled into the field for a rescue. Instead, they'd been sitting at their desks in oblivion while Ember lay dying in a creepy stairwell.

From the way they looked at me and then looked at each other, they knew something had gone wrong, and I had no way to avoid them, as my desk sat directly behind theirs. That didn't mean I had to talk to them though. They both stood as I approached, but I walked in between them without a word, eyes on the floor. Sam Colvin's big brown puppy dog eyes, which made the little Italian look deceptively innocent, implored me to speak to him, but I refused to meet them. His hand grazed the outside of my arm, and he stepped forward as if he meant to follow me, but the voice of reason within our group, Peter Hamlin, reached out to squeeze his shoulder, and Colvin stopped in his tracks. I silently thanked him and willed them both away. A single interruption might cause me to lose it—I required every ounce of resolve to keep it together at this point.

Mercifully, they let me be. I went to my desk and sat down, watched as they knocked on Spade's door and then entered. I glanced around, not entirely sure what to do or where to go next. Everyone else in the room sat hard at work, typing a million words a minute. Oddly, it reminded me of the hospital, where I'd been pretty much invisible. And like the hospital, it wouldn't stay that way for long.

I just knew that I didn't want to still be sitting here when Colvin and Hamlin came back out of Spade's office. My eyes fell on Ember's desk, his laptop sitting on top. Why hadn't he taken it home with him? *Because he was quitting*, I reminded myself. The Sedition-issued laptops all had tracking devices, one role of the *intel bots*, in case of theft. I half thought it was really because The Heads wanted to track *us*, but couldn't do so without it being a direct violation of human rights, one of the very principles they sought to uphold.

When I was absolutely sure no one was watching me, I stealthily crept over to his desk, entered a password I wasn't supposed to know, inserted a drive, and copied the entire contents of his internal hard drive. The Sedition would know I had done this, but not until after I'd gotten what I wanted. I needed to move quickly, for a cleanup crew would be here soon to clear his desk, to erase his entire existence. No one would know he was ever here, and one day someone else would take a seat at his desk, and it would seem as though they'd been there all along. Maybe they would even take his name.

I searched through his drawers and put anything that seemed remotely relevant inside my backpack. Then, I went through everything in the trashcan, and repeated the process at my own desk, leaving my own bot-riddled work laptop behind. I had to take anything that might be useful and leave anything that could be used against me, for the world had gone mad. Charlie Spade had basically placed me on extended leave. When the door opened to his office, I slung the backpack over my shoulder and walked out.

I sat alone in my house for the next few days, waiting for the Sedition to show up and "deactivate" me. Spade called every day to check in on me, to remind me to relax. He was keeping tabs on me, trying to make sure I didn't do anything foolish, which was foolish in and of itself. If I was headed into folly, nothing and no one could stop me. The only one who could have stopped me was now dead, for I was the Sedition wild card. They called me *The Forest Fire*, for more than one reason.

Enough had gone awry in the beginning of my training to make anyone wary. In those days, I often left a trail of disaster in my wake, which usually ended with something on fire, though I hardly ever set the fire myself. Pyrotechnics followed me, as if I were the catalyst in a chain reaction, or the perfect circumstance by which the sun aligns with the Earth to start a bush fire — not exactly inconspicuous, especially for one in the field of espionage.

As Ember proved to be the only one capable of directing me, the Heads paired us together. Our *modus operandi* was similar, but he had learned to control his temperament and taught me to do the same — how to leave no trace, and to dance with the fire instead of being consumed by it.

He'd always been my saving grace, but now that his character was under review, it might not be so cut and dry. He'd acted outside of the Heads, which surely implicated me as well, perhaps even made me the instigator, given my history. Even if they did believe my ignorance, they would logically assume that I'd become unpredictable again and revert to my old ways without him — kind of like the student that takes a turn for the worse when the substitute teacher shows up.

So, I waited for the hit to come while Spade ran damage control, trying to keep me alive, keeping the Heads at bay by pretending to have the same amount of influence over me as Ember. He didn't and he knew it, but the Heads had to think that it was so. He had to convince them that I was not a liability, that I'd taken no part in Ember's rebellion, that I should be regarded as a pawn and reassigned with a new partner, instead of being relocated to an underground plot.

'*He can offer no salvation or protection,*' Ember's ghost reminded me.

At times, death seemed the easier path, but as usual, curiosity won out. I had to know what Ember's personal grant was. If the Sedition came hunting for me in the meantime, I wouldn't make it easy for them. If it came to that, I actually pitied them a bit.

My nights went by sleeplessly, as the hospital haunted me from the time the sun went down to the time it came back up. Ember's own secret grant; us both packing heat; then separating; the disbelief on his face when he ran into me covered in blood.... Now that I thought about it, he was surprised to see me. He wasn't shocked at his own predicament or relieved that I had come back to rescue him; it was fear—fear for *my* life. I wasn't supposed to have come back to join the fight. I was supposed to be far, far away, not witness to something I shouldn't have seen. But why?

Every time I closed my eyelids, his face burned behind them, so placid and serene, the calm in his eyes so accepting and resigned to his fate. He almost seemed to be welcoming it, relieved by it. Why didn't he at least *try* to survive? Bots or no bots, why did he sit there and refuse to come with me? Had he actually *wanted* to die? I feared I might never find a credible answer, and that lack of knowledge would plague me for the rest of my life.

His words from that day resounded in the long, dark halls of my house, not so much because they were his last words, but because they were so unusual. *This is more important... I'm a dead man... you can't get caught... living on borrowed time... don't let me die for nothing.* Had he really died for me?

But the main one that ran over and over in my head on a reel: *The Sedition is no longer safe.* I had clearly missed something big, but if Spade was trustworthy, as Ember had also said, then how was the Sedition no longer safe? Unless there was something Charlie the subordinate didn't know.

I jerked awake, as usual, out of the nightmare of the hospital. The same vision came every night, me trying to save Ember a thousand different ways and failing each time. I tried everything in the dream: a different hall, a different stairwell, injecting the bots anyway, taking the bullets for him. None of it mattered, the end always the same: Ember dead and me devastated.

Routinely, I went and sat down at my personal laptop and stared at the blank screen. I had been through every inch of his computer files, breached every bit of security, and I'd found nothing, no trace of anything unusual, and the drive that he'd pretty much said to guard with my life was completely blank. Maybe he'd handed me the wrong one; perhaps he'd meant to give me the drive containing the ten patient files, and I'd now unwittingly turned it over to the Sedition. Or maybe delusion had taken him as his brain began to shut down; maybe everything he said in those final moments was out of context, the results of the last neurons firing in his brain.

No. I knew—or hoped—in my heart that wasn't true. There had to be something, and I'd just missed it. Hindsight really was 20/20, but I didn't have the liberty, or the time, to let it unfold naturally.

I briefly ran through the patient records again, copies of the ones I'd given to Spade. That's what I'd really done all night after I escaped the hospital. I meticulously went through everything we'd snatched from that God-forsaken place. There wasn't much: a set of blood-splattered scrubs, two guns, three clips, and five drives, all blank except for the one containing the patient files—ten nameless, information-less files. Without names or background, the most I could hope for was that I'd recognize one of them on the street, assuming they weren't all still in the hospital. The same intake date headed each file, just short of a month ago, but there were no release dates. Eight men, two women; three black, seven white; same age range, late-20s to mid-30s—I'd cross referenced all news reports, official and otherwise, with that intake date and found nothing, just the same horrid rush hour traffic and resulting accidents, an update on the pandas in Woodley Park, another murder, or ten, in the southeast. I plugged in Ember's "special" once more, hoping that something would come up, hoping, in short, for a miracle.

Nothing. "What were you looking for, Ember?" I asked the darkness, and his voice echoed in my head, haunting me. *'I'm not leaving you alone.'*

"Well, it sure feels like it," I answered, and crawled back into my bed, resigned to again stare at the ceiling until dawn crept up the walls and lined my periphery.

CHAPTER 10

I walked up the familiar slope of the hill, the sliver of a crescent moon high, the grass already slick with dew. A thick mist rolled in from the east, carpeting the graveyard floor, the absolute definition of eerie. The hour was late, or early, depending on how you looked at it. As usual, I couldn't sleep; in fact, I'd nearly given up on it entirely. After those first few nights, when it became obvious sleep would not grace me with its presence, I went walking. I roamed the city every night, about midnight to three a.m., sometimes until sunrise. The forgotten, deserted cemetery sat atop Cherry Hill, a misnamed mountain on the outskirts, high above the heart of the city. It offered an incredible panoramic view, so I went up to watch the city, not people so much, but cars, the cops patrolling the city. I didn't know what I was watching for, but I knew to watch for *something*.

Tonight, I wasn't alone. Another striker from the Sedition had joined me. Crispin Bishop comprised one fifth of our sister team, in case the job called for reinforcements. He worked with Maren Vancent, the closest thing I had to a girlfriend. Vancent and Bishop made up half a striker team, led by the subordinate Avery. Avery and

Spade reported to the same Sedition Head. As all strikers, I wasn't privy to who he or she was, but ironically, that part had never bothered me. I had trusted Ember, who trusted Spade, and that was enough.

However, Bishop wasn't here playing the part of the concerned friend; he'd be sent on assignment, part of "damage control." I'd wager my inheritance Spade had sent him on this glorified babysitting mission. I'd met Bishop inside the cemetery gates and let him come along on my night hike, partially so that he would report back that I was doing no harm—weird, yes, but not harmful—and partially so he would regret accepting me as an assignment.

Like he had a choice.

In truth, though, Bishop was a friend, tall, dark, and handsome, like most of the boys at the Sedition, but not *too* anything—it didn't pay to stand out at the Sedition. Although... looking at him now, I wondered—skin nearly as black as the night itself, bones an evolutionary masterpiece, and every muscle carved in exquisite perfection. At first glance, it wasn't obvious, as he'd mastered the art of disguise and made himself blend in quite nicely. In another life, he might have been a print model, but he'd chosen differently. We'd all chosen differently.

Bishop and I entered the Sedition in the same year, the same striker class. Of our original class of fourteen, only a little more than half that remained. I can't say I trusted him *completely*, but I did trust him.

I suddenly found myself thinking more than friendly thoughts about him. It had happened before—work related, of course, but nevertheless, it happened. We'd been busted in an exec's office during a midnight soiree and had to improvise as a drunk, lustful couple. My mind wandered.

A little tryst in the cemetery, wouldn't that be exhilarating. Maybe in one of those elaborate mausoleums on top of a crypt. Extra creepy.

That might make his "assignment" worth it.

'Distraction won't help,' a voice in my head spoke. I pushed the impulse aside and led Bishop onto the hilltop, weaving between tombstones, trying to get him to guess at what the hell I was doing. Nearly two weeks of sleep deprivation had interesting effects.

On to me, he stopped quickly, planting himself between two stones. "Your review is at seven tomorrow," he said bluntly.

I paused mid-stride and turned to him, putting my hands on my hips theatrically. "Did you come all the way up here to tell me that? Couldn't Spade have called?" I asked sarcastically.

So, I was due back at the Sedition in the early morning, where I would be reassigned with some other striker and placed back on active status. That was, if they decided to keep me. I very well might be greeted with a bullet to the cerebrum. Heads you win....

I resumed walking, and heard a sigh and then a wet crunch of leaves as he followed.

As I continued musing over my cerebral cortex, Bishop broke the silence. "You know why I'm here. I came to see how you're doing. Ember on your mind?" he asked impatiently. "Or are you high?"

"Tactless as ever, Bishop." I rolled my eyes and sighed. "Yes, Ember's on my mind, and yes, I am high, though not from any drug. I haven't slept well since." I came to a halt beside a headstone and pretended to read the epitaph, but unless I had the eyes of a cat, I wasn't fooling anyone.

Bishop paused beside me and offered that same weird, useless attempt at closure. "I'm sorry, Stone. He was a good man."

Spade had said nearly the same thing in his office, but with Bishop, I allowed a little more emotional margin.

"He was... my friend," I said quietly, keeping my eyes fixed on the headstone.

Bishop fell silent for a moment, and when he spoke, a voice I'd never heard came out of him, the voice he used before the Sedition, when he was just another guy walking down the street. "Stone, I'm your friend, too. I mean that, and I know you've heard this a million times, and it's easy for others to say, but you've got to move past this. You've got to let him go."

I turned to him and looked into his toffee-colored eyes straight on. "It's not him I can't let go of, Bishop," I said in a bare whisper.

"Then what is it?" he nearly pleaded.

"Something is wrong, inherently wrong. Isn't that what we're trying to stop? Stop the world?"

He put his hands on my shoulders and gripped, as though trying to bring me back to reality. "Yes, Stone, of course, but what? What's wrong?"

I dropped my eyes. "I don't know exactly. It's more of a feeling, like a ripple of chaos in the air, the calm before the storm." I thought of telling him of Ember's warning about the Sedition, but decided against it. He very well could be carrying an intel bot, consciously or unconsciously. As they were all beyond microscopic, privacy had been completely eliminated. Even in the field, bots did most of the work for us — spied for us, reducing risk; relayed information, eliminating theft; repaired bodily damage, evading capture. It only required an operator on the other end, the human intellect.

Bishop leaned into me. "Stone, you've got to make a choice here. Either you let it go, or you will be running forever. Catch my drift?"

"I do." I laughed nervously.

"Speaking of which, we should go and get some sleep. It's an early morning tomorrow." He started back down the hill.

I followed and he became conversationally casual. "I've got a review tomorrow too," he said, as though this might lighten my situation.

We've come full circle. How quaint.

"What happened?" I joked. "Did your partner go rogue and then take half a dozen bullets, leaving you to fend for yourself in front of the Sedition inferno?"

He turned to me, half stunned.

I held up my hands lightly. "I'm letting it go, letting *him* go, like you said. That's all. I laugh my way out of it, every time. Seriously, though, what did happen?"

"Broken Novem," he said, continuing down the hill.

"Which one this time?" I grumbled.

Bishop had a pretty stellar reputation for breaking the Novem, though he never caught much flack for it. So, he either had a forked tongue or damn good excuses, and I banked on both. I wondered if he knew just how many Novem Ember and I had recently broken, and that we broke the worst one: *Never begin with excessive force.* I shuddered at the thought of all the holes in Ember, pouring red down his white uniform.

"Met a Ruski twice in a row at the same diner."

"Not just twice, but twice in a *row*?" I shook my head. "I guess tomorrow we'll all know where we stand, huh?"

When we reached the bottom of the hill, I stopped just outside of the two stone pillars that marked the entrance to the graveyard. "I think I'll stay out a little longer, go out on the town perhaps, have a drink or two." I swept my arm in the direction of the neighborhood they called *The War Zone*. The city had tried re-naming the area *The International District* to make it more appealing, but gangbangers didn't change their territory just because some fascist liberal in a tower gave it a fancy name. "Go ahead. You are officially released from duty. Spade will get over it."

Bishop grinned sheepishly, caught on to the fact that I knew Spade had assigned him to watch me. "Are you sure? You'll make it on time tomorrow? I don't want to have to report that I lost you."

"Go on, Bishop, I can handle myself."

"Yeah, I've noticed," he said with a trace of sarcasm, gazing out at the city lights. "There's a rough crowd out tonight, by the way. I can *feel* it." He arched his eyebrows. "Go easy on them, and stay out of trouble." He headed towards the street, but turned to me as he reached the sidewalk. "And good luck tomorrow. We'd like to see your face around again." He laughed, revealing a set of teeth so pearly white, I could see them in the dark. "You keep the spotlight off the rest of us."

"Just you wait," I called after him.

This gave him pause; I had unnerved him. He eyed me warily a moment longer, and then nodded. "Goodnight." He turned his back to me and walked off.

I smiled inwardly at having shaken him, not an easy thing to do, but they'd sent the wrong man. Friendship is a difficult thing to overcome in terms of objectivity. They should have sent Cam; he'd have seen right through me.

CHAPTER 11

As I watched Bishop walk away, the familiar chill of another set of eyes descended upon me. I had been waiting for this, for the watcher to become the watched. I could have called Bishop back easily, but I let him go — this was not his fight. A man stood behind me, to the left, behind one of the stone pillars of the cemetery gates. Only a sliver of his shadow made it into my periphery, but I could feel his eyes boring into my skull. I quickly crossed the street, and after a few moments, he followed.

We began the dance, and I led him deep into the heart of the War Zone, one of the only places left you didn't need a QR code to get into. If I walked, he followed. If I stopped, he stopped. I quickened my pace, and he subtly quickened his. This was a good game, the night finally getting interesting. The streets were busy, with seemingly every lowlife in town out. I couldn't deny that I was ready for a good fight — welcoming one, in fact.

I slipped into a dive bar on my left and stood before the street front window, arms crossed, and waited.

My shadowy stalker appeared a moment later. I made no attempt to hide, and neither did he. The pane of glass between us disappeared as we faced each other. Young, well-dressed, dark-haired, medium height and build... his designer jacket bulged slightly on the right, though he surely had no permit for concealed carry. His gaze burned into my own, and the intensity of his eyes was almost unbearable—even in the dark, they struck me like lightning—but he walked on.

The world froze as a swell of nostalgia swept over me. A memory sat so close, right on the edge of recall, but my intellect couldn't quite grasp it.

I shook it off and turned into the dark and smoky dive. Men on both sides eyed me as I walked the biker gang gauntlet. A smattering of facial piercings and tattoos leered out at me, hulking frames draped in black leather dripping with fringe. Oddly enough, these geniuses never bothered to wear helmets. Pray tell, what good is all that leather, when your brains are smeared across the pavement? Rider ego: the number one cause of all accidents. These guys wanted to be noticed, but wear a helmet and no one recognizes the badass riding the bike. Which is exactly the reason I always wore a helmet; I liked to be anonymous. That and I wanted a chance at staying alive in a wreck.

Inside, I laughed darkly to myself. *I could spin circles around you, all of you.* A few catcalls pursued. *Please,* I thought, *please try it. Give me one reason, just one. Go ahead, reach out and grab my ass, I fucking dare you.*

As if they heard my thoughts, their attention shifted to the next female foolish enough to walk in here. Slightly disappointed I didn't get the excuse to break a wrist, I went to a back table and set in to wait for the man from the street—he'd be in soon enough. I inconspicuously pulled out a revolver from the inside of my coat and held it under the table. I'd carried since the hospital, which would horrify Spade, but I felt strangely comfortable with it. The weight of it in my hands felt good. No longer low profile, it almost seemed like I wanted to be noticed. In any event, I'd at least leveled the playing field with my friend from the street.

I'd switched from the automatic to the revolver, a Smith and Wesson .38, John Lennon's maker. Old fashioned perhaps, with fewer shots, but ultimately more reliable. Automatics and guns with clips are prone to malfunction. If something goes wrong in a revolver, it's usually a problem with the bullet, and there's generally more where they came from. An equipment malfunction is not what you want in a last resort, and I did still consider the gun my last resort. Nonetheless, Ember's little Beretta, all I had left of him, was attached to my ankle for further backup.

I raised my eyes from the table and they met with his, the man from the street. He really could have been called ordinary if it weren't for the eyes — they belonged to a man who had seen too much. Yet he seemed too young to have seen much of anything, which made him an enigma, and I liked to break enigmas, both literally and figuratively.

He sat in a booth about halfway down the bar, to my right, and he'd gotten there without me noticing, an impressive feat. We stared intently at each other and, after a moment, he flicked his eyes to the doorway.

I kept my gaze on him a little longer, and then stole a glance at the front of the bar, where a group of men had entered, seven in total. They were eerily similar: black suits, dark hair, skin as pale as morning frost. Within a minute, they honed right in on my table, as if they had radar tuned just for me, or I was a beacon shining in the dark. Seven pairs of eyes settled on me, eyes as black as the night from my vantage point. One of them mumbled something, his lips barely moving, but the others responded like they were in the stacks of a library at midnight. They traveled in unison, then spread out and headed toward me, very slowly. In their dark eyes gleamed what I saw all too often, the evil eye of the enemy.

The odds are not in my favor.

It would be tricky, but I'd always been lucky. I could take the septuplets, or whatever the hell they were. All I had to do was keep one eye on the strange fellow to the right, the enigma. He would be the real wild card.

The septuplet that had spoken nodded to the others, who all abruptly stopped, and he came straight at me. A gun bulged at his waist under his overcoat. Bold. This would not go quietly. High profile lay only moments away. In turn, my enigma across the room jumped up and pulled his gun from under his jacket, and time, once again, slowed down. Plenty of time for me to make my move, but this time I didn't need the path.

I quickly dove out of my chair, landing on my left and pulling the table onto its side to use as a shield, or at least to slow the bullets down. I zeroed in on the septuplet I'd pegged as the leader, closest to me at this point.

Before I could pull the trigger, a spray of blood erupted out of his chest, and he lurched forward half a step before another bullet took out his left eyeball. Strangely enough, the gunfire broke out between the septuplets and the enigma.

I wasn't in the line of fire at all.

I had obviously missed something. Perhaps this had nothing to do with me at all. Maybe it was all a wild fabrication due to lack of sleep and a worsening case of paranoia. If that was so, the Sedition had every right to exterminate me. No, that wasn't possible. It always had something to do with me.

Watch, Stone, just watch.

The bar turned to chaos as the usual crowd frenzy and mass hysteria set in. The biker boys weren't so tough anymore, and they, along with everyone else, rushed for the front doors. I kept my eyes on the enigma and found him to be extremely agile and efficient, highly trained — no doubt about that. Unbelievably, he wasted no time in taking out the rest of the septuplets. I couldn't have done it better myself. In fact, he had done it *better*.

After the last one fell, he locked eyes with me and began to make his way to my side of the room. I locked onto his chest with the gun, watched the laser-sighting center right over his heart, not caring if anyone saw. He didn't shy away, kept coming, straight and true.

Pull the trigger, Stone. Solve the problem, I told myself, but for the second time in a month, I hesitated. *Put the gun away before you hurt someone.*

He calmly walked over to me, bent down, and put a hand on my shoulder, at which point all thought of killing him disappeared. "Come with me," he said softly.

"Who are you?" I asked, slightly awed, staring at the one-eyed septuplet twitching before me on the floor, a crimson pool spreading beneath him.

"What's relevant is that there will be more of them," he said gently. As if on cue, the front door burst open.

More carbon copies.

"Come on!" he shouted, pulling me up and pushing me towards the alley exit.

I kicked the door open, which was also the emergency exit, and the alarms went off shrilly. The enigma flew out behind me and then stopped to barricade the door, though with what, I couldn't tell.

"Run!" he commanded.

More gunfire came from inside the bar, but it was not meant for us. The cops had arrived. Well, at least the carbons would be distracted.

I took off like wildfire down the alley, with the intent of putting as much distance between myself and *everything*, including the freak behind me. A black BMW blocked the road, and the streetlights reflected a bright orange glare off the windshield. I jumped on the hood on all fours like an animal, and made to go over the roof, but before I had my hands on the roof, my legs were taken out from under me and I landed on the windshield on my stomach with a smack. My head slammed down on the glass and a burst of pain exploded around my right eye. I looked down beneath me, half expecting the orbital bone to have cracked the glass. It was intact, with no blood on it either. Face also intact, but it would leave a mark.

Strong arms flipped me over onto my back and pulled me down the hood of the car. I came up ready to swing, expecting a carbon, but it was him again, the enigma. I now realized how young he was—late twenties, if that.

Just a kid. Well, isn't that the pot calling the kettle black?

His short, dark brown hair looked like the kind that could turn unruly if it wasn't maintained. Electric blue eyes sat above high cheekbones, and there was no malice in them.

"What are you doing?" I demanded, half bewildered, half enraged.

"Get in the car," he ordered.

"Hell no." I shook my head and articulated my words clearly. "I am not going anywhere with you. Thanks for the help, but on top of being a loner, I'm bad luck, as you've probably noticed, so let me do you a favor." He didn't release his grip, so I leaned towards him. "Let me go right now, or your face won't be so pretty anymore."

He dragged me off the hood and threw me up against the bricks of the alley wall.

Normally, I would have dropped to the ground and taken the fight with a low center of gravity, but squeezed between him and alley walls left me no room, so I slammed my fist into his temple.

That shook him. He let go and dropped, but then quick as lightning came back up and regained his hold on me, giving me no time to react. He grabbed my fist as I swung a second time, and held it fast.

He spoke in a soft, measured voice. "Get in the car and *don't* do that again." He looked into my eyes as though searching for something, then jerked open the passenger door and shoved me inside. He slid over the hood to the driver's side, and in just that fraction of a second I could have slipped away, but I lost it due to the childproof locks.

Damn, the man did his homework. He knew I wouldn't go easy.

I reached into my pocket and my fingers closed around a ceramic piece of a spark plug. I always carried one with me in the event I had to break a car window from the inside, but I had always expected this to come in the form of a submerged vehicle. These were strange days indeed. I took a deep breath and mentally rehearsed the next few moments.

Simultaneously elbow him in the face and break the window, open the door from the outside, roll away from the car.

Some will say that breathing is incessant. I beg to differ. There is a pause, however slight, between each inhale and exhale, more noticeable in sleep, but exists in waking, nonetheless. It was at this very moment, at the pause at the top of the inhale, that I hesitated. Hesitation number three. What in the hell was going on?

Stay.

I exhaled and surveyed the man in the driver's seat.

He looked back and seemed to know what I planned to do. "Stay in the car and hold on. We have to move fast." He turned the key in the ignition and put the car in reverse. With one hand gripping my collar and the other hand on the wheel, he stomped on the gas pedal.

Overkill.

The car peeled out of the alley backward, tires squealing. This brought us back to the main street, next to the front of the now demolished bar, where nothing remained of the glass front or the carbons. The cops' heads snapped toward us, but that didn't worry me. What did worry me were the more sinister eyes I could feel watching us as we drove off. He turned a corner, putting us out of their line of sight.

A squall of sirens rose in the distance, and the chase was on.

CHAPTER 12

After a series of evasive techniques and turns that left even me disoriented, we drove in silence with our eyes on the rearview and side mirrors, watching for blue lights. None appeared, and he had done well in choosing a route that would be hard for the law to follow. By the time they got a helicopter out, if they even chose to do so, we'd be well hidden.

I sat, glaring menacingly at my unwanted rescuer, trying my best to convey etheric daggers.

He, in turn, kept his eyes on the road, intense and focused. Though on the leaner side, his strength was a force to be reckoned with and the hard set of his eyes never faltered. They continuously drew me in, hypnotically, shockingly blue.

Just like Ember, I realized, and then pushed the thought out of my mind, feeling like a traitor for some reason.

I considered grabbing the little Beretta above my ankle and changing the power differential, but if I was honest with myself, I didn't think there was much chance in surprising him. He was fucking quick and good at what he did—he'd just given me quite an impressive demonstration. He had even managed to take control of the .38 without me noticing. It now rested in his lap, and I didn't want to be in a position where he had both guns.

No longer in control of the situation, I weighed my options.

There is no control.

Sure, I could cause us to wreck, and possibly escape, but that wouldn't further my situation or result in any kind of clarity. Plus, I'd likely hurt myself in the process. Whoever this guy was, he had an answer for me. I knew that. What the question was, however, I didn't exactly know. A million possibilities ran through my head, but he obviously didn't want me dead, at least not yet.

"Are you hurt?" he finally asked, in the same even tone he'd first used, staring straight ahead at the road.

I didn't answer.

"I'm going to take a device out of my left pocket, a bot tracker. We need to make sure you're not being tapped."

I stiffened at the thought but still didn't answer.

He reached into his pocket slowly, brought out a small black device, pushed a button, and handed it to me.

My infrared image popped up on the screen, a swirling mass of reds and yellows. No blue other than my hair. I was boiling.

"Nano-thermometer," he explained. "Bots will be tiny black dots, if there are any."

I studied the image, searching for the organic creatures, wondering how the hell he got one of these trackers. Nanotechnology wasn't new, but civilians didn't exactly use it in everyday life. I finally shook my head. "None. What would happen if there were?"

"Then I've got a pill for you to take to rid your system of the bots, and I've got no illusions I'd have to incapacitate you to get you to take it. Now scan me and the rest of the car."

"Who the hell are you?" I asked threateningly, leaning toward him slightly, as though I might pounce.

He took a deep breath, and in it, I heard a strange combination of both relief and sadness. "My name is Vail, and you may not believe this, but I'm here to help you."

I didn't offer my name in return. "What happened back there? In the bar?"

"*Gemination*," he said, as though it should all make sense from one nonsensical word.

I gave him a minute, and when it was clear he wasn't going to explain, I pressed him. "I don't know what that—"

"You're the target," he said over me.

"The target of what?"

"I told you," he said patiently. "*Gemination*. They've found you, and they were there to kill you, in case you didn't notice."

"*Gema*-what?"

"*Gemination*," he said for the third time.

"You're talking about the men back there?" I deduced. "The seven freaks you killed?"

He nodded. "Yes, but they're not men, at least not in the way you'd recognize." He ran a hand through his hair and sighed. "You should just let it alone for now. It won't make sense."

I narrowed my eyes at him. "Try me."

He took another deep breath. "We call them *geminates* because they're copies."

"What the hell do you mean 'copies'?"

He stared straight ahead at the road and took a minute while he thought the answer over. "Copies of people." He gritted his teeth. "Clones, in layman's term."

I didn't respond for a moment, not sure I'd heard him right. "Clones?"

"Not just clones," he clarified. "Genetically superior clones."

"What does *that* mean?" This was getting weirder by the second.

"Hell's army in a hand basket, and you have no idea how serious this is. They risked the unfinished ones for you."

"Unfinished ones?" I shook my head. "Aren't clones an outdated conspiracy theory of some sort?"

He cast a sideways glance at me. "Indeed, though not a theory. It's quite real, unfortunately. I'm not here to defend myself. I'm just answering your questions, and just because you don't believe what I'm saying doesn't mean it doesn't exist."

"And just because I don't believe doesn't mean it does exist," I countered philosophically.

"Fair enough," he conceded.

"All right then," I said sarcastically. "Can you tell me why a hoard of super clones is after me?"

He looked over at me sharply. "You tell me, Striker. You've probably got a lot of enemies."

My heart froze. "What did you call me?" I whispered.

"You heard me," he answered evenly.

I began to protest. "Listen, whatever you think you know—"

He held up his hand and cut me off. "Save it, I'm not here to play games, or to fight over what is or isn't.

I know who you are." I read his face and he was not bluffing.

"No, you don't," I said haughtily and looked away. My mind started digging for a repressed memory of meeting this guy before, maybe on some grant that had gone terribly wrong, but there was really only one of those before the hospital, only one that I remembered anyway — Indigo 11, the day I reaped what I'd sown.

This time he laughed. "I know that you can snap my head off whenever you feel like it. I advise you to wait at least until I'm not driving, and it will help us both if you take the hostility down a notch, okay?"

I sighed. "Okay." I relaxed in my seat and stared out the window. "Can you take your hand off my shirt then?"

He released me, straightened up in his seat, and cleared his throat. "It's a real word, by the way."

"Huh?"

"*Geminate*... it's in the dictionary."

"Fantastic," I said cynically. "Where are we going?" I squinted out at the dark streets.

"We need another car. It's unlikely someone got a good look at these plates, but we can't take that chance."

"Whose fault is that? Nice driving." I waited a moment. "Did you kill the person you stole this from?"

He shook his head. "No, he was sleeping."

"Good. Can I have my weapon back?"

"Promise you won't shoot me?"

"No." I smiled. "But I promise we will crash if you don't." He solemnly handed the gun over, and I looked at him until he looked back. "By the way, never, ever touch it again."

He couldn't conceal the smirk that spread across his face. "Since when did you guys start carrying, anyway? Are the Novem just guidelines now?"

I kept the stunned look off my face and didn't answer.

After about half an hour of driving, where we were both apparently contemplating the phrase, *silent as the grave*, a thought dawned on me.

"They put a hit on me." I then realized I'd said it out loud.

I'd given the Sedition the last five years of my life, which was a lot considering I was only twenty-seven. The cowards had decided to take me out a few hours before I was due back in—lame, but not totally unexpected.

"Well, it's about damned time, but why would they go so public? Who were they trying to pin it on?" I frowned, puzzled. "Doesn't make sense...." I wondered if Bishop knew. My mind spun a fantasy about Bishop making the call after he left Cherry Hill, not something I wanted to believe, but I had to admit that the timing was kind of perfect.

"Hold on," Vail said, as he swerved into a parking garage. He parked and then turned to me. "No, the Sedition has not put a hit on you, at least not yet."

The Sedition... how did he know? This time I couldn't keep the stunned look off my face. The only plausible explanation was that he also worked for the Sedition, either a new guy or in a different office, but why wouldn't he have said so? It should have been the first thing out of his mouth.

"Who are you, and why did you help me?"

His eyes went soft for a moment, and then turned to steel again. He chose to answer the latter question. "Because I need your help."

"*My help?* You need *my* help? I don't even know you."

In response, he grabbed a backpack out of the back seat, exited the car, and motioned for me to follow.

I reluctantly obeyed. Half of me wanted to bolt, and the other half still wanted to break the enigma that walked in front of me. Curiosity always got the better of me, and he clearly knew this.

He began the break-in process a few rows down, on an older Lincoln town car, a good choice. Hot-wiring newer cars is tricky, chief among them being "kill switches" that will shut down the engine so that not even a key can start it.

He went old school and pulled what used to be a wire coat hanger out of his backpack. I thought about offering to help, but once again, he was good, and fast, and it took him all of two seconds to unlock the door. I braced myself for the car alarm, but none went off, which seemed not to surprise him. He obviously had a large and varied skill set.

A jack-of-all-trades, but a master of what?

He slid behind the wheel and pulled a flathead screwdriver and a cordless drill out of his backpack and immediately started drilling into the keyhole as though he'd done it a hundred times.

I watched in fascination for a moment, and then walked around and opened the passenger's side door and slid inside. This couldn't be sane.

As soon as I shut the door, he began to talk, in what sounded like a semi-rehearsed speech. "I am from an organization, just like you are... only mine doesn't have a name, but a number. We are called the 19, and you are with the Sedition."

I raised my eyebrows.

"Don't worry, we're not rivals," he said, his eyes shifting around. "We're not even similar. We're a very small task force and we focus only on one thing: Gemination."

"What is Gemination?" *The question of the night.*

His answer hadn't changed, which could be interpreted as a good sign or a bad sign—on the one hand, there was consistency; on the other, delusion. "Like I said, genetically designed and engineered preternatural humans, a race of super humans, if you will."

I shook my head. "I won't, but I'll play for now. Why are they here?"

"Gemination is an education for the masses, a school of hard knocks for the complacent, and a fancy insurance policy for the select few of the developed world."

"Select few? As in the 1%?" Another conspiracy theory wavered on the horizon.

"There's a war going on, a very quiet war. Unknown to most, it's in the preliminary stages, but soon enough it will erupt into a maelstrom. Gemination is at the heart of this war. My organization is trying to stop them before they get started, before it goes public."

"What's the effect?" I asked nonchalantly. The *effect* was the term we used at the Sedition for the end result in any given situation. There were two parts to the *effect*, *rise* and *die*, success and failure. I wanted to gauge just how familiar he was with the Sedition, trying to stump him.

But of course, he knew. "If they *rise*—" He lingered on the word to make sure I knew it wasn't coincidence. "—they establish resolute control and power over the world as we know it. They are demi-gods at the moment. If they *rise*, they become God. If they *die*, life goes on as before and only a few will be the wiser. I'm here to make sure the latter happens."

"Are you saying Gemination is some kind of global fascism?" I asked skeptically.

"I'll get into the long story later, but the short story is, we formed an opposition to try to stop them. We weren't strong enough, though, and we were fighting a losing battle."

The puzzle pieces started to come together. Vail must have come to the Sedition for help. That meant he was high class, very high class.

Prince of Monaco, perhaps? I grinned inwardly at the thought. "I suppose that's where we came in."

"Right, the Sedition allied with us. Well, more specifically, a part of the Sedition allied with us. One team helped us turn it around, brought us back to our full strength, gave us the resources we needed."

I went through my recent memory banks, searching for a rumor of what he talked about at the Sedition. Perhaps something I'd seen or overheard, something someone had mentioned in passing, but after a few minutes, I came up with nothing. "I wasn't involved. Are they mistaking me for someone else?" I thought of Vancent, taller and generally built a little bigger, but people often mistook us for each other.

Vail shook his head. "Not at all."

"Well, which Sedition team are you talking about? What did they look like?" If I could identify the striker team, I'd at least have a direction to go in.

"One was a man whom I recently heard is dead. Can you verify that for me?" He paused and looked at me — that knowing look.

I knew what he was going to say before he said it, but how was it possible? "How could you know — "

He put both hands on my shoulders, locked me in with his eyes, and spoke very slowly. "Is John Ember dead?"

The name still froze the breath inside me. After a moment, I managed to breathe out. "Yes," I whispered. "I was with him."

"The hospital?"

I nodded.

"Tell me everything that happened. Leave out *nothing*," he enunciated, as though he expected me to do just that. He put the car in drive, left the garage, and headed out of the city.

I deliberated for a moment, and then impulsively decided to tell him. I gave him the full story... almost. I left out Ember's critical drive and all reference to the Sedition.

He said nothing while I told my story, listened very patiently, and drove exactly the speed limit. When I finished, he chose his words carefully. "Did he... expire in your presence?"

I thought for a while. "No," I said quietly. "He lost consciousness."

He let his head fall back onto the seat. "Then perhaps he is still alive."

I breathed a sigh of relief I'd been holding since I'd left Ember in that stairwell. I had been waiting for someone, anyone, to hint at that possibility. I latched onto it and exploded in a rush of words. "That's what I've been hoping. I mean, he was *shot* in a *hospital,* but it's been weeks, and I haven't heard or seen anything. To tell you the truth, I've been trying to get back there, but I've been under very strict surveillance." I balled my hands into fists. "But I'll tell you, as soon as they drop their guard, I am going back in."

"No!" Vail yelled at me. He stomped on the brakes and grabbed me by the shoulders again. "You can never go back in there."

The horror in his voice spiked my curiosity. "Why?"

Vail turned back in front of the wheel and sat there quietly.

It all clicked into place; this was all about that damned hospital. This was Ember's personal grant, and this was the guy he'd really died for, whoever the hell he was.

"So you know about the hospital too," I accused. "Well, I'll be damned. You don't want me to go back in there?"

He shook his head vehemently. "No, absolutely not."

I leaned in close to him. "Then are you going to tell me about what's in there? About what I went in there for?" *About what he refused to live for,* my mind added.

"Not yet," he said morosely. "It's not time."

"Then watch me." I'd get the damn answer my damn self, damn it.

"Trust me." The way he said it, so tragic and romantic....

I snorted. "You should be careful. The last person that said that to me was dead within the hour." The raw wound of Ember's death ripped open again like sutures coming undone.

He wasn't fazed. "Well, I'd say that's pretty likely, considering who's after us."

"Us? I thought they were after me." *There's more to the story.*

"Well, you're with me, and they don't exactly discriminate."

They're after him, too.

Of course, they were after him too. It clearly hadn't been his first encounter, and that made us a double target. I tried again. "What's the connection between Gemination and the hospital and Ember?"

"Look, I *will* tell you everything, but we need to go somewhere else first, put some distance between *us* and *them*. That's the priority." He pulled back onto the road and continued to drive away from the city.

I knew he was stalling, but I had something else on my mind. "You said a Sedition *team* allied with you, which means Ember was working with someone else on the sly." I frowned. "And he didn't tell me," I said more to myself, irrationally feeling a bit hurt and jealous of his mystery partner.

"He didn't have to." Vail turned to me again, and a mischievous glint appeared in his eye. "It was you."

I'm sure a vacant look settled on my face for a moment, and then my eyes widened as I uttered a single word. "Impossible."

At that moment, the back window exploded.

I ducked and Vail floored the accelerator. "Head down," he said, slouching low in his seat as we picked up speed.

I kept low until I heard sirens.

"Cops?" I asked, praying for a fire truck.

"Yes," he grunted.

"How many?"

"Two behind us, roadblock ahead." He slowed and reached for his handgun on the dashboard.

I put one hand firmly over his as he took hold of the semi-automatic grip.

He flinched and looked over at me, eyes wide as he came to a stop.

"No, they'll kill you," I said firmly. "This is still the War Zone. You won't get a warning."

He resisted for a moment and then released his hold, but his hand remained resting on the gun.

I curled my fingers into his palm and removed his hand from the dashboard, pressing it firmly into his thigh. "You're no good to me dead. Now get out of the car, and put your hands up."

I opened the car door, slowly stepped out, and raised my hands into the air. "And no matter what, do not tell them the truth... or what you think is the truth."

CHAPTER 13

Unsurprisingly, Vail carried no identification, and they immediately took him into custody. He did not go peacefully. They pulled a U.S. military ID out of my wallet, high clearance with a "do not detain" stamp on it—my get out of jail free card, should I ever encounter the local law, and it had come in handy on multiple occasions. Colvin was on the other end of that call, playing Director of Whatever Was Needed in the Moment.

Colvin broke protocol and asked for me after the cop. "You're on schedule?" he inquired formally. "You'll make the morning meeting?" Not really a question, but a command, a fancy way of saying, *'Wrap it up and don't be late.'*

"Yes," I lied, feeling a twinge of guilt, as that made two of my team members I'd lied to in the span of twelve hours, but I needed as much time as I could get. He would give me a few hours before telling Spade.

"Godspeed then," he replied coolly and hung up on me.

At the station, it seemed most logical to play "kidnapped"—kidnapped by a madman. Not one of the eyewitnesses to the bar shootout had seen a gun in my hands, and I had ditched the S&W along with the Beretta inside the car on the driver's side floor. The cops naturally assumed they both belonged to Vail, and by the time they matched fingerprints and ran ballistics on the guns, and realized they were mine, I would be well on my way.

Both of us. I wasn't leaving without him.

Vail was now a valuable asset, perhaps the only one who could tell me the story Ember had meant to tell. Before that bullet had come through the back window, he'd implicated my direct involvement with Ember's personal grant. Either he was mistaking me for someone else entirely, or I was insane, the only two options I could think of. He also said he'd tell me everything, and I was intent on making that happen, one way or another.

Unexpectedly, Vail read my mind and admitted to kidnapping me before I had the chance to accuse him of it, like we were old childhood friends still finishing each other's sentences. The man was blowing my mind at every corner.

"We're going to interrogate him shortly, and then you'll be free to go," one of the cops said icily and with great reluctance. He clenched his teeth, trying hard to be civil, his giant shaved head glistening with sweat—the sweat of anger.

I glanced at his nametag: Officer Lutz. I had an overwhelming urge to start calling him Occifer Putz but managed to keep it down. Sedition employees by nature had problems with authority. I'd given Putz my statement, and he didn't like my story, but he had to take it—my ID gave him no choice.

I sat there for a moment. "Do you mind if I watch the interrogation? It might help."

He looked as though I'd slapped him in the face. "Absolutely not."

"It was a rhetorical question." I clarified, as though speaking to a child. I couldn't resist.... "Rhetorical means —"

"I know what rhetorical means," he almost yelled. "This is a police matter."

"Then it is my matter. Do I need to remind you of the government tag you pulled off me?" I enunciated my next words very clearly. "I am going to be present for this, for what he has to say, and I've got all night. Do you?" I bluffed. Certainly, I didn't have all night — a few hours at most, as that bullet through the back windshield had come from a carbon. Incarceration would hold them off for a little while, but they'd find a way around it.

He considered this for a moment, his jaw muscles bulging like a pit bull. "You do anything other than watch, and you're out of there. I don't care who you are," he said gruffly.

The voice inside me again said, *thank you, Occifer, can I get you a donut for your troubles?* I smirked and told the voice to shut up.

A few minutes later, I sat behind the two-way mirror watching the man who called himself Vail being interrogated by a couple of fat, pinheaded cops, and a third officer claiming to be a criminal psychologist. The general consensus was that he was nuts, and to be honest, I kind of agreed with them. The fat cops, Tweedle-Dum and Tweedle-Dee, respectively, said nothing, only sat there trying to look intimidating, which was hard considering that they, too, were sweating so profusely.

I didn't feel warm in the slightest. Was it possible, I wondered, to drown in one's own sweat? They looked like a couple of bullies fresh out of high school, overjoyed to have a piece of false power strapped to their hips.

Amateurs.

The cops in this town were as dumb as the criminals, opposite ends of the spectrum. They were overeager for the chance to pounce on Vail, but if he got the chance, Vail would take all three of them, handcuffs or no handcuffs. The criminal psychologist was older but no wiser, and did most of the talking.

"Reports are that you shot seven men dead in a bar on Elm Street, kidnapped a woman, went on a rampage in a stolen car...." He flipped through his file dramatically. "Correction, two stolen cars... and ran from police. What do you have to say about that?"

"I was just trying to help her," Vail said quietly.

"Help her?"

"Those seven "men" *I* killed were there to kill *her.*" He paused for a moment and stole a quick glance around the room.

They didn't know he had done it, but I did. He had just cased the room, searching out the possibility of escape. Judging by the smirk that settled on his face, he found it, but for the life of me, I couldn't see where — four walls, a door, and a thick plane of glass, the room itself opening from the outside exclusively. Maybe he planned to take all three of them and ransom his way out. That or walk through walls.

Then, I'm sure just to spite me, he added, "And they're not men."

I winced and held my breath. Not smart. I caught the eye of Occifer Putz beside me and looked away.

"No? Robots perhaps, then?" mocked Tweedle-Dum ironically, having no clue of the large and varied role robots, *nano-bots*, played behind the scenes in the field of espionage—indeed, in everyday life. A.I. had run the world since Facebook's grand debut. Half a century later, it was no longer Facebook, but there were a million platforms designed to collect data—e.g. spy on the consumer. There was no fighting the algorithm.

"In a way," Vail said abstractly, and then threw them a curveball. "Do you want to know why you can't identify them?"

"Excuse me?" The criminal psychologist asked, taken aback.

"The dead *men*," Vail said condescendingly, and then rolled his eyes. "Try to keep up."

Well, well, Vail and I have something in common after all: a shared disdain for the law.

"We're asking the questions, buddy," said Tweedle-Dee, gripping the sides of his chair with his meaty hands, as though restraining himself from flying into a sweaty rage.

Vail ignored him. "Aside from the fact you don't have the bodies anymore, there is another reason you wouldn't be able to identify them even if you had them. Do you want to know why?"

Tweedle-Dee failed to keep the dumbstruck look off his face. "How do you know we don't have the bodies?"

"Who took them?" Vail asked, looking smug. "The Bureau? The Intelligence Agency?" When Tweedle-Dee didn't respond, Vail leaned towards him. "You'll never know—just some guys in black suits, maybe gray suits. So, I repeat, do you want to know why you couldn't identify the bodies even if you had them?" Vail's eyes had turned deadly, and I was half convinced he might be able to kill with them.

Tweedle-Dum considered this for a moment, and in the end, his curiosity got the better of him. "Sure, enlighten us, please," he said with feigned admiration.

"They don't exist," Vail said nonchalantly, and then yawned and started looking very bored.

"If you're not going to cooperate—"

"Look, all that matters is they want her dead, and there will be more of them," he said with conviction. "In fact, you'd better evacuate this whole station, because if they don't get what they want when they come—and believe me, they won't—they will raze it to the ground. Those lives will be on you." He shrugged. "Assuming you still have yours."

Tweedle-Dum didn't quite know how to respond to this and became very flustered.

Then Vail looked directly at me, clear he knew I sat on the other side of the glass watching. "They're coming. Leave while you can."

CHAPTER 14

I tried to have Vail released to me, but Occifer Putz refused. "Do not detain" got me that far, but I had no power legally to take anyone with me. I tried giving orders, then threatening him, but I didn't have the time to go through the motions, nor would any of this pass a Sedition screening. Colvin would have to relay to the Head on duty, and I couldn't call on the board for help. Oh, they'd help all right, but I had no illusions that I'd only be trading one detention center for another, one where I would also be detained. At least one of us had to stay on the right side of the glass. *Find Spade.* I went immediately to an office and dialed Spade's emergency number.

It rung several times, and then there was some clatter. He hated to be woken up. "Yeah," he answered drowsily.

"I need your help." Right to the point, simple and true.

"Stone?" A tremor of anxiety rang in his voice. "It's two in the morning. Where are you?" he asked strangely, as though he expected me to be calling from a field of flaming wreckage.

"Nothing's on fire," I quickly clarified. "I'm at the damn midtown precinct."

"Ah, Christ, the War Zone." A dresser drawer slammed as he sprang into action. "Damn Bishop," he grumbled. "What did you do?"

"For once, nothing. You'll never believe this. A guy picked me up at a bar... and not in the way you're thinking."

"What happened? Don't tell me you beat some poor guy senseless because he looked at you wrong?" Keys jingled in the background, followed by the sound of a garage door opening.

"It's slightly more complicated than that," I said, giving no further detail. "I just need you to get here and bring the big guns."

"Are you being held?"

"No."

"Well, leave then." An engine revved in the background. "I'll pick you up where Bishop left you."

"I can't. This guy has got to go with me, and I can't call the hotline. I need you to make it happen."

"What the hell are you talking about?"

I glanced around a bit obviously and then whispered into the phone. "This guy... he knows about us, and a lot more. Have you ever heard of a *geminate*, Spade?"

He was silent for a long time. "I'll be there as soon as I can," he finally said, and hung up the phone.

I tried to sit up and wait for Spade, but the lack of sleep over the last few weeks coupled with the exhaustion of the night's prolonged adrenaline rush had me asleep on a couch in the employee break room within minutes. Sleep, now so unfamiliar, was like crawling into a dark void, but it didn't last long. I awoke twenty minutes later and decided to wander out to the lobby, maybe for some bad coffee or a snack poisoned with high fructose corn syrup and red dye #40. What the hell was red dye #40, anyway?

My inconsequential thoughts were interrupted by a very consequential turn of events. Three seconds shy of pushing through the doors that led into the lobby, I looked up through the glass to see two men standing at the front desk talking to one of the dispatchers. *Not men*, Vail whispered in my mind, *geminates*. No doubt two more of the same kind I had encountered a few hours previously, black suits and all. Carbons.

I immediately dropped out of view of the window, but instead of retreating, I cracked the door slightly.

"We'd like to take him into our custody now," one of them said. "We've been after him for some time now, and thanks to the hard work of your officers, we have him and can handle the rest. We have all the necessary documentation." The false admiration in his voice was sickening.

A pause here as the dispatcher, a stout little woman, reviewed the "documentation."

My heart took up a quick pace, but my head remained clear. Who were these people? What did they have that I didn't that would allow them to take him?

The same thing that allowed them to take seven bodies from a crime scene without question, my mind answered.

"I'll have to call one of our officers to take you back and review the paperwork," she said warmly. She clearly saw nothing amiss, which I found alarming; the creep factor in these people was undeniable.

"Much appreciated." Another pause, and then, "Also, it would be helpful if you could provide us with information on how to contact the woman. She might be able to provide us with crucial information."

The dispatcher gave a bubbly laugh. "Ask her yourself. She's still here. You can use one of our conference rooms if you like. Please have a seat, and Officer Lutz will be with you in a moment."

"Thank you so much." His voice dripped sweetness. He was practically salivating like a rabid dog.

I silently closed the door and started back down the hallway. I hadn't made it far when a door opened in front of me, and I sensed the hulking mass of Occifer Putz coming out of it. I quickly ducked into a dark room on the opposite side of the hall, and waited until he passed by the door. I stood rigidly, senses on high alert, as I went back over my mental notes of the layout of the building. Two hallways ran the length of this station, parallel to each other, with one in the middle that ran perpendicular, connecting them. The room I'd been napping in was past the fork in the middle. If they chose to go for me first, which I assumed they would, knowing that Vail was in custody and I was free, they would have to pass all the way to the end of the hall. I decided to stay put and go for the connecting hallway after they entered the break room. The only problem was, I would have to run, as there would be very little time from the moment they entered the break room, realized I wasn't there, and turned back down the hallway. Running draws attention, but I had no choice.

First, however, they would have to pass the room in which I hid and not sense in some freakish way that I was in it, a risk I would have to take. I had no chance to form a backup plan.

Half a minute later, I heard the door to the lobby swing open, followed by footsteps coming down the hallway. I held my breath, afraid they had some form of supersonic hearing, but nothing happened. The two of them chatted amiably with Occifer Putz, his uncharacteristic enthusiasm making it obvious he absolutely delighted in handing me over to them.

When I judged they had passed several doors down, I cracked the door and spied out through the sliver.

No one turned at the opening of the door. They all kept walking, passed the connecting hallway on the left, walked all the way to the end of the hall, and turned right into the break room.

I bolted from the room and down the hall, keeping my eyes on the break room door at the far end, half expecting someone to open a door into me. I took a left into the connecting hallway and slowed my pace to a fast walk. I didn't look back, for some reason sure I would sense them if they happened to get behind me. As I neared the fork, I picked up my pace again, anxious to get out of the danger zone.

No doubt by now they had found the break room empty and would start to panic, and the calm demeanor would give way to a deadly one.

A gunshot far behind confirmed my suspicions, and I broke into a dead run. Poor Putz was an idiot, but he didn't deserve to die. I decided to go right instead of left, hoping for an emergency exit, as I didn't want to chance the front door. There would have to be an exit down there somewhere, or the building wouldn't have passed code. As I rounded the corner, I literally ran right into Vail.

"How the hell did you get out?" I staggered back a few steps and then quickly resumed my pace.

"Doesn't matter. They're here. Let's go." Vail fell into stride with me.

"How do you know they're here?" I asked incredulously.

"I told you they were coming. I wasn't fucking around. If you were smart you would have left me here... but then, you've never been good at following orders."

His words flustered me so much I couldn't speak. How would he know that?

He opened the door to a stairwell and glanced through it. "Follow me." He began to walk forward and then paused. "Oh, here you go." He reached into each pocket, pulled out the S&W and the Beretta, and handed them over.

I put them back inside my jacket and said, "Thanks," not bothering to ask how he got them. I noticed he also had his gun, upon closer inspection a Colt .45, under his jacket again.

Vail led the way out, incredibly avoiding all human contact, and we ended up right at the back emergency exit. He studied it a moment, then glanced back the way we'd come. "I don't think we have time to disable it, so we're going to have to make some noise." More gunshots behind us only hastened his decision. "I warned them. This is their fight now." With that, he kicked the door open, and the alarms went off, breaking the ominous silence of the world outside.

In back of the police station, Vail quickly and quietly jacked another car, and we tried to leave stealthily. Once again, however, a gang of carbons keeping watch outside spotted and fired on us.

I hit the seat as a bullet shattered the front passenger window, putting a hand on the side of my head to make sure there wasn't a hole in it. A dull smack, followed by a gasp, resounded close by, and I knew what had happened before I looked up: Vail had been hit. I put one hand out to steady the wheel, but the car didn't swerve.

My head still on the seat, I asked him, "How bad?" *Severity.*

"Not bad."

"Where?" *Location.*

"Arm."

"Pressure." *Control.*

"Got it." He clamped his left hand over the wound.

"You sure?" *Affirmation.*

Without realizing it, I'd run through the Sedition protocol for wound evaluation in the field, and he hadn't missed a beat. In fact, it was like we'd done it a hundred times.

"Yes, damn it," he muttered, annoyed.

"Let me drive."

He shook his head. "Not until we put some distance between us and them."

"What if you pass out?"

Vail ignored my statement. "We've got to get out of the city."

I nodded. "I kind of hate to say it, but I think we should head for the Sedition." *Again.*

My review loomed on the horizon, but that wasn't why I wanted to go back. Those chasing me were proving to be worthy adversaries. Maybe the Sedition wasn't what I thought, but nothing could get through those walls. Spade's voice had wavered after I mentioned the word *geminate* on the phone. He was part of this; I knew it. Remembering that last exchange in his office, when he bizarrely asked about my sleep, it was obvious now. I needed them both, Vail and Spade.

"The Sedition," Vail agreed.

I nodded again. "Hopefully, they won't overreact, and by overreact, I mean kill us. But I need to go there." For what, I didn't tell him. "Anyway, the geminates...." I felt ridiculous even saying the word. "The geminates can't follow us in there. We'll be safe."

"Don't bet on that," Vail said doubtfully.

I ignored him. "It's the best place to go."

He sighed and ran a hand through his hair. "You're probably right, even if they're not entirely trustworthy."

"What makes you say that?" The statement triggered the echo of Ember in the hospital. *The Sedition is no longer safe.*

"A hunch." As usual, he gave no explanation, and then only silence.

I rolled my eyes and said, "All right then, keep a sharp eye. I'll lead you to it."

He shrugged. "Not necessary, I know where it is."

"Of course you do," I said cynically, no longer shocked by anything that came out of his mouth.

CHAPTER 15

I sat in the car in silence, internally attempting to rationalize this recent turn of events. *I'm out of my goddamned mind*, I thought. *I can't show up at the Sedition with this nutbag. I won't be able to explain it.* They'd have him in solitary confinement immediately, and maybe that's where I'd be too, but I had to talk to Spade, and in person. He was hiding something from me, that much was clear. Upon finding the police station empty... or gored to a crimson death, he would return to the Sedition and wait for me, as he had after the hospital debacle.

I glanced at my watch: nearly four a.m., my review only another three hours away. No way in hell was I walking into that interrogation room now. That gave me about two hours to get in, talk to Spade, and get out. I had to take the chance. Plus, it was *early* Sunday, still staffed, but at this hour, there wouldn't be quite as many people working.

I stole a glance at Vail, who stared out at the road with the same deadpan expression on his face. He surely had a few screws loose, but had such resolute conviction that I almost believed him... almost. On top of that, I couldn't even begin to guess who he was or where he came from. Nearly a blank slate, it was as though he'd materialized on the planet, rather than been born here. Whoever he worked with and for had trained him well, his skill level on par with that of Sedition employees. I'd yet to encounter another organization of that caliber. Of course, I'd always thought we weren't the only ones out there playing world police.

The only hint came from a dull flame that sat just behind his cold eyes, like a smoldering fire. It told me one thing about him: Vail had been sown, reaped, and spit out again. Whether by his own hand or someone else's, I couldn't say, but he'd seen true hell. He'd battled demons, been on the brink, and dug himself back up from the muck to stand on top. I'd searched all visible skin for scars, but his skin was perfect, so I'd ruled torture out—physical torture, anyway. Mentally, it was a different story—intense, hyper vigilant, devoid of emotions—but in the center of that flame, a flicker of sadness burned constant, as though whatever softness he had left converged there.

I shook my head, tried to clear it, admitting to myself that I had been weak ever since the hospital, not an easy thing to come to terms with. Maybe Vail was the enemy, one from the hospital to repay my invasion, perhaps one of those who had killed Ember. He would know I was weakened without my partner, and now planned to infiltrate the Sedition with the weak link, just as I had done with the guard at the hospital. Maybe it was *his* hospital.

No, I couldn't find that plausible. Besides, just how the hell did he know where the Sedition was, and so much about the Sedition in general? The only thing I could think of was ex-Sedition, and that had already been ruled out, unless he was lying. The Sedition didn't even tell its own people much, and they certainly weren't in the habit of divulging information to those whose cases they'd decided to take on.

After about fifteen minutes, he pulled off into the woods. "Do you think anyone's following us?"

I glanced at the darkness behind us. "I'd say no. Why are we stopping?"

"I need you to drive now. My arm is killing me."

We got out of the car and met in front of the headlights to swap places. He held his arm against his chest and a dark patch stained his jacket where the blood had soaked through it. It ran down to the elbow and dripped onto the pavement.

I stopped in front of him. "Okay, I think this requires some attention. Let me wrap it."

He shook his head. "Forget it. There's no time, and the headlights will draw attention. You drive. I'll wrap it."

I stole a look back down the road, empty and dark as far as the eye could see. "No, I'll wrap it and I'll drive. I'll do a better job, and if someone does come, I'll have us out of here quick. Take that off." I gestured to his jacket, and took off one of my own shirts and started ripping it into wide strips.

Looking partially annoyed, he took the jacket off, revealing more skin, but as the rest, it too, was flawless. He took off his t-shirt and threw it to the side, again showing no signs of physical abuse or scars other than his most recent acquisition. The hole sat above his elbow on his right arm, close to his shoulder. He'd taken it from the side, and it had smashed into the flesh just below the deltoid muscle. Before I could get my hands on him, he'd pulled a knife off his belt and dug the bullet out, barely making a sound. More blood gushed as the bullet-casing hit the pavement with a *chink*. I gawked for a minute at what he'd just done, and he held his arms out, as if saying, *'Well, come on, don't just stand there and let me bleed out.'*

"I can't clean it," I said hastily, taking hold of his arm. "But I can at least stop the bleeding. You'll pass out otherwise and I can't have that. Like I said, you're no good to me dead. I'm already kind of fucked at the Sedition. I need to at least have something to show for it."

Education is what you remember after you've forgotten what you've learned. *Direct pressure, elevation, pressure bandage,* dug itself up from what had become my education from the field emergency basics class five years ago, the order to go in when dealing with virtually any wound. It required not just direct pressure, but *well-aimed* direct pressure. It had been well over two years since the last time I'd done a field dressing. I flashed back briefly to the last time Ember had been seriously injured. That one had been bad, the bullet having hit Ember's femoral artery, and I'd nearly lost him, even had to give him an infield blood transfusion, despite Hamlin's bot work, to get him back to the Sedition alive. He'd been nicked by a bullet a few times since then, but none required more than direct pressure. In the hospital, I never got past direct pressure.

I returned my attention to Vail, who waited impatiently, so I skipped the first two steps and started a pressure bandage. I folded the wide strips of my shirt into tightly packed squares and placed them directly over the hole, using a few narrower strips to tie them on firmly, not worrying if I cut off his circulation. It wasn't pretty, but it would do for now, and one of the nurses could redress it in the Sedition's infirmary. I had a feeling he'd refuse any kind of Sedition med bot.

He drew in a sharp breath the first time I pulled the bandage tight, the knot right over the wound. I looked up into that flicker of desolation in his eyes. Nostalgia, now too close, returned and gave me pause.

"What?" he asked, searching my face, a little uncomfortable with the level of attention.

"Nothing. You just...." I looked down awkwardly and resumed bandaging his arm.

"Remind you of Ember?" he finished knowingly.

I sighed and stepped back from him, looked at him head on. "Yes, you do. I don't know why. You don't look like him." I paused. "How did you know what I was thinking, that I was thinking about Ember?"

"Because you used to look at me like that and tell me just that, that Ember and I had the same eyes — color, I mean... the same shade of blue."

This was absolute madness. I'd never said such things, never spoken to him in my life, but I refused to argue now. He believed his madness, and there's no talking to people when they don't know they're mad. An old proverb from one of my teachers came into my head: *'A madman does not know he is mad. Once he realizes the madness, the madness goes away.'*

Vail clearly did not know he was mad, so that madness would not go away.

"This is sick," I said, referring to his arm, among other things.

"Soft stomach for a Striker, huh?" he asked half-mockingly.

No use in denying it. "I've never been shot."

"Never?"

"Never."

"How is that?"

I shrugged. "I don't know. I just know where to put my body and where not to." Of course, how I *knew* in the first place was something no one would believe. In fact, I'm not sure I even did.

"Made of *Stone*, I guess, huh?" There it was, he knew my name — my Sedition name.

I stepped back from him again. "How is it possible that you know me and I don't know you?" *Anything is possible.*

"Ember."

"What?" I gritted my teeth.

"He told me about you."

"That's not what I meant." I returned to his arm with one last long strip of cloth. "It's cold as hell out here. I hate winter. A job on a Caribbean island would have been a better choice," I muttered.

"Cold as hell?" He raised an eyebrow quizzically, and almost seemed sincere about it.

I rolled my eyes. "Never mind the oxymoron. Tell me about the Ember you knew, *if* you knew him." *Ah, I'll give him a test to fail to ease my mind.*

Vail seemed to know what I was doing, but he played along. "Well, he's a dark angel all around — that's most obvious, though you wouldn't expect it from him. A powerful force, yes, but a powerful force to be reckoned with, not so much. Comes off like a joker, but is serious beyond measure. He was crazy about you, on and off record."

"How would you know *that*?"

It was true. Ember and I were bound together, though not by blood. We'd never taken it beyond the job, but we'd played house a time or two on a grant, and neither of us had any trouble with it. One didn't indulge in romantic relationships at the Sedition, as that was a good way to get whoever you loved killed, but we were still human, so in the field, the Heads gave us free reign to make the grant look as realistic as possible, and then some. Lust, love's evil twin, would not be denied. A lot of pent up energy came out when the sun went down, and Ember had been damn good at it. Of course, we were all trained to be good at it.

His classic, husky voice in my ear whispered, *'This is really why I work here,'* backed up by a set of smoldering eyes. Those eyes killed me, mesmerizing pools of stardust and blue drop heroin. Luckily, he'd kept it professional and chosen not to destroy me with them.

I'd played house with Colvin and Hamlin too, but neither of them came naturally. They looked all right, but didn't feel good — fairly boring, actually. Colvin and I weren't compatible, and Hamlin didn't like women — not his fault. Ember had been easy, and in every way imaginable. I hadn't thought of it before now, but my physical outlet had also been removed from this plane of existence. Insult to injury.

I jerked the bandage hard for the final knot, and Vail winced. Our eyes met again and he smiled.

"What?" Somehow, I resisted screaming it at him.

He laughed softly. "Ember and I have the same eyes? Well, you and Ember have the same look — the same will."

"Will?" *Back to Madman Land.*

"The will is that which pulls you through a situation you would otherwise die in. It's invisible to most, but you both have that quite strongly. I can see it in the *stone* of determination in your eyes." He leaned closer, searching my eyes further. "And your will is particularly interesting, and well suited to your line of work."

I stepped back from him, thrown by his last statement, suddenly wishing I had a cigarette even though I didn't smoke. "We all have the same eyes, don't we?" I finally said. "Eyes of the damned." Then, I exploded in a burst of run-on sentences. "Do you know how fucking mental this is? I do not trust anyone, and if you know anything about my line of work, you know that, but for some insane reason, I'm standing in the middle of nowhere in the middle of the night bandaging the arm of some guy I've never seen before, who, by the way, I'm about to take to one of the most unofficial headquarters in the world, and I'm being chased by an army of freaks that I have nothing to do with. Could you please explain to me how I had anything to do with this, because I have no memory of it! What the hell am I supposed to think about all this?" Any moment, I would rip my shirt off and burst out of my skin like The Hulk.

I stopped, trying to still myself, breathing heavily as the adrenaline coursed through my system and then drained away.

Vail stood there very calmly and we stared at each other, just as we had at the window of the bar four hours ago. Had it only been four hours? It seemed like a millennium ago. Time certainly remained the trickiest adversary I had ever come up against.

As if in response, the world froze again, and this time, I froze with it.

CHAPTER 16

I stood, suspended, for some unknown length of time. Then, all of a sudden, the answer hit me like a Mack truck. "Mother fucker!" I almost laughed and my knees nearly buckled. I leaned against the hood of the car for support. "I do know you, don't I? I feel like I've known you all my life. That's why you're still alive. Ember didn't tell you about me, I did. I know you, but I don't remember you." A thought dawned on me, an uncomfortable thought that something was terribly wrong with me, that something had gone awry in my brain. "What's happening?"

I said it mostly to myself, staring out towards the trees. The smell of wet leaves and cedar hung heavy in the air, and the deafening roar of the cicadas flooded my ears. Fireflies lit up the darkness with tiny pinpricks of light, as though the fabric of reality was wearing thin. I remembered running around in the night as a child, catching the little creatures and hiding from the world. Even then, I had been more comfortable in the dark. It offered solace and a deep companionship I'd never found anywhere else, or in any living creature... except for Ben. Maybe I could just walk into the night and disappear. Forget.

Vail put his hands on his knees and leaned towards me, the moon reflected in his eyes. "Yes, Stone, you're right. You do know me. We met a long time ago." His voice dropped an octave. "In a dream of sorts, a dream of chance. Perhaps only a shadow of what it once was remains, but that shadow may be all we need."

"Nothing makes sense," I complained, absolutely exasperated.

"That's because you don't remember. You said it yourself. All will be revealed, I promise."

"When? Can you give me anything?" I nearly pleaded. God, I wished Ember were alive.

He paused and ran his hands through his hair. "It's not simple, but since we don't know what's really going to happen when we walk through the Sedition doors, I'll try to condense it for you. If we get separated, you'll at least have a little more of the puzzle to go on."

"A little more of the puzzle? How about *all of it*?" I countered angrily.

He looked up the road in the direction we were headed, and then down at his watch. "As much as time allows. I know we're close, and I know you're working under a deadline, so I'll give you the most important details first."

I hadn't told him about the review, but realized he'd been privy to Bishop's and my conservation. He'd eavesdropped without either of us noticing. With each passing moment, I realized more and more the extent of his expertise.

I nodded, at a loss for words, and decided to listen and let him tell his story. I would sort out later whether I believed it or not.

He began. "A certain part of your memory has been, for lack of a better word, lost. As I said before, a while ago a team from the Sedition allied with us against Gemination—your team. As far as I know, the alliance had formed in secret, and Spade never gave out the full detail to the Heads."

The mention of Spade's name and the Heads flustered me, but I held my tongue.

"Half the team wasn't directly involved, so they only followed orders. I'm talking, of course, about Colvin and Hamlin, acting as the technicians."

Another ruffling of the feathers that left me feeling like a defensive peacock. I forced myself to take a few deep breaths. At this rate, an aneurysm seemed imminent.

"Only three knew the full detail of the grant: you, Ember, and Spade. Spade and Ember set up the logistics and did the outside work. You worked on the inside, as the liaison, the only true connection, but you were like a ghost, a shadow. Ember and Spade worked in the light, and you worked in the dark. However, you were all working on the sly, helping us, the 19."

Interesting.

"A few weeks ago, something went wrong. Gemination managed to locate us and flattened our operation. There's no one left—well, just me. I escaped because Ember showed up at the last minute."

"The knife wound," I remembered, thinking back to the hospital. The cut above his hip had been fresh.

Vail nodded. "Yeah, the guy sliced him before Ember put him down. The rest of my team is either dead or admitted," he said bitterly.

At first, I wasn't sure what he meant by admitted, but then it finally clicked. The hospital and the ten patient files. "Ember was looking for them," I said. "Those are your people."

Now it made sense why Ember had insisted on being the dead man on the table. Even though it was my turn to play opossum, they were hunting *him*. The guard *had* recognized him. I felt like a fool for not seeing it sooner.

"Yes, the hospital belongs to Gemination, and they did not know you were part of this, not until you pushed Ember in on that gurney. Now, you're also in the light—shadows no more."

I'm being hunted by the people who hunted and killed John Ember.

If that was so, I didn't stand a chance. Ember had been nearly indestructible. He could bounce a bullet like Superman, and I'd been so sure he could do it one more time.

Sat there... he just sat there.

I shook my head. "So... what? You're telling me I've got amnesia? Some kind of partial amnesia that's extremely intelligent?" I asked quietly. "Like I was in an accident of some sort and blocked out the memories related to the trauma?" Surely Vail was talking about the attack. Had I been there? Had I taken a hit to the head?

"Something like that, except you weren't in an accident."

"And Spade knows all this?" I clarified again. "Why wouldn't he tell me?"

Vail shrugged and pulled his jacket back on, leaving the crumpled, bloody T-shirt on the ground. "Why *would* he tell you? When we were attacked and then Ember died, it was over—no evidence of his team's involvement. With the grant itself effectively on the *die*, you were now all safe from the repercussions of the Sedition. Hamlin and Colvin oblivious, Ember dead, you didn't remember... problem solved. It was easier to forget, to let it go, and only Spade would be the wiser. As far as he's concerned, the grant is over. It failed."

"What happened to make me forget?"

He continued, not answering. "But as usual, there's a hitch. Because your face accompanied Ember's in the hospital, Gemination knows they missed something, but not *missed* so much as *found*, and... found something for which they'd been looking for a long time," he said obscurely. "With your identity revealed, we are the last people on their hit list. Ember told me that if he fell, I was to keep you alive."

I sighed. "Ember turned out to be the real wild card. When was the attack? I'm assuming this is about the time I blacked out."

"Yes, a week ago."

"A week ago, Ember and I went to the hospital."

"Two days after the attack, to be precise."

"You knew?" *Why didn't he go with Ember? Why take the one who's only got half her memory?* I somehow immediately knew the answer. *Because you were the one they didn't know. Vail couldn't have wheeled Ember in. It had to be me.*

He nodded.

"Was I there?" I asked him directly. "With you, at the attack?"

He shook his head.

"So, what happened to me then?" I repeated.

He shook his head again. "I honestly don't know. You were *supposed* to be there, but Ember got wind of the invasion right before it happened, and ordered you away." A strange expression came over Vail's face. "And you listened for once. We feared it might mean that you too had been taken, but you showed up for work the next day at the Sedition. I guess you picked the right time to follow orders, but something must have happened to you, because you lost your memory that night."

Something in his statement didn't sound right. "How about Spade? Does he know what happened to me?"

"I don't know that either. I haven't spoken with him."

"In how long?" I asked slowly.

"Since I met him. I only had contact with him once. Ember too, up until the invasion."

Something else clicked: my role in all this. "What did you mean when you said I was the liaison?"

"Simple: you were the go between, our only means of communication."

I looked at him curiously. "For how long?"

He paused as if considering whether or not to tell me. "Six months."

Six months. Christ. "And what were you to me exactly?"

He stared at me, and for the first time, something different lit up behind his eyes, a spark of anticipation. When he spoke, his voice was quiet. "I was, *I am*, your right hand, Stone. You trusted me with your life, which is why you trust me now, without even consciously knowing who I am. When the plan went astray, I knew the next time I saw you, you might not know who I was."

"Did you know I wouldn't kill you?"

"No, but I hoped and had faith that you wouldn't." He stopped here, and searched my eyes for a moment. "Do you remember me? Anything at all?"

I searched him in return and eventually shook my head. "Nothing." *Though, there is something....*

A silence grew between us. We looked out beyond the road into the trees, the cicadas fading, the first traces of dawn lighting up the woods.

Mental, absolutely mental.

We needed to move on, but I couldn't tear myself away, and most disturbing, I was beginning to believe him.

"What's next?" I sighed. "Why exactly has Ember charged you with keeping me alive?"

Vail's eyes had the glint of a madman, which didn't seem like a good sign. "Understand, Stone, we have to carry on. We must build the counter alliance once again and finish what we started, to destroy Gemination. Believe me, Ember wanted nothing more."

"And why am I so crucial?"

"Other than Spade, we're the last two walking out around here free. And honestly, I can't do this alone. You're part of the alliance, part of this war."

"I'm part of Spade's striker team," I reminded him.

"In some ways." An odd smile appeared on Vail's face, and his voice took on that same obscure tone as before. "But it would be helpful if you remembered the other side as well."

All I could think to say was, "I can't go on borrowed memories."

Vail checked his watch. "Come on." He turned back toward the car. "We'll have an hour at the Sedition, no more. I assume we're going in there to find Spade, but don't mention Gemination or my name directly to him, and don't talk to anyone else."

CHAPTER 17

By the time we reached the Sedition, it was nearly six in the morning. I'd taken a few extra precautions to make absolutely sure we weren't being followed and herded into a trap.

"So, you've been here before? Inside?" I asked as I pulled up to the paper mill.

"No, but I've known where it is," he answered. "Just in case."

"In case of what?"

"Times like this," he said vaguely. "Ember brought me here a few weeks ago, right before the raid."

"Great."

I realized I hadn't really thought much about how I was going to get Vail inside unnoticed, especially without any form of identification, but the guard only gave me a form to fill out and sign. A conservative-looking young man wearing square glasses sat in the security booth, and he seemed completely uninterested in us. He gave the car a cursory sweep with his own bot tracker and waved us in.

I parked the Lincoln in the lot and led Vail in.

As soon as the wall slid shut behind us, he became extremely tense. "I'm a little claustrophobic," he whispered.

So he was an idiosyncratic human after all. "Not in here, you're not." We couldn't afford to draw any attention *at all*, not to mention *unnecessary* attention. "Relax. That's a direct order."

Luckily, few people milled about, the night shift still on duty. The changing of the guards wouldn't come for another hour, and I planned to be long gone before then.

As expected, but much to my dismay, Spade was already in his office waiting for me, so I pushed the door open just as I had after returning from the hospital.

Charlie Spade stood in the center of the room, mid-pace, a mad glint in his eyes, and something else: worry. He turned on me. "Stone, what the hell? I show up at the damn mid-town precinct three hours ago, which, by the way, is absolutely destroyed and —" He caught sight of Vail and stopped abruptly, and his jaw dropped open.

"I didn't do it," I said calmly.

"Oh yeah? Who then? Him?" He jerked his head at Vail.

"You know who," Vail said icily.

This seemed to shake Spade for a moment, but he quickly rebounded. "What the hell are you doing here? Have you completely lost it?"

"We need to talk," Vail said, and flicked his head towards the door.

"You." Spade pointed a finger at him. "You are leaving right now if you know what's good for you."

Vail shrugged. "I won't and I don't."

"Then you are going with my colleague here." Behind him, the young man with the square glasses from the guard booth appeared, leaning casually in the doorframe. "And you are not to say a *word*, you are to be silent as the grave, understood?"

For a second I thought it might turn ugly, and held my breath.

Spade's "colleague" was the only one completely unconcerned, yawning as though bored. He seemed a bit sociopathic to me.

But Vail only nodded and the young man moved forward to escort Vail to who knew where, one of the elusive holding cells probably. I had been right; the only question now was if I would be joining him shortly.

Vail jerked away from him. "I'll take myself out," he said, throwing me one last look that warned, *'Be careful,'* before he slammed the door.

Spade wheeled on me. "Stone! Where the hell did you find him?"

"*He* found *me*, and actually, Spade, he saved my life. I about got jumped by seven of them, and honestly, I don't know if I could have taken them by myself."

"That's very touching," he said cynically. "So... what... you brought him here for his reward? Don't you remember that you're not supposed to bring civilians here?"

"He already knew the location," I said patiently. "I didn't show him anything, and what else was I supposed to do? Wait for you downtown somewhere? You saw what happened. Also, he's not a civilian, and I think you know that." I stepped up to him. "I know you know him, Spade. I can see it in your eyes. Hearing you think isn't the only thing I'm capable of."

He deflected the question and threw his watch in front of my face. "What the hell are you going to tell the Heads? You have less than an hour until the review. This is extremely bad timing."

"Don't worry, I'll think of something," I said a little too quickly. I still wasn't going to that damn meeting, but I didn't want to give Spade's a heads-up. He'd lock me down for sure if he knew I planned to run, and with each second, it became more and more apparent where exactly I should run to.

He spoke in a voice barely a whisper, ominous. "This is dangerous, Stone, more dangerous than you could ever imagine." He looked up at the ceiling and grabbed his hair with both hands, a wild look about him: fear—something I'd never seen on Spade's face before. There was no doubt about Vail's importance, as I'd never seen anyone get a rise out of Spade like this. "I have to go... fucking damage control," he said abruptly, and furiously started for the door. "Again."

I called after him, his last chance to stop me from doing something rash. "What is in that hospital?" I asked again. "It's not even a hospital, is it?"

Spade wheeled around and grabbed my arm, sending a jolt through me. I'd only been grabbed like that twice, and both times I was in mortal peril. It triggered the memory of Mack's cold grip on my arm before he turned me into the only survivor of Indigo 11. A death grip like that is unforgettable.

He bent down and brought his lips very close to my ear. "Do not mention the hospital again. This is not the time or the place. Tread carefully. Just for once, do as I say," he begged. "And we might live."

His voice, so chilling, caused me to wonder if I should share his fear.

One thing was clear: while they were obviously not the best of friends, neither Vail nor Spade had any interest in telling me the truth about the hospital, which made my next decision quite easy.

With Vail preoccupied with the mystery of the square glasses, and Spade busy with "damage control," it was my one chance. While Spade covered my trail, pulling surveillance tracks from the last twenty minutes, no doubt, I found a new, clean set of scrubs in the laundry room, and a new car in the lot, and set back down the road from whence I came—back to the hospital.

CHAPTER 18

I chose what I judged to be the least trafficked entrance, with an employee going in or out roughly every ten minutes—ironically, the same door I'd fled from last time. To get into the heart of the hospital, I would have to pass through the stairwell where Ember had met his maker.

He lost consciousness, I reminded myself, remembering Vail's words, *so perhaps he is still alive.*

I had to know. I told Ember I would carry his dead body out, and I meant to do it. If it came to it, I'd wheel him back out on the gurney he'd come in on.

I took a deep breath and prayed that some force, whether divine or demonic, would allow me back inside the hospital, but I needn't have worried. Security was even easier this time, with no guard at the door, and my security key still worked. Seemed counterintuitive, but this was actually a common occurrence—security always dropped its defenses after a breach. Initially, it heightened, but after a few days or so of "normal activity," security subconsciously got lax, thinking that no one would dare another attempt so quickly.

I shivered as I passed the landing where Ember and I had our final conversation, half expecting a splatter of blood to still be on the wall as an ominous reminder, but the walls had been scrubbed clean. I cracked the door to the west wing and looked out to find the hall empty and eerily quiet.

Forward ho.

I hustled back to the data lab and began looking for information on medical procedures, recent deaths, anything that would tell me where Ember was or what had happened to him. It took me longer to hack in than Ember, but I eventually made it.

I felt their eyes before I heard anything.

"Looking for something?" a voice asked from behind me. It sounded strange, metallic.

I froze, fighting the impulse to turn around.

"Stand up and turn around slowly," another voice rasped, as though he had throat cancer.

I stretched my peripheral vision as far as it could go and judged there were about three or four of them, five at most. A click echoed as one of them thumbed the hammer of a gun back.

Not even an attempt at diplomacy; how barbaric. Well, when in Rome....

I curled my left hand around the object concealed in my sleeve, and glanced down at the .38 on my hip, as if to make sure it was still there. Then I stood and resolutely turned around, not so slowly. "You boys sure are sneaky."

More carbons, all right—no mistaking them. I thought briefly about how odd they looked: anything but inconspicuous. If they were actually clones, technology had a long way to go before they blended in.

"You'll be coming with us," the metallic voice said.

"Wait," I said, my voice dangerously soft. "Let me explain," I began, and then pulled the pin out of the flash-bang one handed and let it clatter to the floor. At the same time, I swiftly threw myself back onto the table I'd been sitting at only a moment before. I hooked the table with my right hand as I slid off and pulled it onto its side, using it as a shield. The monitor crashed to the floor, and I kicked it across the room to draw their attention away. Lying on the ground, I curled into a fetal position and stuffed two plugs from my shirt pocket into my ears and clapped my hands over them. Squeezing my eyes shut as tight as they would go, I brought my elbows together in front of my face.

The flash-bang grenade was meant to stun, not kill. It only temporarily disoriented those at close range, causing blindness and deafness for a few moments. It took five seconds from the time I dropped it to go off. Plenty of time for me but, I hoped, with the element of surprise, not enough time for them.

As soon as the grenade went off, which sounded to me like a muffled gunshot, I rolled over and glanced around the end of the table. Complete disorientation ensued as they careened around like men in a blinding sand storm, but it wouldn't last long. I'd have only a ten-second window, fifteen if I was lucky, before their senses righted themselves, so I pulled the revolver out of my belt and turned the room into a roar, dropping most of them with the first shots.

In any given situation, there is often the exception, as if part of the order of chaos, entropy. So it was now. One of the carbons opened fire and a searing pain exploded in my left shoulder. I ducked back behind the table, and then flipped it upright with a struggling effort. His next shot hit the top of the table, and I took out his knees from under the table, and when he dropped to the floor, I put a bullet in his head.

I picked myself up off ground and stumbled out of the lab. As badly as I had wanted to get back into the hospital, I now wanted out—the irony of the situation was tangible. I hastily wound a piece of cloth ripped from the back of a carbon around my arm, but the blood dripped from the tip of my elbow as I hugged my arm into my chest. The bullet had smashed head on into the deltoid muscle and embedded itself in the flesh, but I sure as hell wasn't going to dig it out like Vail had.

Out in the hallway, I weighed my options. I didn't have much time left before the blood loss put me out. The way I had come in was too far, I surely couldn't go out the front door in my condition, and I'd never make the back door. That left me only one choice: the stairwell directly centered between data and medical, which led to the basement—the stairwell Ember and I had originally chosen as our escape route until things went south. In the basement, I would at least have some protection, a place to hide where I could make a real dressing of some sort. From there, I'd make my way to the underground parking garage.

With the hospital schematics still fresh in my mind, I plunged down the stairs into the shadows, refusing to turn on any lights to aid what was surely coming from them, but once in the warren of dark halls, my cognitive ability began to malfunction and I lost my sense of direction, blindly moving forward. I placed one foot in front of the other, but I couldn't think of what came next. I came across several bare rooms that looked to me like prisoner holding cells, and stared into them blankly.

Why would there be prisoner holding cells in a hospital? Because this isn't just a hospital.

My peripheral vision grew dim and everything slowed, and not in the way that would be helpful to me. I became audibly aware of the laborious shallowness of my breath. The hall went sideways as I collapsed and began the descent into unconsciousness.

Nearly on the other side, someone bent over me. "Stone," a familiar voice said.

"Vail," I breathed. Even in my semi-conscious state, I recognized him.

"What the hell happened?" Through a dream, I felt him take my arm.

"Just let me lie here for a few days and I'll be fine," I mumbled. Sarcasm: my only ally in the face of death, or what felt like death. Sounds came in the hallway, which I vaguely identified as people drawing closer.

"Come on, you've got to get up." Vail helped me off the ground and pulled me along behind him. After some unknown length of time, he set me down against a wall and took the key from around my neck. "Stay here and stay awake." His footsteps faded away.

I fought to open my heavy eyelids and saw only blur out of them. I focused and managed to clear most of it, and took in my surroundings — just a dark hall, no orientation whatsoever.

A few seconds later, Vail came back, breathing heavily this time. He grabbed me around the waist and dragged me at breakneck speed down the hall. He busted through the door and daylight flooded.

Something exploded close by, and a ringing in my head followed. Then, the world faded, and I heard no more.

CHAPTER 19

I awoke, disoriented and numb, lying on my back in an infirmary, staring at a white ceiling. For a moment, I wondered why I was here. Then memories of the hospital flooded back and I saw the man, or non-man, that had blown my shoulder open. *Damn.*

A tiny pinprick marked the back of my right hand, where an IV had administered a drug, likely a sedative, a pain killer, or both. My shoulder, now cleanly dressed, ached, though distantly. I touched the wound tentatively, the flesh around it numb—local anesthesia, lidocaine.

Vail sat across the room, and it dawned on me that this wasn't just an infirmary, it was *the* infirmary, the Sedition Infirmary. *Fuck, it's all downhill from here.*

The door opened and Spade walked in. He and Vail had obviously been waiting, a bit anxiously, it seemed, for me to come around. I glanced at the clock on the wall: three p.m. I'd left for the hospital just before seven a.m., and I couldn't have been there for more than two hours. Had I been out that long?

"Striker Stone," Spade said grimly, coming beside me. "You don't know when to quit, do you?"

"Obviously not," I agreed, a bit depressed and embarrassed, to say the least. I hadn't done anything so unprofessional that had gone so wrong in years, maybe ever. "Have I really been out that long?"

Spade ran a hand through his hair nervously. "Your deltoid muscle took the full force of the bullet. We pulled it out."

"What do you mean 'we'?"

He rolled his eyes. "When I say 'we', I mean 'we.' I couldn't bloody well pull in a surgeon. We were trying *not* to draw attention."

"So, what the hell am I doing *here* then?" Vail might as well have let me bleed to death, the Sedition being no safer at this point. I'd have to go in for a review now, and I would not come back out.

Spade ignored me. "We dosed you up on morphine and Valium and removed the bullet. Well, Vail removed the bullet—turns out he makes a pretty damn good surgeon."

I eyed Vail, remembering how he'd dug that bullet out of his own flesh as though he were paring an apple.

Valium.... No wonder it had taken me so long to come around. "What was wrong with ketamine? Were you out?"

"I told you, Stone, we're not doctors. We didn't want to risk you waking up in the middle of it."

"Well, you certainly didn't have to worry about that," I said sarcastically.

"Or experiencing pain in your unconscious state," Vail added.

"Thanks for that," I said honestly, but the note of sarcasm had not left my voice.

Spade pulled up a chair by the bed and lowered his voice. "I've cut the monitors in here, but we're still going to keep it down."

"Cut the monitors? I wasn't aware you held that much authority."

"I don't." He sighed, the resignation in his voice unmistakable. "The hospital was the last place you should have gone. You're lucky you're not dead, but that's the least of your worries now. To the Heads, it will look like you've really gone rogue, skipping a review to go to the very place you're being reviewed for."

The way he talked about it, it seemed it hadn't happened yet. "Wait a minute... the Heads don't know I'm here?" I asked in a bare whisper, as though if spoken loudly, it would cause them to come storming into the infirmary and formally assassinate me.

Spade shook his head. "The Heads left when you ditched the review. I'd have put a bullet in you myself on that one, if you hadn't shown up with one." He laughed bitterly. "Vail decided this was the last place they'd look for you right now. So far, it's proven to have been a good choice. No alarm has been raised, I've made sure of it, and no one has contacted me about your most recent extracurricular activities, but it will come out soon."

"Well then, I shall rid them of myself first," I said defiantly, sitting up. "I quit."

"You know damn well you can't just quit," Spade said angrily, giving my good shoulder a shove, which put me flat on my back again. "Look at Ember, dead before he even handed in his resignation. They'll find you."

"Well, they've got some healthy competition now, don't they?" Despite all that had happened, I found this amusing. The Heads would be furious if someone beat them to my murder.

"What do you mean?" Spade asked slowly.

I looked at him incredulously. Was he still playing this game? "Uh, the carbons... those creepy bastards that keep trying to kill me.... According to him—" I jerked my head in Vail's direction and ignored his former instruction. "—Geminates."

"Oh, Christ!" Spade clapped a hand to his forehead.

"Don't play dumb," Vail said from across the room, and then gave me a harsh glance. "And you, shut up."

Spade shot him a daggered look. "Keep your voices down," he hissed, looking around wildly as if making sure no one else was in the room acting as a fly on the wall. He turned back to me. "We can talk, just not here."

"Where? And when?" If I didn't get an answer soon, there was no telling what would happen next—arson, most likely.

Spade cast me an icy stare. "When I say and where I say. I have a plan, and you'd better not screw it up. The Heads will be back within the hour, if they're not already milling about somewhere. I'm going to leave now. I need a few minutes to cover us. It's my curse. I'm too good at it, but I'll make sure we get the green all the way out. Leave in ten, but first put on some clean clothes and stock up on supplies." He gestured to my arm. "We can't risk a med bot in there, so you're going to have to heal the old-fashioned way, on your own." He set down a keycard on the table in front of me. "There's an elevator at the back of one of the walk-in fridges in the kitchen, the one on the right."

"An elevator?" *How did I not know that?*

"Pay attention," he hissed. "Take the elevator down to the 3rd level of the parking deck. I'll be waiting for you at my car, a white VW Golf. If I'm not there or don't arrive within five minutes, steal it, as you've clearly no problem doing, and go." He stood and headed for the door.

It then dawned on me how far this had gone. I'd somehow held out hope that this whole situation could be righted, but I'd made that choice when I let Bishop walk away from me last night.

"This is it, then. I'm never coming back, am I?" I asked when he was half way to the door.

He turned back around, his eyes pleading with me to listen. Not just pleading; it was desperate. It gave me chills, as he was not a man that pleaded with anyone or acted out of desperation. I realized then that I might be completely fucked, no matter what, with or without him. He gave a slight shake of his head. "Not on your own terms. Don't look back."

I only nodded and dropped my gaze to the floor. The onset of an unidentified emotion rose within me, neither good nor bad, but if the emotional cauldron boiled over this time, I wasn't sure what would happen. I quickly rubbed my eyes and the emotion dissolved. Compartmentalization certainly came in handy sometimes.

Spade stalked out of the room.

Vail still sat across the room staring at me curiously, with a hint of wonder.

"What?" I asked, a little annoyed, though I shouldn't have been, considering I'd have been dead without him, maybe now Ember's neighbor in the morgue. Or worse.

"I thought you never got shot."

What a bizarre fucking comment. "Huh, well, first time for everything, you know," I said cynically.

He walked over and took the seat Spade had been sitting in, and we stared at each other in silence for a bit—for some reason, I was determined not to look away first. "What were you looking for?" he finally asked, dropping his gaze to the floor.

I snapped my fingers in his line of vision. "You know exactly what I was looking for."

He looked up sharply. "Listen, even if you did find Ember, you would not find the man you once knew. You don't want to find him alive, Stone. Trust me."

"What the hell does that mean?" At this point, I knew there wasn't much chance in it, but I wanted to find Ember alive more than anything.

He glanced up at the clock on the wall, said, "Seven minutes," then stood and left the room.

"God damn it," I muttered, left there by myself. "Now what? Am I even awake? Or have I gone totally insane?" *Yes and no.*

I sat for another minute testing my shoulder— limited range of motion. True to what Spade had said, I was dosed pretty good, so no pain. *Fine by me.*

I swung out of the bed, wobbling slightly as I stood up. I dressed one-handed, my second set of clean scrubs for the day, though these were navy blue instead of white, and paid a visit to the medicine cabinet to stock a small backpack with dressings and pain medication, anything I might need for my arm in the next week or two. I wiped out the entire supply of liquid morphine but left the Valium behind—no way I could function on that. I ransacked the drawer next to the refrigerator and grabbed all of the epinephrine, injectors, and ampoules. It always came in handy down the line.

Like when you're frozen in limbo, my mind said, thinking of that last day with Ember. The image of him on the gurney invaded my mind: the jet-black hair, the skin tinged blue from cyanosis. How ironic that I witnessed him as a dead man on the day he died, but *before* he died. He at least wore death well.

I slung the backpack over my good shoulder and slowly walked out of the room. *One foot in front of the other, keep your balance, nonchalant and inconspicuous.*

The Sedition buzzed loudly in the full swing of the day but, absorbed in their own tasks, no one paid any attention to me. Seemingly, no one knew anything was amiss. I kept walking, slow and steady toward the kitchen. I didn't know where the hell Vail had gone. *Fine time to disappear.*

The kitchen, mercifully empty at this hour, sat farthest away from the employee entrance, which unnerved me quite a bit. If Spade's key didn't work, I'd have to walk the gauntlet to get out of here. I pulled out the key, held it up to the sensor in front of the giant, silver cooler door, and held my breath. A click registered as it unhinged, and I exhaled with relief, stepped into the cold room, and breathed out frosted air. A couple of chairs sat in the middle of the room, a drain on the floor between them—no food at all; the fridge was a complete decoy. This was probably where the Sedition interrogated people, brought them up through the elevator and into a cold room to make them sweat.

The elevator sat in the very back behind a curtain, to which Spade's magical key again gave me access. The silver doors opened, but before my foot hit the elevator floor, movement to my right made me jump.

Vail stepped in immediately after me, just a fraction of a second behind, as close to me as my own shadow.

"Christ, Vail!" I whispered. I hadn't even noticed him behind me, which was strange. Was I that drugged?

"Sorry," he said. "Not like I have a pass to get out."

"Well, perhaps we should have gone together. Where did you go, anyway?" I pressed the P3 button, 3rd level of the parking deck.

He didn't answer, and we both stood inside the elevator awkwardly staring at each other, while some blasted Muzak chirped away in the background.

Elevator music to relax the captives? Get them into the mood to reveal?

It seemed an eternity before the P3 button lit up and the doors slid apart. Vail nodded, and we walked toward the back of the parking deck where a rather beat-up-looking Golf sat in the corner.

Spade sat behind the wheel, the car not running, and rolled down the windows as we approached. "You in the front," he said to me. "You in the back," he told Vail.

I got in and buckled my seat belt, such a ridiculous, mundane action given the seriousness of it all, as if I were going on a field trip or something.

Vail's clicked in the back.

"Not a word," Spade said, and I nodded an affirmation. He started the car, backed out of his space, and began to ascend the ramp, spiraling several times. We came up inside one of the paper mill's garages, and Spade clicked a button on his key chain to open the garage door, and turned toward the security booth.

I held my breath and looked straight ahead. There would be a different guard on duty at this time of the day, one who would perhaps not be so lenient and would insist on identification from all parties in the car.

Spade rolled down his window just enough to slip his hand out and onto the scanner. The guard smiled and waved him on, Spade nodded in return. He rolled forward and took a right out of the paper mill, bringing us back to the highway.

We drove in silence for several miles. Spade constantly flicked his eyes to the rearview mirror, but no alarm registered in them, meaning no one followed us.

I finally broke the silence. "So, I'm unofficially on the run."

Spade immediately turned on the radio, declining to speak.

For a few moments, we all listened to some horrid, unbefitting pop song, where the world is all players and haters. If only it were that simple.

When I could bear it no longer, I switched it off. "Why? Why am I on the run for something Ember did?"

Spade kept his eyes on the road in front of him. "Because you are loyal to him, and the Sedition is no longer a friend of Ember's. This is the beginning of a long time coming. There's a massive shift going on among the Heads — been happening for a while. They're starting to split into two camps, and one group is much bigger than the other, but no matter what the outcome, there will be no victors from this. We will all lose something. Ember was the first to die, but I guarantee he won't be the last."

If Ember was dead because of some high-level bickering, I swore to myself I'd bring an end to it, and swiftly — an end by lead poisoning.

Quiet for a moment, Spade looked over at me and began a briefing, as he'd done with me nearly every day for the past five years. "The Sedition is enemy ground for you now and they will be hunting you. All I can do is to give you a good head start." He looked in the rear-view mirror at Vail. "Both of you. I have left Colvin and Hamlin specific instructions, and they should be able to give you at least twenty-four hours."

Both of you. The way Spade had said it, it sounded like Vail and I were supposed to go on the run together. Had that been Ember's original plan? Meet up with Vail after the hospital? If Ember had been alive, with me, I'd have felt better, but truthfully, I didn't want to be on the run at all. The Sedition had been my home, for good or ill. Suddenly terrified of being with this so-called Vail, I glanced at him in the backseat staring out the window. I didn't know him, and he hadn't said a word thus far. Panic crept into my periphery, and I quickly beat it back. Emotional involvement would not help.

Spade let out a long sigh and muttered under his breath, "Jesus," and let his head fall back into the headrest.

"What?"

He groaned. "I had this same damn conversation with Ember two weeks ago."

Finally, I knew with certainty the reason for his odd behavior when I'd returned to the Sedition without Ember. *He already knew.* "He told you he was leaving. I thought so."

Spade nodded. "Understand, I couldn't tell you before. Our cover depended on it. The Sedition may officially be a mostly bot-free zone, but you never know."

Ironically, the advances in nanotech had rendered places like the Sedition incapable of using that same technology in their inner sanctums. There were four types of bots: cyber, intelligence, medical, and security, each with a different task and frequency, but there was no way to distinguish between a foreign and domestic bot, so everyone played it safe with the old-school surveillance systems, cameras, and tracks. They allowed only med bots and security bots, with security bots responsible for sweeping the house clean of cyber and intel bots.

"This car may even be bugged, but I doubt that." As if testing his theory, he banged on the dashboard with his fist.

Vail pulled out his bot tracker, much more pragmatic.

Our cover. Vail had said it, but I wanted to hear it from Spade's mouth. "You were in on it, weren't you? Ember's grant?" I looked back at Vail. "All three of you, actually."

"Yeah," Spade affirmed, as he exchanged an uncomfortable glance with Vail in the rearview mirror.

"So, what was the grant?"

Spade shook his head. "I will tell you soon, Stone, but not here."

"You know, Ember said the same thing." For all I knew, the carbons targeted us right now, and the next altercation would leave Vail and Spade dead, and me with no sources of information. I had two *right now.*

"It has to be," Spade answered rigidly.

I knew better than to press him. "When, then, and where are we going?" From what I could tell, we were skirting the city in a great arc.

"A safe house. Vail and I will bring you up to speed there."

"How long?"

"An hour or so. Get some rest. You're going to need it."

I happily nodded in agreement, and pulled a syringe and an ampoule of morphine out of the confiscated backpack. My arm ached again, so I injected myself through the same vein on the back of my hand, and then laid my seat back. The last thing I saw before dozing off was Vail looking down at me with those wild blue eyes. Right as my eyelids shut for the final journey into dreamland, he became Ember.

CHAPTER 20

Hospital. Empty. Silent. I'm clad in white, *running through white corridors looking for Ember. The sterility of the lighting blinds me. I reach the doors of the morgue and enter against my will, an unseen force driving me, a phantom. A ledger hangs on the wall to the left, holding the names of those entombed. As I scan down the list of names, one I don't recognize stops me, but I know that it's Ember's real name. It tells me which compartment he's in. I know how this ends.*

I try to flee the morgue but am compelled to go on. I have no choice but to open the drawer that holds him. My shaking hands pull the tray out, and Ember lies on top, looking exactly like he did when we first came here, when he was simulating death. Now he is really dead. The irony of it hits me.

Mysteriously released from the phantom's hold, I turn to walk away. I've only made it a few steps when an icy hand wraps around my wrist. I pull away and turn towards the hand simultaneously.

Ember's blue eyes are wide open and his fingers, so cold, hold my wrist in a near death grip. I can't speak, but he can. He breathes out frosted air as he says, "Pay attention to the name."

The door behind me swings open, and footsteps echo as someone or something enters the room, but before I can turn around, the light switch clicks, and an instant later the room plunges into darkness.

CHAPTER 21

I awoke in a dimly lit parking garage, under a dilapidated apartment building on the southern edge of the city, or so my internal compass told me.

"The Sedition went all out for this one," I said sarcastically, squinting as I gazed around. "I see where all my money has been going." The neon glare of the fluorescent tubing hurt my eyes, reminded me of the hospital.

"Oh, it's not the Sedition's. This one is all mine," Spade said proudly. He got out of the car, walked around to open my door for me, and extended a hand down.

I stared up at him, suspicious, as this wasn't like him. "Well, well, I guess chivalry isn't dead." I took his hand and he pulled me to my feet. "Why do you have a personal safe house?"

"Because I'm smart," he answered haughtily. He went to the trunk and took out a large and heavy duffel bag.

I stood and stretched, and noticed Vail on the other side of the car doing the same thing.

"What's in the bag?" he asked Spade.

"The last resort," Spade answered. "Come on."

We climbed the stairwell to the fifth floor and turned left at the top of the stairs. It was a damned noisy building, the tenants all in a constant state of either fighting or partying. The first door on the left stood wide-open, harsh music blasting out of it. A fat, bald punk in a wife beater, with tattoos all over his neck and head, stood in the doorway talking to someone presumably in the living room, but he looked drugged out of his mind, and very well may have been talking to himself. He leered at me as I walked by, but I was too tired to care. Farther down, a woman screamed inane profanities, accompanied by simultaneous shattering, as though she were throwing dishes against a wall. Then there were the obvious sounds of a couple screwing.

Classic. God help the children who grow up in this place.

Spade fished a key out of his pocket and opened the door to apartment 505, though a key was hardly necessary; a little bit of force could easily have broken the rusted lock and busted down the thin door. Spade grinned. "I left everything the same so the place would not arouse suspicion."

The inside matched the outside, repulsive and shabby. Walls that had once been white were now off-white — *way* off-white. The apartment door opened into a small and grimy kitchen with hideous orange counters and dull yellow appliances. A round wooden table and four chairs with peeling varnish sat in the middle of the room on top of a sagging, yellowing linoleum floor. Green shag carpeting lay straight ahead beyond the archway to the living room. God knew what lived in that. An open door to the right led into the bathroom and, by extension, the bedroom.

Vail pulled his little bot tracker out again.

"Well, it worked. No bugs, huh, Spade?" I glanced at Vail, and he nodded an affirmation.

"No, not necessary, other than the bugs already living here, of course."

Spade, the comedian.... I rolled my eyes.

He slid the duffel under the table with a metallic clunk, and pulled three of the busted chairs closer to the kitchen table. "Sit," he said amiably, as if the three of us were about to have afternoon tea.

Vail and I both dropped into chairs, causing the seats to slant a little further and the floor to sag a little more.

Spade then filled three glasses from the tap and set a glass of water in front of everyone. "Hydrate," he commanded, a little more harshly.

Vail and Spade remained eerily quiet, sipping their glasses of water absurdly.

I held mine up to the light and examined the contents, the water remarkably clear from having come through such rusted pipes, or so I assumed, as this was an extremely old building and I doubted upkeep was a high priority. It was perhaps the only thing out of character. I gulped my glass down and set it back on the table with a little more force than I meant to use, and the glass shattered, causing Vail and Spade to wince. The drugs had made me clumsy, but I couldn't just blame it on that; my nerves were completely and utterly shot. I swept the broken shards into a little pile and then sat there for only a moment before charging in like a cutthroat CEO.

"Okay," I said. "Listen, before either of you says anything, I would like to make a few things clear. One, you are going to tell me what I want to know. Two, I would appreciate it if the two of you would stop talking in riddles. It's making me crazy. Three, you will begin with telling me what the fuck is going on in that god-damned hospital. Everyone seems to know but me, and if you don't tell me, I will find a way to go back in there and find out for myself, or die trying." I paused for effect. "Again."

"That's actually not a bad idea," Spade said. "Then I won't feel so guilty when the Sedition kills you."

"That's not funny," Vail growled.

"They're going to kill you too." Spade gave Vail a cold look. "And probably me. We're all pretty much fucked at this point." He looked accusingly at Vail and slowly spun his glass around on the table. "How do I know you are who you *say* you are?"

"You don't," Vail said indifferently. "And I can't prove it to you."

"And who is it *you're* supposed to be?" I interrupted.

Spade and Vail both regarded me with pitying eyes, which made my blood boil.

"This really isn't the best way, you know," Spade spoke to Vail. "Can't you... you know... like was done before."

"Be my guest," Vail said, with a theatric flourish of his arm in my direction.

Spade huffed. "What do you mean, *be my guest*? I can't do it."

"Well, neither can I."

"What the fuck?" Spade's voice dripped with disbelief. He and Vail looked at each other for a while, clearly communicating telepathically. "How can it be that neither of us knows how?"

"Do you think that if I knew how, we'd be in this situation? With bullet holes in two out of three of us?" Vail asked sarcastically.

"Why would Ember leave us in the dark on this one?"

"It doesn't matter," Vail said bluntly. "It is what it is, and she hasn't been sleeping anyway. Even if we knew how, we couldn't."

I nearly gasped involuntarily. How the hell did Vail know I hadn't been sleeping? And what the hell did that have to do with anything? *Everything.*

Vail threw a cautious eye in my direction and took a deep breath. "I waited for her to make contact, sure Ember had given her some sort of instruction, but she never showed. I had to grab her at the last minute before they did. So, we'll have to tell her like this." Vail spoke low to Spade, his mouth hanging open, beyond stunned. "Listen," he whispered. "Ember is gone and she's in the open now. We need to think about what to do next."

"And just what the hell is it that neither of you can do?" I interrupted again.

They ignored me.

"This is suicide," Spade warned.

"So be it." Vail's face was grave. "What else can we do?"

"We walk away," Spade said definitively. "Disappear."

"No, the 19 moves forward. We're only down two." Vail looked at me with such intensity that I became extremely uncomfortable. "Well, one and a half, and we can get that half back with time."

"Down two?" Spade mocked. "The entire 19 is entombed in that hospital, or what's left of them."

Vail shook his head. "We can get them back. They're alive."

"No, we walk away," Spade snapped. "It's over. We tried, we failed, and we accept this. Ember is dead, and if we don't want to meet that same fate, we close up shop: new names, new faces, new countries. I've tied up all the loose ends."

"Ember died for this," Vail said patiently.

"That's very romantic of you," Spade said cynically. "What the hell do you think this is?"

"What's your solution, then? Look over your shoulder while you're running for the rest of your life? How is that even a remote possibility? Stand still for even a moment and *they'll* find you. You won't be able to get comfortable and hide somewhere. None of us will."

Vail had hit home, as yet another thing I'd never seen lit up in Spade's eyes: defeat.

"Besides, if it's over, then we're *all* over." Vail paused and looked at me again, searching. "Her death warrant has been signed, more than once, especially after the incident."

My shoulder ached at the memory of my most recent trip to the hospital, and I fought the impulse to inject another little vial of morphine. I was making my best attempt to follow, but despite my orders, the riddle speaking had not stopped. Morphine would not help.

Vail continued on. "So, I'll ask you this: are you coming with us, or are you going to turn tail?" He waited a long moment and then said, "We need you, Spade. This is why you went to work for the Sedition in the first place—same reason Ember did, same reason she did." He nodded at me.

"Protect life, destroy evil," Spade muttered absently, running a hand over his face. "Well, here's the first of the big decisions that will result in imminent death. How do you propose we do this?"

"First, we lay it all out for her. Everyone else knows who she is. It's time we let Leyla Stone in on it. Then we make a new game plan."

"Wait a damn minute." I held up my hands. "Let *me* in on it? Let *me* in on *my* own life?" I felt a mental break coming on. I watched Spade roll this option around in his head and became infuriated, about to burst out of my skin. "I don't have time for you to think," I finally said. "Is it true, Spade? All the *nonsense* coming out of his mouth?"

Spade sighed and resignation settled on his face. "It's all true, every word of it."

I threw my hands in the air and crossed them, leaned back in the chair, and broke a spindle behind my back. "Okay, then like the madman who isn't mad said, *lay it out for me*, in great detail."

Vail is telling the whole *truth. Un-fucking-believable!*

"Great detail," Spade repeated, his eyes widening slightly. "Where do we even begin?"

"Well, the most pressing thing," I began sarcastically, "is what the hell you two are talking about, and why I don't understand any of it. How am I involved in something I don't know about? And don't tell me it's fucking amnesia or repressed bullshit something-or-other. I remember every god-damned second of my life here, and I've had plenty of reasons to repress or to forget, but I never have. There's not one gap... not one." I waited.

Spade ran his fingers through his hair and said, "It's complicated." He finally looked up at me. "Very complicated."

My eyes tried their best to burn a hole the size of a smoking crater into his mind. "Try me."

"Go on, Spade," Vail urged.

CHAPTER 22

Spade first rose and refilled his water glass. I didn't know if he was stalling, but he was definitely nervous, that much I could tell. The slightest tremor moved through his hands, and I reflected on how unusual his behavior had been in the last few days. In the five years I'd known him, I'd never seen him like this. He'd always been so even-keeled.

He sat back down and turned his chair to face me, then leaned forward and rested his elbows on his knees. "There are two parts to this."

"Pick one," I enunciated a little too clearly.

Spade stared at me icily. "I'm getting to that. Are you going to be quiet and let me talk?"

Fine. I glared at him.

Spade looked from me to Vail, and back again. He took a deep breath, blew it out, and his hands stilled. "Population control... it's all about population control. War, I mean. Few wars occur naturally. Yes, it's part of the human condition to fight, but most war is contrived, in order to reduce our planet's population and to gain control over our most valuable resource. The reasons are all just propaganda."

"As in natural resources? Oil? Natural gas?" I thought of all those crazy million-dollar-cowboys out there fracking—modern day gold mining.

"No, you're thinking a little too literally. Think about what really keeps the system running. The most important *current* resource on this planet has very little to do with what was already on it. In this day and age, our most valuable natural resource is...." He paused here to let me fill in the blank.

I narrowed my eyes at him, in no mood for being treated like a student.

"Us," he said plainly. "Humans. Our most valuable natural resource is human life. There are now over nine billion humans on Earth, and the world is multiplying, and multiplying fast."

And then suddenly, Spade gave me a history lesson. I don't know what I expected, but it wasn't that.

"In 1350, at the end of the Great Famine and Black Death, world population was 370 million. It has continued to grow since then, picking up speed like a runaway freight train. It wasn't until 1804 that the world population reached one billion. It was another one hundred and twenty-three years before it reached two billion in 1927, but it took only thirty-three years to reach three billion in 1960. Four billion a mere fourteen years later in 1974, five billion in 1987, six billion in 1999, seven billion in 2011, eight billion in 2024, nine billion in 2037. We're now roughly a decade past that and we haven't slowed down."

I had to admit that did seem like an accelerated world growth rate, but failed to see the point.

Spade continued. "Now, it used to be that the days of divide and conquer kept the population down, but we've become a bit too civilized." He said this last part with a trace of an English accent, and I wondered if Spade might actually be British. My eyes again fell on his faux wedding band. "Acts of genocide aren't quite so common, nor are they accepted as acts of divine will. The age where kings were regarded as gods is over. War is now engineered by an elitist group."

"Like the Sedition?" I asked with a note of revulsion, surprised at how quickly I had turned on them.

"Not quite. I'm talking about the elitist of the elite."

The elitest of the elite? I snorted. "Don't tell me it's the fucking Illuminati and we're the Dragon Family," I scoffed, close to retracting my earlier statement about Vail not being a madman. If the conversation was heading in that direction, I would take my chances with the Sedition.

He leaned closer to me. "Oh, they're real all right, they're just not called the Illuminati, a clever diversion."

My mind spun. "It's the fucking Russians then, isn't it?" I always knew the world's underdog would come back around. I had become fluent in Russian for that express purpose.

"No," he said bluntly. "It's not a border matter."

I leaned even closer, not to hear him better, but in defiance. "Who are they, then?" I mocked.

A satisfied smile lit up his face. "That's the problem. *They.* No one knows who *they* are, yet we talk about it all the time. We use the word *they* so often in daily life, without even knowing to whom we're really referring. Do me a favor one day: pay attention and count how many times you use the word *they* in any given sentence. Most people would say that *they* are the government." He laughed. "That gives the government entirely too much credit. Those fools couldn't organize their way out of a paper bag, which, as you know, is why the Sedition exists in the first place."

They? This all still sounded pretty paranoid to me. I glanced over at the door and tried to determine whether I could overpower both of them and get out of here.

Spade continued. "The real *they* make no public appearances. *They* are the puppeteers behind the scenes, pulling the strings of politics, economics, globalization, you name it. *They* are the parent company of the parent company of the parent company. There only a handful of people that rule this world. We're not in Washington because of the western governments. We're in Washington because *they* control the governments." He again went back to the history lesson. "Now, the old *they* were fairly public. You know them as Rockefeller, Carnegie, Hyde, Vanderbilt, Morgan, Warburg, DuBignon... to name a few. The Jekyll Island boys laid the foundation of the system we're currently entrenched in today, started the Federal Reserve, all that good stuff. The *they* of today, however, are far more private and far more international. Some of the big names are the same, but for the most part, we don't know who *they* are. We call *them* the Faction."

"The Faction," I repeated to myself, almost involuntarily, and something in the name clicked inside my head. I searched my database of past grants and came up with nothing, but if not from there, where? I felt a flutter of movement behind my eyes, but as quick as it came, it stilled. I shook my head, chalked it up to being beyond tired and confused.

Vail cocked his head and looked at me strangely.

"The Faction," Spade said again, as though he knew what was happening in my brain and trying to root it there. "*They* have done an excellent job of making you think you're free, that you have power over your daily life, that you have choice. All *they* have really done is brainwashed you to insert yourself into the forty-hour work week to chase the almighty dollar, and then to pump every cent of it right back into *their* system on the weekend. This starts when you're a child, going to school Monday through Friday like a good soldier, having the weekend off. Before long you're another worker drone. You don't question, you just do your job and pretend you don't hate it. You pretend that it's important, and it *is* important, but to whom and why? To the Faction, your job is important because you're the cog that turns the wheel, or the hamster that turns the wheel, to be more precise."

The tremor in his hands returned, and his voice rose as he picked up speed. "You spend your so-called free time shopping where everyone else shops, those uniform strip malls where everything you 'need' is conveniently all in the same place, at a handful of different stores, but even that is an illusion. Different stores?" He shook his head. "No, all the same. The parent company of the parent company of the parent company owns them all. Monopolies are illegal? That's bullshit. The world is one big monopoly." Spade was fully rambling at this point. "You get home from your job and plop yourself in front of a box designed for your complacent entertainment, until you fall asleep, and then you wake up and do it all over again. Anytime your body or mind tries to tell you something is wrong, *their* pharmaceutical industry pumps you full of toxic, tissue-damaging drugs to keep you numb, docile, and dependent."

Spade paused here and drummed his fingers on the table, talking to himself. "Actually, *they've* got a pretty clever form of slave labor going on. Well, I guess *they* had to come up with something after the abolition of—"

"Get off your soap box, Charlie," I cut him off. "You're preaching to the converted here. That's why I work—" I again noticed Vail looking at me curiously, and I corrected myself. "—worked... for the Sedition. I'm well aware of men in black suits."

Spade raised his hands. "No, you don't understand. These are not just men in black suits. These are *the* men in *the* black suits." The rant clearly wasn't over. "You vote and have the choice over who's president?" He shook his head. "It's the illusion of choice. This is no democracy. Hell, it's not even a constitutional federal republic anymore."

"You sound like an anarchist, Spade."

He shook his head vehemently. "No, I'm the opposite, I'm a patriot. The choice between the lesser of two evils is not a choice, especially when it's between two men, both controlled by the same faction, *the* Faction," he repeated emphatically. "The Sedition's main enemy."

I looked at him dubiously. "Main enemy? Really? Why have I never heard about the Faction?"

Spade returned my stare just as suspiciously. "You know the answer to that, Striker. Hear no more than you need to hear."

"See no more than you need to see," continued Vail.

"Speak no more than you need to speak," I finished—the Sedition's unofficial mantra, a spin on Japan's three wise monkeys. "Of course, in your case, it is tell no more than you need to tell."

Spade shot me a cold look. "Returning to population control... there are too many people in the developed world."

I tried to bring the focus back to reason. "Listen, we've thought this for centuries, that there are too many of us, that the Earth won't be able to support us. Isn't it human nature to think that the end is nigh?"

He nodded in agreement. "It's true that we always think the end is coming, but even that human trait has been exploited. Actually, directed is a better word for it. The media, which operates hand in hand with the Faction, tells us everything we need to think, what we should like, but mostly what we need to be afraid of. This greatest fear is presented in different ways, but at its heart, it's always the same. We are to fear *each other*, the true divide and conquer. On top of that, infuse us with a little paranoia... and we enthusiastically become sheeple."

"And conspiracy theory?" I raised an eyebrow.

"Also a manipulation. The Faction's greatest power lies not in stopping or squashing rumor and dissonance, but in perpetuating it. *They* are like cancer, absorbing whatever energy comes at it and growing stronger. *They* don't deny conspiracy theory. They use it to their advantage. Anytime someone gets close to the truth and starts spouting it, *they* spin it, hype it up, make it a movement, make it a protest. The media goes crazy, people go crazy, like sharks in a feeding frenzy, but after a little while, the media slyly shifts its attention and, with the ever-decreasing attention span of the developed world, the hype wears off, and it's on to the next big thing." He snapped his fingers. "It's like clockwork, and every now and then, *they* throw out some biblical stuff to please the bible thumpers — a few prophets, some rapture-like stuff."

At the mention of religion, I felt a bible thumper rant coming on, and wasn't sure if I could handle it.

Mercifully, Spade bypassed that topic. "But what I'm talking about is something different. This idea of population control is not in reaction to some kind of scarcity fear. The Faction is not creating war to reduce the planet's population because *they* think the Earth can't handle us. There's a much more immediate problem. This is about control—control of the world, not the end of the world—and time is running short, relatively speaking. The masses of the developed worlds are starting to wake up. People are starting to piece the Faction's system together, and they're realizing that they're not as free as they think. Before long, there will be too many *awake* people for the Faction to control. So, the Faction is making a pre-emptive strike to stop the problem before it even becomes one, to maintain control. *They* are starting a war, and Gemination is the army."

"I don't quite follow... the army against what?"

Spade said it so softly, I almost didn't hear him. "Free will."

"How can you launch a war on free will?"

"Very subtly," Spade said in a bare whisper.

An awkward pause followed, and I used it as an excuse to go the bathroom. I had to be alone for a few minutes or something bad was going to happen, as in, something was probably going to catch on fire. The faulty wiring in the building would finally spark to life or the refrigerator would melt down or the toaster would blow up... it was about that time.

I took my bag with me and sat on the floor on some filthy rug, my back against the sink cabinets, feet on the smudged and dented wall in front of me, finally breaking down and shooting up with some morphine like a junkie. I'd shot up a lot of stuff before, but this was the first time I felt like I needed it, both physically and mentally.

I relaxed immediately, never happier to stare at a wall in all my life. It was blank, a canvas on which to paint anything. I leaned back and closed my eyes, trying to absorb Spade's speech by osmosis. A war on free will? I knew what that looked like: communism, fascism, subtle and cunning. But what Spade talked about was more than that; it was apocalyptic. The part about the Faction really wasn't so hard to believe—another clandestine organization of the same caliber, only on the far end of the spectrum, the Sedition's archenemy. I just thought that perhaps, since I was the field agent, the Heads would have given me every advantage in knowing who I was dealing with. Their effectiveness depended on it.

Guess I was wrong. Very wrong.

CHAPTER 23

He rolled to his side and spat out a bloody glob. Pain shot through his head and he tried to open his eyes, but they were either gone or the room pitch black. He lay on something soft, his arms unrestrained. He felt along its sides and found them narrow, like a hospital bed. He was about to wonder where he was when he realized something even more out of place; he was *alive*.

John Ember tentatively felt down his chest, finding patches of stickiness all over the place—*five* patches. He felt under a shirt that wasn't his, and found his torso tightly wrapped in very thick gauze. The stickiness was blood seeping through the gauze. He knew better than to try to stand up, as that would tear every wound open as fresh as they day they'd been made, whenever that was. He had no sense of time. The bleeding was minimal at the moment, and could be handled, so long as he was careful.

A blinding light clicked on overhead and he heard a door open. He breathed a sigh of relief that his eyes still sat in their sockets and his ears worked. His three most important senses still functioned; he could deal without the other two. Footsteps drew closer, the scraping sound of a chair being dragged across the floor just behind them, followed by a shuffling of papers, and then the door closed. He kept his eyes squeezed shut and then slowly allowed light in, little by little. It seemed he had gone a long time without it.

Steadily, the haze lifted and he lay staring at the man who'd surely put him here: a Sedition man.

Ember slowly pushed himself to a sitting position, and blood began to trickle down his chest. "How in the hell am I alive?" he asked, regretting it instantly; it hurt to talk. Not only was his voice hoarse and his throat raw, but the words coming from inside him vibrated against the wounds, pressing on them uncomfortably.

"We've got good surgeons. We could keep anyone alive, short of a decapitation." The man tossed him a clean towel.

Ember caught it with a grimace and wiped the blood off his mouth. "Modern day Frankenstein.... How long have I been out?"

"Over a week."

"What happened to her?"

"Your 'nurse'?" The Sedition man mocked. "Oh, she's fine, but we've got a problem."

"Thank you, Captain Obvious." Ember smirked. "Only one?"

"Her other half has gone completely off the grid. The Sedition hasn't figured it out yet, but she's definitely gone dark."

"Well, it's not like they're all that bright."

The man smiled. "We'll change that soon enough."

"Yes, I'm sure we will."

"Are you ready?" As if awaiting the words, the door opened and one of the staff brought in a wheelchair.

Ember smiled genuinely in return, and a trickle of blood ran off his teeth, making him feel like a cannibal. "As sure as the day I was born."

CHAPTER 24

I'd fallen asleep — no idea for how long — and awoke to the faint sounds of struggle coming from beyond the bathroom door. I achingly got to my feet, feeling twice my age. I was about to step out of the bathroom, thinking Vail and Spade had finally gone at it, when it dawned on me that there were more than two voices outside, and footsteps quickly approaching the bathroom door. I shook the morphine cloud off as best I could, quickly stepped behind the mildewed shower curtain, and pulled it a quarter closed, just enough to hide.

The bathroom door opened and I braced myself. The footsteps drew closer, but then the person opened the door to the bedroom, and the footsteps faded.

Amateur! Didn't even look behind the shower curtain.

"Where is she?" a voice asked from the living room.

Silence ensued, followed by a dull smack.

I peeked around the shower curtain to see the door leading to the kitchen now wide open, and Spade's cache of firearms under the kitchen table grabbed my attention — *the last resort,* now my first resort. I stepped out of the shower, crept up to the bedroom door, and spied through the bedroom into the living room.

Two carbons had Vail and Spade pinned, one each, while a third stood in the middle of the living room with his back to me, asking questions.

I caught Vail's eye, and then quietly closed the gap to the kitchen.

Vail started to struggle wildly as a diversion, provoking another beating.

I bent my will to be as invisible and silent as possible, crawled to the kitchen table, and dragged the bag of guns back to the bathroom with me. I swiftly took out four guns, and shoved two of them into the backside of my pants, gangbanger style. I stepped into the bedroom and then glanced into the living room.

Spade sat on the couch, his carbon towering over him and pointing a gun at the back of his head. Behind him, pinned against the wall, a trickle of fresh blood ran down Vail's forehead, dripping into his eyes, a gun dug in under his chin, a carbon finger on the trigger. I would have shot the bastard in the back of the head, but I worried its gun would go off and send Vail to the Promised Land.

Instead, I stood in the doorframe and leveled the two guns in my hands at Vail's carbon and the interrogator standing in the middle of the room. My shoulder screamed, but I ignored it. "Put the guns down," I said calmly. "And don't turn around." The opposite of what they'd said in the hospital.

For a moment, no one moved or spoke. "Put the fucking guns down," I tried again. *What am I going to do if they don't?*

"Miss Stone, I presume," the interrogating carbon said. "Boys, you heard the lady."

Both guns went down on the floor.

"Kick them to the side," I ordered.

Both guns clattered against the wall.

"Your turn," the one in the middle mocked.

"Not a chance."

"Too bad you don't have a third arm," he sneered.

I smiled. "All I need is one."

"Not with us," he said darkly. He spun on his heels to face me.

Vail launched himself into his carbon, and Spade dove off the couch for one of the guns.

I squeezed off a round and hit the interrogator, who'd now halved the distance between us with alarming speed, in the thigh. He barely flinched, so I put a bullet in his other thigh, which he also ignored. Hell bent on taking at least one of them prisoner and having an interrogation of my own, I landed three more shots in non-crucial areas. He jerked back a little with each hit, but it didn't deter him.

Before I knew it, he'd slapped both guns out of my hands, grabbed me by the collar, and dragged me back towards the apartment door. He shouted for the others to finish up.

In response, shots rang out behind me, followed by the sickening realization that I'd just gotten Vail and Spade killed. Blood dripped onto my clothes from the holes in the carbon, but it wasn't near the amount of blood that should have been coming out of him. On level with the kitchen table, I managed to snatch one of the shards of my broken glass and sliced his wrist as deeply as I could, not so much to wound him as to distract him. Blood spurted from the artery, and when it had his full attention, I pulled a gun out of the back of my waistband, brought it up against his chest, and fired as many times as I could.

He dropped me onto the kitchen floor hard, but didn't immediately fall himself, just kind of stood there frozen, his eyes all glassy, unseeing.

I stared up at him, entranced.

Then a heavy boot kicked him over, and Vail took the gun from my hand and put a bullet in his right eye. And then the left... for good measure.

Spade stood in the doorway, breathing hard.

They were both alive. I couldn't believe it.

"Okay, you've got my attention," I heaved. Though still not totally on board with the cloning theory, I was ready to listen, and listen good.

Vail held out his hand, I thought to help me up, but instead, a small blue pill sat in the palm of his hand.

I didn't take it immediately.

"You've got to," he reasoned. "We all do. We don't know how they found us." He handed one to Spade. "In case the Faction somehow found a way to make the bots invisible and they managed to get inside of us, this will rid the system all the way out to the aura. Even if they are invisible, they're not invincible."

"Invisible bots," Spade said, as though it were a death sentence. "If that's the case, then the game just got a whole lot harder. Make sure you crush it before you swallow it." He filled a glass of water from the kitchen and took his pill.

Vail crunched down on his, then swallowed it dry.

After a moment, I did the same.

"Go out in the hall and keep watch," Spade said to me, wasting no time. He and Vail hefted the carbon in the kitchen between them.

I did as he asked. The complex now sat eerily quiet after the gunshots. Before long, the whole building would be crawling with cops.

Spade and Vail carried the bodies, one by one, to the trash chute. Probably wouldn't be any different than what the trash collector usually picked up from this hellhole.

Spade slung the duffel over his shoulder and motioned for us to follow, and we climbed two more sets of stairs to apartment 703. "Always have a Plan B," he said, opening the door and ushering us inside — same exact layout, but with a different, though equally hideous, decor. Patches of disintegrating floral wallpaper dotted the kitchen walls, and scuffed pine covered the floor.

Spade crossed to a big bay window in the living room and pulled the curtain aside.

I peeked over his shoulder and involuntarily gasped. The most dangerous ghetto in the city sprawled before us. "Valley Gardens? Are you fucking kidding me?" Worse than the War Zone, Valley Gardens was a place where even a Sedition agent didn't want to be caught after dark. My internal compass had unfortunately been correct, but I hadn't expected to be in this particular 'neighborhood.' "Why isn't our 'Plan B' to leave?"

Residents streamed out of the building below.

"Their pals are watching for just that." Spade shoved aside the couch and peeled back the carpet, revealing an almost completely unnoticeable trap door in the floor, as though it had been cut with a laser. "We're all going in to wait it out. First, the cops will come, and then the geminates."

"And if they find us?"

"If they find us, it means the whole building is compromised." He handed me two semi-automatics. "And we'll be ready for them."

"Go for an eye," Vail said. "It's the only thing that puts them down." He pulled back the slide on his gun and popped the first round into the chamber.

CHAPTER 25

The three of us lay under the floorboards in the dark, little bits of light filtering in from the cracks. Sandwiched between Vail and Spade, I tried not to think about what else might be moving around down here. No doubt a host of critters had taken up residence between floors.

It didn't take long for the cops to show, which meant they'd put one team on each floor. They came and went quickly, but the geminates were not so speedy, waiting in hopes of lulling us into a false sense of security.

I fell asleep again, until my protesting shoulder woke me up, requesting another dose of morphine. I was trying to figure out how to get the backpack from my feet up to my head when the apartment door creaked open. Footsteps crossed the living room, raining dust down on us. I closed my eyes.

One of them, closer to the door, spoke. "They blipped out right around here."

So, invisible bots are possible. That isn't good.

Another farther down the hall answered. "The car is still in the garage."

"On foot then?" the one over our heads asked.

"Most likely," said the one at the door. "Maybe went down the trash chute after the others."

Yes, I willed them. *That's what we did. Believe it.*

"Keep an eye on the exits, and monitor the car if it moves."

I felt Spade stiffen beside me with rage, and could almost feel the heat coming off of him. The one on top of us faded away and the door slammed shut.

When the sounds of tenants returning to their apartments drifted through the door, we emerged from the floorboards.

"God damn it," Spade muttered through gritted teeth. "*They* bugged the car, which bugged us." Then he smiled, and it was scary.

I, myself, was eager to return to the conversation. "Gemination... give it to me," I demanded. I wanted more answers. Now. I knew I'd only gotten the tip of the iceberg. I took a seat at the kitchen table in hopes that they would do the same.

Vail followed, but not Spade.

Spade continued to smile maniacally. "I have a wild goose chase to begin and some work to do at the Sedition." Night had long since fallen. "By now, no doubt, word of your extracurricular activities this morning has reached the Heads. They will know that you left the Sedition... with me."

"You're going back?" I asked in disbelief.

"My work there is not done... just following orders. Something you are very bad at," he chastised.

"Something I'm very proud of," I retorted.

He ignored me. "I appear loyal to the Sedition Heads, but in truth, I am loyal to the Sedition *cause*."

"What are you going to tell them?" I couldn't see how he could possibly cover himself for receiving us from the hospital and then helping us leave the Sedition.

He addressed me as though speaking to the board. "Whatever I have to. I have to make them believe that everything I did was to win your confidence and your trust. I'll make them believe that you two are sitting ducks."

"Which we are," I added. I did not like the idea of waiting for Spade to come back. Though impatient by nature, it seemed intrinsically wrong in this situation. We'd already been busted once, and for me, waiting here felt like waiting to be killed. "What about the geminates? They're watching your car."

"Oh, I'll take care of them," he said vaguely. "I'll draw them off, and be back tomorrow, late morning or early afternoon, and hopefully not alone."

"Hamlin and Colvin?" I asked expectantly. I'd feel much better if they were with me, and felt pretty bad about snubbing them on my last day at the Sedition.

He shook his head. "They're with us, but they're staying in. We need a few on the inside." His thoughts shifted, and he put a hand on my bad shoulder and squeezed, just hard enough to make me wince. "Speaking of inside... stay here, Stone."

I fought the urge to slap his hand.

"Get some sleep, but make sure one of you keeps an eye out."

"You said there were two parts to this. What about the second part?" I pressed.

He winked. "Incentive that you'll be here when I get back."

Damn it.

"And to fully understand Gemination, you must first understand the 19."

"The 19?" *Vail's organization, targeting Gemination.*

Or so I thought; Spade had a different take on it. "Kind of the secret service of the Faction."

Vail shot him a dangerous look.

"Relax." Spade put his hands up. "The 19 are *the* elite force — the crème de la crème — and just like us, they officially don't exist. They're the would-be enforcers of population control, but not in the way you think. And since we have one of them here —" He swept his other arm toward Vail. " — I'll let him tell you about it." He released his grip and patted my shoulder affectionately, as though he were a kind uncle. "Also, if I don't come back by tomorrow evening, go. Don't look back... and don't come looking for me."

With that, he took his coat and hat and walked out the door.

CHAPTER 26

Vail stared at the door after Spade for a moment, and then slowly turned to me. "The 19 *were* the personal henchmen of the Faction," he took over. "Anything that needed to be done with the utmost secrecy and concealment was done by us. Who shot JFK? The 19, that's who."

"Is that so? You hold your age well," I teased.

He shot me an annoyed look. "No questions, no records, no witnesses. Always silent, always a first class exit, always a scapegoat. We were ghosts. The Faction, as an organization, is ruthless, but not everyone can pull a trigger. Some only want to push buttons or throw money. A soul can be bought easily and often for a low price. We did what others could not do or did not want to do themselves."

"Well, that sounds familiar," I said cynically, thinking back on how many covert grants I'd pulled for the Sedition so the Heads didn't have to get their hands messy.

Vail continued. "A few years ago, the Faction decided to try out a rather unorthodox method to deal with the projected future problem of population control.

Stem cell research and genome mapping have paved the way for other avenues, avenues that are not so straightforward."

"The road to hell is paved with good intentions," I said absently. "I gather this is where the cloning comes in — reproductive cloning, specifically." It still sounded ridiculous.

He nodded. "For decades, the Faction has been collecting embryonic stem cells."

"From where, exactly?" I didn't like where this was going. It opened up a whole new possibility of horrors, as original embryos were destroyed in the process of stem cell extraction. Stem cells were only totipotent, capable of developing a fetus, at the very beginning of embryonic fertilization. But why go to the trouble? Why not just steal the fertilized eggs? Or artificially inseminate them?

But that wasn't what Vail was talking about. "The Faction laboratory succeeded in creating embryonic clones out of DNA." His face grew dark. "And since the 19 didn't technically exist, *they* picked us as the pilot group — more than picked, snatched. No longer the owners of our lives, we became Faction property, the same as a piece of machinery or a gun." His voice became bitter, resentful. "The cloning was not only successful but genetically enhanced. The clones were stronger, faster, and virtually indestructible. We were the best of the best, but they were better, and they replaced us."

"You're saying you've got a double out there? All 19 of you?" I remembered Spade's doubt of who Vail was.

He nodded. "A geminate."

My mind reeled away from him. "But this isn't the future of warfare," my ego argued. "The future of warfare lies in the bots, nanotechnology. Right now, the bots are doing half the work for us. Intel bots just have to get close enough to the target, cyber bots ride in on a drive. Eventually, there will be no need for the agent to even get it there. My job won't exist in another twenty years."

"No," Vail countered. "You can't take humanity out of the equation. There's no replacement for the brain, no matter how sophisticated the tech. It's impossible."

I crossed my arms. "So, a clone is considered as intelligent as the real deal then?"

"I'll let you decide that for yourself," he said cryptically. "But in nature, stem cells clone themselves without losing any energy at all. Therefore, the clone has the same potential as the original."

True. Now I waited for the explanation of all explanations.

Vail didn't disappoint. "Gemination is a cloned army designed to destroy half of the developed world's population via contrived war, and take control of all remaining resources, natural and human. It's self-preservation for the Faction."

In my mind, my jaw dropped to the floor. Then suddenly, my grandmother on autopilot took over. "Do you want some tea?" That had been her response to any stressful situation—amusing to watch at times, but not so funny now.

"Sure," Vail responded slowly. "I suppose so." He eyed me oddly.

I had no choice but to go along with what I'd just offered, so I stood up to boil some water. I had to light the stove with a match; so archaic. That showed what kind of world I'd been living in.

I stood with my back to him while the tea boiled. *If I can't see him, he doesn't exist.* This was all some kind of weird, surreal story. I couldn't be entirely sure that it was real, and it wouldn't be the first time I thought maybe I was in dreamland, or in some parallel universe. I thought that every time I slid onto that weird, protective plane. Though now used to it, the first time it happened I was sure I had died and my soul had become stuck in some sort of purgatory. Perhaps I had been right, and I was still there. Maybe I had died on Indigo 11.

I half considered reaching out to touch the teakettle, just to see if I could be burned, but then I decided, real or unreal, it was irrelevant. If I was dreaming, I had to go through the dream. Only then could I wake up. But in this dream, I had to be very careful not to die, for if I died here, I was sure I'd never wake up on the other side. An odd sort of resignation had settled in, and it hadn't taken too long. Perhaps, when you don't know things that you know, they're not too hard to accept when you realize you know them, even when you still don't.

As if that makes any sense.

I shook my head and tried to clear it, but what I really needed to do was bash it against the wall. The teakettle whistled, which felt even more surreal. I stared at it screaming for a while before I took it off the heat. I poured the tea, another mundane action that felt ridiculous, and turned back to the table.

I handed Vail his cup, which he accepted without a word, and sat down opposite him once again. Clearly neither of us wanted the tea, and our cups just sat in front of us steaming. Even after they had cooled, they remained untouched.

A war on free will, across the globe. I shoved aside the fact that Spade had confirmed Vail's story, and searched his face for incredibility, some trace of wavering countenance that would be incongruous to his words. I found none, but couldn't let it go. It was too complicated. My mind ran through a million scenarios and landed on one that seemed plausible.

"In fifty years," I finally said, "a two percent rise in global temperature will cause mass destruction of eco-systems and will kill off about a fifth of the population. Why go to the trouble of cloning an army to do something that's going to happen anyway?"

Vail scoffed. "Listen, the Faction isn't going to bother with tribal Africa or the Islanders of the South Pacific, and look at the Middle East—they did an excellent job of killing themselves. Palestine and Israel are now two giant, radioactive smoking craters. The third world is not a threat. They can barely keep themselves alive as it is. It's the people of the developed world that are a menace. They don't live hand to mouth, but paycheck to paycheck."

"What about biological warfare then? That test pandemic when I was a kid went pretty well."

"All we learned was that control through fear as a tactic works even better than anyone could ever imagine."

I continued, determined to find a chink in the armor. "How about Cohen's neutron bomb, finally perfected."

"Neither are specific enough. You still need enough crew to run the ship. The potential mutineers are just being tossed overboard."

"But how the hell can cloning more people solve a population problem?"

Vail shrugged. "They're expendable assets with an extremely low life expectancy." He then eyed the door.

"And speaking of expendable assets, do you think we can trust him?"

It took a minute for the impact of his statement to sink in. "Spade?"

Vail nodded.

Good damn question. "In the hospital, Ember said he was trustworthy. He also said that Spade would not be able to hold back the Sedition."

"Should we make a plan in case he doesn't come back?"

"We're not going anywhere," I said stubbornly. Spade had the other half of my story, so I'd fight another round of carbons if I had to.

"You think we should at least lock up?" Vail gestured at the apartment door.

I glanced over at the rusted deadbolt. "I suppose so, though it will do little good, just a formality really, which we just learned." I stood up and crossed to lock the door.

When I turned around, Vail was gone.

CHAPTER 27

Charlie Spade drove back through the city to his house, cursing himself for not *bot bombing* the car in the first place. He should have done it upon leaving the Sedition. He glanced in the rearview mirror, knowing geminates were in the background somewhere, monitoring him from a far, following him at what *they* thought was a safe distance.

After about an hour of meandering, he tossed a ball roughly the size of a cherry bomb in the backseat, but instead of exploding it merely started blinking, emitting a frequency that would disable any bot in his car. Then he took another pill for good measure and blinked out of existence. But how had *they* gotten to his car in the first place? When he and Ember first met with *them* at the hospital, they'd driven this car but bombed it immediately after leaving. Only two options remained, either at his house or the Sedition. He wasn't sure which he preferred, but he'd know by the end of the night if they came hunting for him. Good thing they'd used the girl for communication.

Spade pulled into his garage and hurried inside, where he knew a Sedition tail would pick him up, but that was all right, just as long as they did not know where he was coming from. Inside, he phoned the Sedition review room, interrupting a Head meeting, and told them he would be coming in early the next morning for an urgent meeting.

"It concerns Emissary Leyla Stone, whom I'm sure all of you are curious about." He tried to sound cocky and impatient, as though he expected to be named Head the next day, and he apparently succeeded, as they didn't demand anything more from him.

Then he went to sleep... with one eye open and his shoes on.

CHAPTER 28

The man was the definition of stealth.

"I'm in the living room," Vail called out as if expecting my surprise.

Has to be slowness due to the morphine, surely. I paused in the threshold, the room dark, Vail silhouetted in front of the big bay window watching the rainfall. Torn between engagement and withdrawal, the former eventually won out and I took a seat in the bay of the window.

After a while, he sat down too.

We sat in silence staring out into the rain, only it wasn't so much rain as what I called a Godless drizzle — no thunder, no lightning, but raining just hard enough to deter an outing. Color abandoned the world in those moments, leaving only a gray smear across the sky in its wake.

I glanced at Vail every now and then, trying to force my memory to bring him back into focus. I couldn't come up with anything consciously, but the blank slate was loaded. An invisible thread of some sort tied me to him, a sense memory of the strongest kind, though I had no visual to accompany it. I wanted to ask him, but I couldn't formulate the question. Even if I had the question, I lacked the courage to ask it, which kind of annoyed me. Strange to lack courage in the face of the unknown.

Or is it?

"Thanks for coming for me," I said after a moment, never having properly thanked him for extracting me from the hospital.

He slowly shifted his eyes over to meet mine.

"If you hadn't, I don't know what would have happened. I suppose I'd have bled to death."

"If you were lucky."

"How did you find me?"

He looked at me with a slightly incredulous expression. "I followed your trail of blood."

God damn, how unprofessional. "Oh."

"I was outside when I heard the shots. By the time I got into the lab, there were just little spots of blood leading down to the basement, and then I found you lying on the floor. Scared the hell out of me." He swallowed, choked back an emotion I couldn't place.

"How did we get out?"

"The underground parking garage. It took me a minute to find it. By that time, someone else was on your trail, literally. I threw the other flash-bang from your pocket when we hit the pavement outside."

"Smart," I said, having completely forgotten I'd brought two.

"Good thing I got to your trail of blood first."

"No kidding." I was still embarrassed, but at this point, it didn't matter. "How did you get out of the Sedition anyway?"

"Walked right out the front door. Like I said, I'm good at not being seen — very good."

"Apparently. I guess you can walk through walls too, right? Superhero style?"

He looked at me slyly. "By the way, how is it that before yesterday you'd never been shot?"

I shrugged.

"What happens?" he persisted.

"Who says anything happens?" I shot back. "Maybe I'm lucky."

He shook his head. "It's not luck. Maybe evading one bullet would be luck, but several? No. So... what happens?" he pressed. "How did Ember end up being the jack of all trades and you a master of none?"

The weird analogy gave me pause. I'd never told a soul about the strange occurrences that accompanied me in stressful situations, not even Ember. It was the only thing I'd kept from him. I always chalked it up to luck, and others seemed to think I was just that good, but Vail was right. It was not luck. Far from it.

I always imagined telling the truth to the Sedition board, and them saying, "Interesting... we'd like to run a few tests." Seemed like something that would get me into trouble, or turn me into a science experiment.

I sighed. "It's going to sound really weird." I would have added *crazy*, but Vail and I didn't have the same definition of crazy.

"Weirder than an army of superhuman clones?" He raised an eyebrow.

Fair enough. "Well, it's hard to explain, but when the situation turns and it comes to blows, and then the bullets start flying, it's like I'm not really conscious at the time, or maybe I'm overly conscious. I remember it later, but it's a distant memory, or someone else's memory, one that I have, but it doesn't seem real — it feels like someone put it there, like an implant. It must be some self-defense mechanism to detach myself from the situation." I paused, not sure how much further to go. "Strange things happen," I said superficially.

"Give an example," he pushed.

I took a deep breath. "Time seems to alter, and gets really slow, as though it isn't consistent, but no one else notices, which gives me extra time. I seem to be outside of it, separate, a witnessing entity of some sort. And then there's this path—it's sort of colored, wispy, illuminated, not real of course, kind of like a tracer from acid. It's got this gravitational force, and I just end up on it." I shrugged in conclusion. "And so far, it's never led me wrong."

"Not until yesterday," Vail added.

His tone made me curious. "Right, this time there was no path. I suppose it only exists without the element of surprise," I guessed.

"Who surprised you at the hospital?"

"The carbons." Vail didn't know that was my own term for geminates, but he seemed to understand.

His tone became stranger. "Why did you get shot?"

"Well, obviously, I was a bit in over my head, returning to the scene of the crime, as you said, but mostly, I just didn't hear them."

Stranger tone still.... "You didn't hear them? Why not?"

"I don't know," I shot back, annoyed with the third degree. I gazed off into the distance at the approaching dark thunderheads. It wouldn't drizzle for long. Zeus and Poseidon were going at it on Mount Olympus. Lightning lit up the pitch-black sky in brilliant flashes. Thunder rolled like cannons on some lost and forgotten, antiquated battlefield.

Vail wouldn't give it up. He shifted to sit in front of me, uncomfortably close. "In five years, you've never been hit, and then you don't *hear* your assailants?"

"No. How many times do you want me to repeat it?"

"Put it together, Stone," he ordered like a commanding officer.

I quit speaking and glared at him, feeling dangerously close to hitting him. I began to get up, done with the game, but he grabbed my wrist, and his touch sent a jolt through me.

"Hold on," he said.

I reluctantly sat back down.

He paused, clearly waiting for something to turn over in my brain, which I found extremely annoying. How the hell anyone could expect my head to work at this point in the game was ridiculous.

A few minutes later, he sighed and put his head in his hands. Then he looked up in disbelief. "Stone, don't you know why you were shot? Because you were dealing with geminates, and they have unparalleled senses. You said yourself you didn't hear them come up on you. They're very good at being stealthy."

Of course, it was obvious now. No ordinary person could have snuck up on me. "Yeah," I said, and that was all I had.

He settled back into his seat across from me. "Now you have some idea of what you're dealing with."

I have a really damned good idea. I remembered the carbon—no, *geminate*—I'd shot nearly a dozen times two floors beneath us. I leaned back against the wall and closed my eyes.

"How's the arm?"

"Hurts like hell." The morphine had long worn off, but I wasn't too eager to take more. I didn't like being slow. Pain at least kept me alert and awake.

"Tired?" he asked, as if reading my thoughts.

"You have no idea," I said, without opening my eyes. "But I'm not going to sleep yet," I added hastily, anticipating his next question.

The next few hours passed quietly, but pleasantly. We developed a comfortable space with each other and I felt content to sit beside him. Outside, the rain changed from a drizzle into a downpour, replete with thunder and lightning. The storm blotted out the moon and moved in from the horizon, right up to the thin panes of glass that separated us from it. I stared out into the deluge, totally entranced, and the world slipped out of focus.

The seed that Vail had planted about Spade's reliability sprouted. I tried not to question his loyalty, but the more I tried, the more it came. Though Ember had said to trust him, the game had changed, had it not? There may have been things Ember had not known, or perhaps things had changed after he moved on—I refused to use the word *died*. And if it weren't for Vail, Spade would have buried the grant and all thoughts of the 19.

A second seed sprouted that was much worse. "Am I losing it?" It came out of my mouth before I could stop it.

Vail thought for a moment. "Time does get slow." He continued to stare out the window at the dark world outside, head leaning back against the wall.

I turned towards him. Surely, I hadn't heard him right. "Come again?"

He didn't look back. "What you said about time slowing down is true. It's not consistent. We only think it is, mostly because we've been told it is, and we live our lives by it. In actuality, time is a living entity that's entirely whimsical in nature... on purpose. How you act with time changes it—a simple law of attraction."

"Law of attraction?" I thought that applied to relationships, not physics.

"Bored? Time slows almost unbearably. Running late? I guarantee that rushing speeds it up. For most of us, it's always a race against time, one way or another. But not you. You're not detaching from the situation. Quite the opposite, you're engaging, fully immersing yourself in it. You're bending it with your will. Amazing." He chuckled. "Time waits for no man, but it waits for you."

"How can that be?" I couldn't believe he was actually validating what I'd just said. *Yes, different ideas of* crazy, *indeed.*

"I'm sure some quantum physicist can explain it, but I can't. We all experience this, subjectively, of course. We experience time dragging on and time flying by. A second can be as long or as short as it wants, and as far as I can tell, time inconsistency is something you're either sensitive enough to pick up on or dull enough to ignore."

I shook my head. It couldn't be.

"It's all relative, not absolute," he continued. "Your Einstein was a genius, but your Sir Isaac Newton...?" He pronounced Isaac as *I-sack* for some reason. "Time marches on? Only if it wants to."

"Einstein also said that if you can't explain a concept to a six- year-old, then you don't fully understand it."

"I never said I fully understood it. It's just what is. And 'what is' is usually not good enough for the western mind, but it's good enough for mine."

The pain in my shoulder eventually became unbearable, and I had to keep myself dosed on morphine, but only enough to leave me just short of developing a tolerance. This was dangerous, as my reaction time and judgment would be impaired if another set of geminates burst through the door. In apartment 505, I'd had some real luck, but the only consistent thing about luck is that it always runs out. In the scope of pharmaceuticals, morphine was one of the lesser drugs in terms of altering mental cognition, but sometimes life came down to a second.

About two in the morning, I couldn't keep my eyes open anymore. Vail insisted I get some sleep, that he would take the first watch, and I didn't have the strength to argue. I trudged into the bedroom and collapsed on top of the bed. I'd say I was out before my head hit the pillow, but I don't think I even made it that far.

CHAPTER 29

The next morning, Spade arrived in the boardroom at precisely 7:00 a.m. He made sure to not so much as glance at the Heads seated around the oval table as he made his way to his seat. He focused instead on the nondescript gray walls, as though they were particularly fascinating, fancying himself in an art gallery — as if he gave a damn about art. Still, he kept his eyes on the splendid works of Monet and especially avoided eye contact toward the head of the table, not because the Director of the Sedition sat there, but because the guest of the day, and possibly many more days to come, sat there as well. He did not care for the man at all.

He'd solved one mystery, though: the bots in his car had not come from his house; no huntsmen had visited him in his sleep. That meant the Sedition might be riddled with bots it didn't even know about. This possibility horrified Spade, as it meant the Sedition security bots were either defective or there was a new player in the game, bots that didn't show up on a tracker, as he'd just experienced. What next?

Two of the heads were out of the gate before he even sat down.

"What the hell is going on?" asked a small man with rimmed spectacles, behind which sat shrewd, narrow eyes.

"Where is she?" demanded a stern-looking woman wearing a pale gray pantsuit. She had an oval face with pale white skin to match, and wore her dull brown hair tied back so tightly it pulled the edges of her eyes back. One word for her: severe.

Jesus Christ, Spade thought, *if she doesn't loosen her hair it's going to pull her face off. It's a miracle she has use of her eyes right now.*

"Manners, manners," came a deep voice from the head of the table.

The voice made Spade cringe internally, though he made sure to betray no emotion on the outside. It belonged to Clive Jackander, the Sedition Director, and today, his voice sounded particularly dangerous.

"Come now, we are not so uncivilized," he admonished, drawing out the last syllable with the hiss of a snake. The two Heads stared down at the table and became silent. "Let's first introduce our guest. Charles Spade, this is Ansel Trenholm."

"Sure, you are," Spade muttered, allowing a cursory glance towards the head of the table. From the corner of his eye, he saw Clive Jackander raise his eyebrows, and smiled internally at having caught the Director's attention. *First order of business done.*

"Good morning," Spade said cheerily, turning to address the whole table. "Don't worry, Mr. Taylor, all is going according to plan. And, Ms. Van Dorn, she's safe and sound, waiting for your *eventual* arrival."

Edmund Taylor and Kendall Van Dorn again launched into a tirade against Spade's cynicism like a couple of fighting pit bulls.

He sat there impassively for a few moments, and then dismissed them with a wave of his hand. "Now, now, one at a time. We are not so uncivilized, as the Director has pointed out."

Van Dorn nodded curtly, and Taylor started first. "How the hell are things going according to plan? She escaped again."

Spade flared. "Is it my problem that they can't catch her? I've goaded her twice into that hospital, and it seems a whole army of your very best—" He now allowed himself to look at the guest at the head of the table. " —can't catch one little girl."

A cruel smile spread out on the lips of the Sedition guest, but he remained silent.

The calm man... there's always got to be a calm man, the most dangerous kind.

Spade turned back to Taylor and snapped, "What else do you want me to do? I've handed her to you twice."

Taylor narrowed his eyes. "And she was here yesterday, *twice*," he spat. "Why the hell didn't you lock her down? You even helped her leave, and after she ditched the review, no less."

"Turns out I'm not finished with her," Spade said, offering no further explanation.

Edmund Taylor leaned across the table, inches from Spade's face. "Since when do you make decisions?"

Spade stared back at him unflinchingly. "Since John Ember died, making me default Head. It's in your best interest, Edmund."

Taylor spluttered at being addressed by his first name. "What in the hell does that mean?"

"It means I have a plan, and a good one at that."

A rather large fellow seated halfway down the table pounded a meaty fist on the table with dramatic flair.

"Damn John Ember and damn this girl! She's been trouble from the beginning." He obviously wanted to say something to feel important, and the entirety of the oval table turned to look at him.

What the hell does he think this is, a movie? "As I recall, Mr. Baker, you know nothing of that time period. She was here before you. Do not speak on things of which you know nothing," he snapped.

Mr. Baker positively growled at Spade, and opened his mouth to retort, but one withering look from the Sedition Director and he shut it.

Adrian Baker, the newest and youngest addition to the Sedition Heads, had lots of money but was short on brains, a barely disguised meathead. He decided to make himself busy by brushing imaginary specks of dust off the shoulder of his navy-blue suit.

Taylor looked up towards the Director. "Let's just send Thacker's team after her. It won't take him any time at all, especially since Leyla Stone is partial to one of his strikers."

"And his partner is hell bent on her destruction, generally speaking," Van Dorn snickered.

Spade shook his head at both of them. "You do not want to get Leyla Stone's hackles up more than they already are," he warned. "Before Ember died, he told her not to trust the Sedition, and we all know her loyalty to him. There's no telling the amount of damage she would do. How many of your strikers are you willing to lose? We can't go after her, or she will disappear, and then she will pick us off one by one. We trained her too well."

"You mean Ember trained her too well," Taylor clarified.

"She's different," the guest at the head of the table said calmly, breaking into the conversation.

Spade gave him a hard look. "Different, indeed." He eyed Van Dorn. "That being said, she trusts me, which is how we have to keep it. She's in the same place I took Ember." He looked to Taylor. "She's there with the asset, and they're waiting, as per my instructions."

"Ha! She's scared," the young lady sitting to the left of Adrian Baker blurted out shrilly, the jarring note in her voice both foolish and immature. Again, everyone turned to stare, this time at Madison Page, another relatively new Sedition Head who was older than Baker, but no wiser.

So, it's true what they say about blondes. Technically, Page was a brunette, but he had a sneaking suspicion she dyed her hair as an attempt to look smarter — a wasted effort. At least she was more pleasing to look at than the oaf sitting beside her. He wondered how many people she'd screwed to get here — normally an impossibility at the Sedition, but these days, nothing would surprise him. Her air was one of a typical southern, orthorexic California girl, although, if she had been a true Cali girl, the word *like* would have gone between *she's* and *scared.*

Madison Page looked at everyone expectantly, as though waiting for approval.

What the hell is this, frat row? We've got one frat boy and one cheerleader. Spade shot her a cold look. "Miss Page, I presume. I want to make one thing very clear to your pretty blonde head. Leyla Stone is not scared. Leyla Stone is never scared. She has no use for fear, therefore she never indulges it." He addressed the table. "But, at the moment, she is unsure. She's waiting to see how things play out, and is undecided on her next move."

The expression on Madison Page's face was one of outright disgust at the way Spade had addressed her, and that pleased him very much.

The Sedition Director, who had at first watched this interaction with dark amusement that had given way to irritation, stood up. A formidable tower of a man, he intimidated most everyone he worked with. "Well, what are we waiting for?" He began gathering his papers. "Let's get this over with. Let the one she knows as Cam seduce her back to us, then we can feed her to his jealous partner. Spade, you can brief Thacker's team yourself." He clearly meant to dismiss the meeting and go on with his day.

The others rose, but Spade stayed put. "Very admirable, Mr. Jackander, but I don't think that will work."

The Sedition Director sharply looked up from his papers. "And why not?"

"She will know you're coming."

Jackander slowly lowered himself back to his seat, and the others followed him like dogs. "Go on."

Spade looked at the Sedition guest, who had also remained seated, and tried not to shiver. "Like our guest said, she's different." He scanned the table, made eye contact with each person. "Look, you all might not want to admit it, but Leyla Stone has some sort of strange, unparalleled sense. Call it intuition, call it telepathy... I don't care what you call it. All I can say, is she often knows things that she shouldn't know, that she *couldn't* know. It's like she plucks thoughts and vibrations out of thin air."

An eerie silence fell over the room. Leyla Stone had been no man's land. Though younger than most, Ember had been a second generation Head the longest, and he'd been very territorial about her. They'd all left her alone, even Jackander, but now that Ember was gone, they were eager to clean house.

"We need to know where she is," Van Dorn began in a strident voice. "So, we can at least monitor from a distance." She turned to Spade. "Where is she?"

He shook his head and bit his lip. "I can't tell you."

Her mouth turned into a puckered apple. "Why not?"

"Because, Kendall," he drawled, as though he were talking to a two-year old. "If I tell you, she will know that I told you, and if she becomes suspicious of me, you will never have her."

"He's telling the truth," the guest said. "She is intuition combined with equilibrium."

Van Dorn continued. "We at least send in intel, then."

Spade looked at her incredulously. "Are you really not paying attention? She would have picked up the bots as soon as she entered the room, and then put a bullet in my head and vanished."

"Not a bad idea," Baker sneered, his ego no doubt recovered.

"Shut up, Adrian," Jackander snapped. "No more."

The smile dropped off Baker's face.

The guest at the end of the table again spoke, his voice chilling. "What do you propose?"

"I need two days," Spade said. "I can bring her in voluntarily."

"Absolutely not," began Jackander angrily, looking rather like an ogre.

"That's how much time it will take me. Take it or leave it." Charlie Spade stood and turned to go, leaving the rest of the board aghast.

But Spade had piqued Jackander's curiosity. "Keeping secrets, Spade? Surely not."

Jackander was a keen man, and Spade had counted on that. He relented and sat back down. "There's something in her house I need her to go back for."

Jackander stood and began to circle the table. He appeared to be enjoying himself.

Spade recognized the danger and fought to react against it. He gripped the underside of the table to steady himself. Jackander brought his hands together as though he were praying at the altar and brought them to his lips. "And are you sure this 'something' is in her house?"

"It's not on her, that much I am certain of."

"Hmmm," Jackander purred, drawing closer to Spade's seat. "And would we not be able to find this 'something' if we were to search her house?"

"It is highly improbable we could find it in a timely manner. It's a damn big place, and she might be keeping it outside somewhere on her two-hundred-acre property."

Jackander came to a stop directly behind Spade, the atmosphere extremely tense. The rest of the heads watched in raptured silence, waiting to see if the Director would make a snap decision to break Charlie Spade's neck, and take his chances finding Leyla Stone. "And what is this 'something' you need from her house?"

The moment Spade had been waiting for.... "Ask him," Spade said, nodding to the Sedition guest and breathing a silent sigh of relief as the attention shifted away.

All heads turned, but the guest once again smiled and said nothing.

Spade continued. "When Leyla Stone returned from the hospital, she brought physical intel on recent patients acquired there, a total of ten patient files, but she held something back. It's the first time she's ever withheld evidence from me, and I doubt she even knows what to do with it, but I guarantee she'll go back for it."

The guest pressed his fingertips together and seemed to think this over. "Do *you* know what it is, specifically?"

"No, I don't, but neither does she."

Clive Jackander, who had returned to his seat, jarred him back to the present. "Do you?" he asked the guest, one eyebrow arched high.

The guest smiled. "Let's just say that I'll take Leyla Stone off your hands forever in exchange for what she stole from *me*."

"Done," Jackander said without hesitation, and turned to Spade. "You have forty-eight hours, no more."

"I'll have it done in thirty-six," Spade said, taking his opportunity to get the hell out of the conference room.

After Spade left the room, all eyes turned to the Director, awaiting further instruction. "Tail him, no exceptions," Jackander said. He did not entirely trust Spade, but he would never voice this fear to the others — tailing was merely protocol. He grabbed the folder in front of his seat, signaling the end of the meeting.

As they all rose to leave, Jackander turned to the guest. "Make no mistake: we're doing this as a *favor to you*." He had caught the inflection in his guest's tone and was unmoved by his little speech. "I never want to see her again. Understand? I would have dusted her a year ago if it had been up to me."

Leyla Stone had been Ember's problem. Ember had kept her reined in, but he'd ended up joining a pseudo striker team and becoming her partner, having to babysit her through every grant just to make sure she didn't "accidentally" blow something up.

Lord, Indigo 11 had been a disaster.

True, she'd proven her worth, never linking the Sedition to the accident, and retrieving crucial information at a critical time. She'd been the only survivor, and she hadn't exposed them since. Nevertheless, Jackander wasn't willing to take over as her steward. He had no clue why she had been so important to Ember, and now that Ember was dead, he really didn't care. A clear threat to the anonymity of the Sedition, Leyla Stone had become an intolerable risk.

"Well, I'm glad it wasn't *your* decision," the guest said brazenly, straightening his cuffs.

Jackander narrowed his eyes. He did not care for arrogance from his subordinates, or those he thought to be his subordinates. He moved closer to the Sedition guest. "Just take her and then get the hell out of my Sedition."

He glanced down the table at Adrian Baker, visibly hitting on Madison Page. *I can't believe this bastard is one of us,* thought Jackander. *He's a moron. The girl too. How in the hell did Lockwood and Ellis choose these guys? That was one piece of Sedition protocol that needed updating.*

Jackander brushed by the Sedition guest on his way out, bumping him ever so slightly, but with enough force to let him know it wasn't a mishap. "Baker, my office," he said bluntly.

The guest caught Adrian Baker's eye and exchanged a glance that suggested, *'play nice, these days*

are almost over. It's only a game, after all'. Baker smiled and followed Jackander out of the room. Jackander had no way of knowing what was about to happen, no way of knowing that the Sedition was nearly no longer his.

The guest eyed the seat where Charlie Spade had been sitting. *Patient Zero*, he whispered inside his head. So the boy had gotten Patient Zero into Leyla Stone's hands. Foreign bots in the mainframe were automatically destroyed, but of course, the boy knew that. The file itself had been coded, on the extremely unlikely event that it was stolen.

Not so unlikely now. Very unfortunate, but very fortunate that she had been unable to break into the file.

If she had, he wouldn't be sitting here right now. It would only be a matter of time, however, especially since she had taken up with that Marcus Hunn creature. If that happened, the detriment to his plan would be paramount. He could not risk the identity of Patient Zero out in the open, as he was still outnumbered. The retrieval of the drive became the new priority. After that, it would be a cakewalk.

One Sedition Head had not spoken at all during this entire exchange, quite young, a handsome, bookish look about him, if such looks existed, neatly trimmed with square glasses.

He still did not speak, just hurried off to arrange "the tail" that was to follow Charlie Spade.

CHAPTER 30

The Sedition guest confronted Spade at his office door. This disarmed him, but the guest left him no time for thought.

"You will deliver the girl and what she carries to me, unexamined, understand?"

Spade turned and met the guest's eyes — black ice in hell.

"I report to the Director, not to you," Spade said evenly. *Since when are Sedition guests allowed to roam at will? And who the hell told him where to find my office?*

"John Ember was your superior."

It wasn't a question, so Spade didn't respond.

"Leyla Stone was your charge." Another statement.

"I'm very busy," Spade said in response. "If you'd like, schedule an appointment with the receptionist." He made to go around him.

The guest grabbed his arm. "If you don't want Leyla Stone to meet the same fate as her partner, you will do exactly as I say."

Spade pushed back into him. "And what makes you think I give a damn about Leyla Stone?"

The smile came again that chilled Spade to the bone.

"Everything about you," the guest articulated.

Spade held his gaze a moment longer and then shook loose the guest's grip. He continued on to his office, mere steps away.

So, the guest is a bully. He'd counted on this also.

Jase Avery had been eavesdropping. It wasn't in his nature, but he'd been instructed to do so by his boss. Granted, the rumors were that his boss now slept with the fishes, and he'd soon have a new one, but he didn't care. He would stick by John Ember long after his death, for he, too, had felt the uncomfortable stirrings within the Sedition, and, from what he'd heard, they were far from over.

Through sheer luck, wind of an early morning meeting had reached his ears just the evening before, thanks to one of his old classmates, Lincoln Decker, the evening doorman. He'd been working late, the last one in the bullpen, and Deck had asked him to keep an eye on the door while he set up one of the conference rooms. Instead, he discretely followed his colleague to pinpoint the exact room, and he'd placed a very old-school bug, not a bot, inside the room before he left.

He'd returned "to work" very early and found a closet to hole up in. After dozing for a few hours, the earpiece crackled to life, and what he heard did not make him happy. Many voices, he recognized, thought he couldn't put a face to them if his life depended on it. There was one he knew very well, however: Charlie Spade, the head of his sister team.

When the meeting disbanded, he made a beeline for Charlie Spade's office and waited.

When Spade walked in, it annoyed him to see Avery sitting in his chair, but he wasn't exactly surprised. "What are you doing, Avery?" he asked with a yawn, feeling beyond haggard.

"I could ask you the same thing." Avery sat up and leaned forward.

"I was in a meeting, Avery, which I'm sure you know all about." He tossed the little bug on the table. "Very foolish, by the way. It's a miracle no one noticed. Just shows how slack things have gotten. Ember was right."

"Is it true, Charlie? Is he dead?" Avery asked quietly.

"Looks that way," Spade answered absentmindedly, as he began gathering his personal effects.

Jase Avery was known as being a hot-headed brute, but underneath all that testosterone lay a fiercely emotive man, and one loyal to a fault.

"How can you do this to her, Spade?" Avery whispered. "You know as well as I do that something's wrong here, and she's in the middle of it. My whole team feels it, Bishop—"

Spade dropped his briefcase and exploded. "Shut up, Avery! Shut up right now! You don't know the full story. You can *follow me* if you want, but don't you dare stand in my way. *I'm leaving.*"

Avery almost missed it—anyone else would have—but before their respective assignments to emissary subordinates, they'd been partners. In the field, as any good team, they'd rarely had to speak to communicate. Spade held eye contact for a moment and raised an eyebrow.

After a moment, Avery nodded an affirmation he had caught the difference in his outburst.

Spade then leaned in close and offered one last bit of advice. "Do not let your emotional liability get the best of you." He then whirled around and walked out the door.

Avery stood frozen for a moment, alone in Spade's office. It seemed that perhaps Charlie Spade was leaving for good, and if that was so, things were about to get particularly dangerous. An ominous warning went off in his head. It was finally happening — all that Ember prophesized about, sometimes obsessively so, was now taking place.

With Ember dead, he would have to act independently, but he needed to take his strikers with him. He would not leave them here. Besides, he had a feeling that Leyla Stone would need them *all* before the end.

How could he follow Charlie Spade without drawing attention? Simple: it needed to be part of his job. Charlie would have a tail no doubt, and who would the tail be? A striker team, no less — *his* striker team.

He hurried out of Spade's office in hopes that the tail would not have been assigned and off already. Rehearsing his speech in his head about why he should be the tail without sounding attached, he had hardly gotten around the corner when he nearly collided with a young man wearing square glasses. He had seen him many times before but did not know his name.

The young man, however, knew his name. "Jase Avery," he stated.

This flustered him a bit. "Yes, and who — "

"You have a new assignment. Come with me."

CHAPTER 31

Charlie Spade unlocked the door of his second refuge to find the apartment empty. He sighed and closed the door behind him.

"Damn it, Stone," he muttered under his breath. "You're always a toss-up." At that moment, the audible click of a hammer being thumbed back froze him.

"Forgot to check your corners," I remarked.

Spade slowly turned around, looking quite relieved.

"And you have no faith in me."

"Sure, I do." He smiled. "But you usually don't wait for me. How's the arm?"

"It's okay. A night of rest did it good." Vail hadn't just taken the first watch, he'd taken the *entire* watch, and I'd actually slept for several consecutive hours. I chalked it up to the madness of the last two weeks, and though partially true, it meant one other thing, one potentially dangerous thing: part of me had begun to rely on Vail.

As soon as sleep becomes sound around others, the defenses have been lowered — the subconscious has decided they're in. Normally, this kind of comfort level takes a long time, but I'd been with Vail less than forty-eight hours. The only person I'd slept around was Ember, after a damned long time of extracurricular "trust-building" activities. This, in and of itself, unnerved me. If I didn't get my memory back at some point, I'd lose it. An insane asylum loomed on the horizon.

I put the gun away as Vail emerged from the living room. "You're right," I said. "I would normally be gone by now, but I really do want to hear the rest of this."

I motioned to the kitchen table, already set with glasses of water and a pitcher, and we all took a seat in a repeat of yesterday—minus the geminate insurgency, hopefully.

Vail had spent the morning filling me in on what he called "current events," although this all seemed to have gone down about six months ago. Eleven of the 19 escaped the Gemination facilities and then set up shop, hell-bent on taking the Faction down. They'd watched the hospital day and night, and then two men showed up they recognized as outsiders, Ember and Spade. The Faction had unwittingly called upon the Sedition for outside help, to find the remnants of the escaped 19, as well as support for their continued experiments. What bad luck, though good luck for the rest of us. After the meeting, the 19 confronted the strikers and told the other side of the story. Ember and Spade made the snap decision to make the call on the grant themselves, rather than bring it home to the Sedition: death to the hospital; death to Gemination.

"Why didn't you tell the Sedition about the grant?" I asked Spade. "Stopping detrimental organizations from proliferating is what the Sedition does. Hell, I've made a career out of hunting organizations like the

Faction. We all have." Between the cartels and the mafia, I'd shut down a baker's dozen of operations. "Yesterday, you said the Faction was their main enemy."

An awkward silence followed as Spade dropped his gaze to the floor.

I kicked his chair, in no mood for elusiveness, and he looked up.

"You're right," he admitted. "Until recently, it was the job of the Sedition to hunt people like this, to assassinate them, and stop them."

"Until recently...." I trailed off realizing that there was more to Ember's statement: *'The Sedition is no longer safe.'* It wasn't a simple matter of Ember disobeying them; it ran much deeper than that. "Why is the Sedition no longer safe, Spade? What happened?"

He eyed me cautiously. "There is something else you did not know about Ember."

"Big surprise," I scoffed. "Seems like there are many things I did not know about Ember."

Spade smiled. "Not so many, but a few. Ember was more than a striker, more than the other half of your team. Ember was a Sedition Head."

"A Sedition Head..." I began, dumbfounded.

Spade held up a hand. "Let me finish, Stone. Ember was a Sedition Head, and the youngest one to ever be appointed, at that. When you showed up for training, he took particular interest in you. The rest of the Heads thought you were too rash, too unpredictable, and in the end, they decided that you would not make a good emissary. You were a rule breaker, which made you a liability, but you already knew too much, and there was some debate over what to do with you. Ember became your saving grace, convincing the other Heads to keep you. You would be his responsibility alone, and he would keep you out of trouble, train you himself. They reluctantly agreed. Of course, 'Indigo 11' helped."

I winced at the name: Indigo 11, the day I'd totally lost my innocence. It wasn't the first time I'd seen death, but death on a horrific, mass scale.

Spade continued. "So, Ember inserted himself into one of his striker teams. Originally, he slated me to be your partner and him the subordinate, but in the end, he wanted to be as close to you as possible, so we switched. Ember placed me at the head of the pairs, over himself, or so it would appear. Like you said before, Stone, we were a team, but we all know who was really in charge."

"I'll be damned," I said, to no one in particular. Ember had been one of my class instructors, whom I ended up with one-on-one quite often before being assigned to him, but I would never have guessed him to be a Head.

"A few years after you arrived," Spade said, "Ember began to notice a shift in thinking within the Sedition, a shift toward self-preservation. The original Heads had all been replaced, and most of the second-gen Heads were more concerned with themselves than the rest of the world. They mistook the medium for the message. Egos soared, conflicts rose, and Ember began to repeatedly find himself in the minority when it came to choosing and not choosing grants. He started to build an alliance, those that were loyal to the *cause* of the Sedition, not simply the Sedition itself."

Spade made a circular motion in the air with his finger. "Flash forward: when we're called to this meeting, Ember instantly recognizes the Faction undertones in the background. The fact that this meeting even took place has a grave nature, for the

Faction to be calling on the Sedition is like the Joker calling on Batman for help with some evil scheme. The Faction, the very people we hunt, are trying to ally with us, but for their own gain. Ember is terrified, for he's seen the power of the Faction up close."

"Did the Faction know who they were calling on?" I glanced at Vail.

He watched Spade impassively, and almost looked bored.

"I honestly don't know." Spade bowed his head. "I do know this is the crucial moment Ember came to believe that the Sedition was lost. He believed certain Sedition heads would support Gemination, and knew he would be outnumbered when it came down to a vote. The only solution, he said, was to stall the effect and counter Gemination before they called on the Sedition for an answer. The Sedition and the Faction combined would be unstoppable — no more checks and balances on a global scale. The world would be completely dominated."

"Completely dominated?" I repeated. "Those are some pretty strong words."

"Not nearly strong enough," Vail put in.

I shook my head. "There's no way in hell the Sedition, no matter how skewed the vision has become, would support the genocide of the 'lessers' of the developed world."

"Do you really think that the Faction would put all their cards face up on the table?" Vail asked, shaking his head in return. "They'd pick a version of the truth, one that the Sedition would find appealing. Their job is to sell lies, and they're damned good at it," he said harshly.

Spade went on. "We're walking away from the complex, and Ember's swearing under his breath, talking like a madman, saying we have to disable the whole place immediately and bury it deep, when we notice we're being followed. This fine young fellow — " He clapped Vail on the back hard. " — steps out of the shadows with a shotgun pointed at Ember's face, and asks if he could have a word with us. I am initially confused, thinking it's an ambush. Ember understands immediately, knowing he's part of the escaped 19."

I eyed Vail, and he lazily saluted me.

"Ember is thrilled. He now has an immediate force to work with to ensure that an environment is not created in which Gemination will rise. We stall for time — stall the Faction, stall the Sedition — and begin our work, but there's a glitch. We still have to go to work at the Sedition and maintain 'normal' lives, so the Sedition doesn't know anything is amiss... meaning we can't physically work for the 19. We can't be involved at all — no memory." He tapped his temple. "Too dangerous. What we need is a liaison, but a liaison incapable of leading back to us."

He said this last sentence with a measured evenness. "And this is where you come in."

CHAPTER 32

"This is where she came in." The head of security pointed to a monitor. On it, a white-clad nurse wheeled a gurney into the lobby.

"Came in right through the fucking front door," Black Suit remarked, inwardly furious but semi-impressed at the same time. "Unbelievable! At least we have a face to go with the ghost now." He pushed the pause button and froze the frame right over the girl's face. Truly unremarkable, as the guard had said, but the eyes told a different story, a story the guard would never have been able to read: highly trained and lethal. "You're sure it's Leyla Stone? Sedition emissary?"

"We've only got the face to go off," the head of security said, which made the probability of positive identification improbable, as appearance meant nothing at this point. "She left no prints anywhere."

"Of course not. She's not an amateur." They'd tailed her meticulously months ago and she'd turned up squeaky clean. Black Suit was beginning to believe that perhaps he'd met his match, but he might be able to use that to his advantage.

CHAPTER 33

"What do you mean, *'this is* where I come in'?" I asked slowly.

Vail and Spade both stared at me intently, and Vail's hands curled into fists under the table.

What do they think is going to happen?

Spade turned his chair so that he directly faced me. "This is where it gets tricky, so I need your absolute, undivided attention. This is the other half of the story, the other side of the coin, and it goes way back—before the hospital, before Gemination—but this is the reason you have no recollection of the things we're talking about, even though you know of them in great detail."

"That makes no sense." I started to feel kind of edgy.

Spade ignored me and began. "Since the beginning of Ember's and my time at the Sedition, years before you came to work, we've had a joint project together. We've been working on the creation of the infallible emissary. Now, Stone, what is espionage's greatest tool?"

I thought for a moment, expecting a trick question, but the answer was obvious. "The agent."

He nodded. "In particular, the mind of the agent—successful or unsuccessful control of the mind is what makes or breaks us. Control isn't really a good word, however, because control implies effort, and what we want is *effortless*." A strange expression settled on Spade's face. "All emissaries have their breaking point. Everyone breaks. But... what if that was impossible? What if there was no breaking point?"

"No breaking point," I repeated. "How?"

Spade leaned in close to me. "This is where you need to pay very close attention, Leyla Stone. What if the agent could do things that he was unaware of, things his conscious didn't know about? If the agent didn't remember something he'd done, how could he incriminate himself? And how could an agent give up pertinent information if he didn't even know he had it? What if you could truly compartmentalize the mind, lock up secrets in different areas, so that the conscious mind was not privy to everything? Only with the right key, the right catalyst, could it be unlocked." Spade touched his index finger to his temple. "Psychological warfare, with a twist that has never been done or even thought of before."

"Sounds like brainwashing."

"No, brainwashing implies a lack of control. Do you remember the case of Chris Costner back in the 1950s? It became a book, *The Three Faces of Eve*."

The static in the atmosphere cranked up a notch, and Spade and Vail fixated on me like rabid dogs.

I hadn't read the book, but I had seen the movie. "Yes, about the woman with the mental disorder, dissociative identity disorder...." I flashed back to Psychology 101, freshman year. "What does that have to do with it?"

"Everything," Spade said gravely, his face growing dark. "Ember and I sought to create an emissary, a striker, who would be unbreakable. We sought to fortify the walls of the mind, so that nothing would be able to penetrate it, not even the one who occupied the mind."

A strange feeling welled up from the deep within me, like a bright orb rising from the depths of the sea, and came to rest right behind my eyes, in the optic chiasm.

The chasm where I lie in wait, the chasm where I will be reborn, the chasm where I will remember who I am.

The morphine cloud began to puff up again, but I chased it away.

Spade tapped my wrist, as if sensing I was about to float off. "You remember I said Ember took particular interest in you? Do you want to know why?"

I swallowed. "Maybe."

"Well, not just anyone could be the infallible emissary. It takes a very specific, yet very rare, set of genes. The mind has to be both pliable and stable, kind of an oxymoron. Ember and his geneticist, Daniel Rutger, had been looking for this specific genetic combination in an individual for a long time, and they found it in you."

"Me?" I repeated.

"You are the archetype. You are the greatest agent the world has ever seen. You are the greatest because you do not know it. You are not conscious of it, not aware. It is simply what is."

I had heard enough. "Look, I don't have chunks of time that are blank. There are no gaping holes in my memory. I remember everything." I almost yelled it.

"Tell me, Stone," Spade turned on me coldly. "Do you? Do you remember every dream you have, the moments after you go to sleep, the moments before you wake up? Have you ever wondered what goes on in those periods between dreaming and waking?"

"What are you saying?"

"I am saying that we found a way to involve you fully conscious, but unconsciously so."

I shook my head at him in disbelief.

"Tell me the last dream you had."

I sat there, thinking. I delved deep inside my head, to flashbacks of all the dreams in my life flowing through the synapses of my brain. I had always been an avid dreamer, and the dream world had never disappointed: vivid, always in color, epic even. Apocalyptic. The childhood nightmares of wolves devouring my family... always being chased, always being hunted, always right on the brink... learning to fly... learning to lucid dream and turning the tide, battle and victory... but....

Lately? Nothing. How odd that I didn't notice.

"Stone... Stone? Stone!" Spade jarred me back to life.

Doubt of the self set in. "I don't remember. It's as though I haven't dreamed in a long time," I whispered.

"I know."

"How would you know?"

A cruel smile touched Spade's lips. "It's my job, remember?"

"Are you saying that I did all this in my sleep?" I asked cynically.

"Oh no, you were awake, but you weren't yourself."

"As in?" Dread filled the pit of my stomach like a lead weight, as it all began to come together.

"Same person, different identity." He waited.

For some reason, I looked to Vail for explanation.

"This is what it comes down to," Vail said. "They induced another personality out of your mind, the one that would remember, who's talking to me right now, and the one that would not, sitting somewhere quietly behind your eyes, watching. You work in the light, and she works in the dark."

The room stilled. Crickets would have been appropriate.

"What?" I said softly, as full comprehension dawned on me. I'd been dissected like a frog in high school anatomy. "You bastards gave me a fucking mental disorder!" I screamed, and the glass in front of me shattered as it had the day before — from my voice or hand, I wasn't sure. "Is that what you're saying?"

"I wouldn't call it a disorder, but... yes," said Vail calmly.

"That's impossible."

"No, it's not."

I searched his face and body language for lies, and found none. "What the fuck is the matter with you people?" I stood and started backing away.

"Easy," Vail said calmly, and stood too.

"Get the fuck away from me!" I pushed my chair towards him, and stood poised like a wild cat weighing its options for escape. If I bolted for the door, they would be on me too quickly. I'd waited too long, lost the element of surprise. Curiosity might really kill the cat this time.

"Oh, come off it, Stone." Spade suddenly jumped up from his chair. "You're already half crazy. It didn't take much. You have every predisposition for a mental disorder. Do you want to know what you got on your psyche evaluation? Indigo 11 wasn't the only reason the

Sedition didn't want you, initially. The eval revealed too much contradiction in your personality. Not to mention, you flat out carry the gene for mental illness—it's hereditary, all over your family! Your mother...." Spade trailed off and collected himself. "We found a way to stabilize the gene." He said the next few words slowly and deliberately. "You are not ill."

"So, you're telling me I've got two god-damned people inside of me right now?" I regretted not letting the Geminates kill them.

"Yes, but one of you is awake and the other is lying dormant. You trade off, so both of you are never active, thus there's no schism."

"You bastards! Who the hell did this?" I couldn't believe it.

"The psychological warfare project team, chief among them, your pal, Nicholai Bachman. He's the hypnotherapist."

"Nico?" I had no clue Nico was anything beyond a cosmologist, always in the library poring over his books, talking to himself. I called him the professor. "What did he give me, schizophrenia?" I thought of the blonde in the *Three Faces of Eve*, Eve White and Eve Black and a third one I couldn't remember.

"It's a stabilized, intelligent version of dissociative identity disorder."

That sounded even worse. "I'm going to kill them, all of them."

"What about Ember?"

"It's good he's already dead." I rued the words as soon as I said them. I put my hands on either side of my head, eyes roving wild. "All those sessions with the hypnotherapist, the psychiatrist...." I had no recollection that Nico had been the hypnotherapist. In fact, I couldn't see a face at all when I thought of the hypnotherapist, or the psychiatrist.

My God, I've been severely tampered with.

"We told you those sessions would help you to become a better striker, and it was the truth."

"But you didn't tell me the whole truth!"

"We couldn't. That would have defeated the purpose! You are one of a kind, the next jump in evolution, mentally. Ember had been looking for you for a long, long time. What would you have chosen if you had known the full truth?"

I'd heard enough. I stalked into the bedroom, slammed the door, sat on the edge of the bed, shot up with some morphine, and shut my eyes.

Spade and Vail were at least smart enough not to follow me.

I remained still for a long time, all of it too wild to believe, too wrong on so many levels. I didn't even know where to start. Vail had just talked about being turned into a science experiment, and I would never have guessed that the same had happened to me.

What would I have chosen if I had known the full truth?

If Ember had offered me the choice to become the most effective, efficient emissary in the Sedition, on the *planet,* in *history*, what would I have said?

After fighting it for a while, I had to admit that Spade was right. I would have chosen to go through with it, even if I had known. At least I thought I would have, but I would never really know, as this was all hypothetical. That moment had never come, and never would.

I stared down at the hideous shag carpeting under my feet, probably put down in the 1970's. I remembered lying on a floor like this after drinking a tea brewed from poppies, lying next to Camden, drowning in those hazel eyes of his, both of us laced with quelling calm from the opium. *Camden Grace.* I hardly recognized him by that name anymore. He'd become Nate Tyson, but he'd always just be Cam to me.

I still remembered that feeling, one of unconditional love for all things great and small. The nicest high I'd ever had, it made me love the world for all its infinite perfections and imperfections. That was back in boarding school, when things had been much simpler, innocent—no Sedition, no Faction, no Geminates. I felt disdain for the world now, for allowing so much evil to run amuck, but I had a choice to make: turn tail and run, or carry on with what had already begun.

Our entire lives come down to just one moment. Unnoticed by most, it often passes us by without so much as a nod, but there is a pivotal moment, no matter how great or small, in each of our lives that turns the tide, for good or ill. I call this the crossroads, the life path, and this was *her* crossroads. She finally knew the truth.

I peered out from behind those eyes, right into the face of Devlin Vail, against all odds alive. For the time being, anyway, and that made me exceptionally happy.

I normally didn't interfere when Stone was in control. I watched her go about her day, listened to the people she talked to, keep a lookout for anything unusual, but when it all went haywire and I ended up on the inside permanently, I couldn't sit by idly.

As the subconscious half of us, I'm fully aware of... well, pretty much everything. I almost feel sorry for her, but what's done is done.

I walked away from John Ember that night knowing the game had changed. The next time I saw him, he was giving her orders to create false passes to gain entry into the hospital, and I assumed the worst; the 19 was over. When Ember and Stone split up in the hospital, I pushed for her to go back and find him. She listened, though it did little good.

I knew I had to go dark when he died, but with her sleep schedule, she didn't give me a chance to get out anyway. The patient files afforded me a brief moment of hope, until I realized Vail wasn't among them. Either he had escaped or he was dead, and I had no way of finding out which. For two maddening weeks, I sat, waiting for a sign, from friend or foe. When he followed her from the cemetery, I couldn't have been happier, but a few minutes later, when I found myself surrounded by dead geminates and staring down the barrel of a gun aimed at him, I threw everything I had at her to stop her from pulling the trigger. It worked, so at least I knew I could turn the tide when it came down to it—down to the most crucial moment.

Normally, each of us hits the crossroads around age twenty-seven; well, twenty-seven and a half to be exact. It begins with a voice that starts telling us we had better figure out just what in the hell we're doing here. A fairly unpleasant period is followed by an abrupt halt, as the path suddenly becomes unclear. When you hit the crossroads, there are five choices. The sweet inertia of the path you're on makes it easy to continue forward. You just better hope you can discern whether you're on the path of integration or the path of fragmentation. You deviate to either side in the crossroads and your life changes considerably. Or you retreat, and go back from whence you came, and live complacently, comfortably numb. And the fifth? You stand right where you are, and do nothing, because you are afraid. You freeze, and the wave of time destroys you in its aftermath.

The girl I knew as Leyla Stone had buried her brother, and then taken up with a band of vagrant vigilantes. Now that was crashing down, and she found herself in a place that was all too familiar. It wasn't her first crossroads, and I didn't think it would be her last. I only hoped there wouldn't be too many more to come, for the crossroads is a dangerous game. Making too many turns will eventually get you killed, and since my fate was bound with hers, I was quite curious to see what she would choose.

The last time we come upon the crossroads is in death, and it may not seem like it, but there are choices then, too.

She was now twenty-seven and a half.

So... what are we going to do?

CHAPTER 34

There is *truth* **and then there** is *Truth*. Capital "T" *Truth* is the only real choice, but it's a terribly subjective matter. In my heart of hearts, I knew there was no going back and no choice, only the illusion of one, as Spade suggested. From the macrocosm to the microcosm, it was in my blood, for better or worse. Returning to ignorance would be a sin, not to mention impossible, and running would solve nothing. Evil would exist independently of me. What exactly was I prepared to do about it?

I rose from the bed, pushed the door open, and leaned against the door frame casually. Spade and Vail hadn't left their seats, but the shards of my broken glass had been removed from the table, as though they anticipated me using them as a weapon, as I had with the geminate. The thought hadn't even crossed my mind, but the fact that it crossed theirs left me incensed. I crossed my arms in front of me, on the defensive.

"Then what?" I asked through gritted teeth, determined to hear the rest of it out.

Spade patted the seat next to him, overeager to resume this maddening conversation.

I glared at him and didn't move.

He shrugged and raised an eyebrow at Vail, who didn't return the gesture. "You, the new method of psychological warfare, were ready long before that meeting with Gemination, but Ember had been waiting for the right situation to put it into play. I don't suppose he ever expected to use it against the Sedition. Ironically, that's how it turned out. Talk about a classic case of biting the hand that feeds you... but they brought it upon themselves."

Use it, as in, *use me.* Now that was fucked up. That's what I was to them: a weapon, an object.

"After that first encounter with the 19, all further dealings were done through a middle man, or in this case, a middle woman. Understand, Stone, this is only the second time Vail and I have met."

"What else did you *use* me for?" I asked, knowing there was more.

"Reconnaissance," Spade answered flatly.

I imagined some bizarre parallel universe shadow of me prowling through the night like a ninja, the other half of the other half.

Ridiculous. That wasn't me. "How did it work? How did you get me to go dormant and someone else to show up?"

"I'll get to that in a moment, but I can't give you a geneticist's explanation. You'll have to wait for Rutger on that one."

"Fucking great," I muttered, getting a new glass from the cabinet and dropping back down into my chair. Vail immediately filled it from the pitcher, which I eyed warily.

Paranoia infiltrated my mind. What if they had drugged it in my absence? At this point, I didn't put anything past anyone. I pretended to drink it to gauge a reaction, but there was none.

Spade continued. "But first, let me clarify something that will help you. Ember *did* ask you. In a deep hypnotic state, he explained the situation and asked your subconscious, and you agreed."

"That doesn't fucking count," I snapped. "Asking me when I'm completely out of it... like I said, the road to hell is paved with good intentions."

"No, Stone, listen. In this state, the subconscious will not agree to anything that it would not agree to consciously. You would also have consciously chosen this, which is why we found it ethically acceptable."

"Whatever." Small explosions rippled across the surface of my brain.

"Listen, there are many examples of mental illness, but what makes them illnesses is that they're unstable. The illness prevents people from discerning between reality and fantasy, or right from wrong. Schizophrenia, anti-personality disorder—"

"Dissociative identity disorder," I interrupted. No way in hell I'd be convinced they'd found a way to make that okay.

He ignored me. "As I said, the psychological warfare crew found a way to stabilize the gene through a form of compartmentalization."

I found myself unable to move my eyes from the floor, fearing that if I did, the world might shatter. Spade waited and, after a moment, I forced myself to look at him.

"It worked brilliantly," he said, and there was no mistaking the awe in his voice. "Mental stability, perfect duality...."

The world did not shatter, and time continued on as it always had and always would, regardless if we were part of it or not, despite what Vail had said the previous evening. Irrationally, I tried to freeze it, but nothing happened.

I glanced over at Vail. *Liar.* He pierced me back with those damn blue eyes, and I looked away.

Spade continued on with that ridiculous voice of wonderment, sounding like a mad scientist, which made me want to punch him in the face. "It's not as crazy as it sounds. It's still you, simply a different facet of your mind."

I tried my best to look as unimpressed as possible.

"Okay, think of it like this." He spread his arms wide. "Think of the mind as a vast lake. On the surface, a very small portion of the lake, is the conscious, but the subconscious lies in the deep, where there is nearly infinite space. The subconscious is an alternative storehouse of one's knowledge and prior experience, and it has a powerful awareness." He winked absurdly. "Imagine waking that up."

"And what happens now that my conscious knows? Kind of defeats the purpose, huh?"

Spade and Vail exchanged glances. "Well, it certainly loses the element of surprise, but I think it will still work."

"You think?" *No way in fuck will I ever see a "specialist" of any kind ever again. Fool me once, shame on you. Fool me twice, I'll put a bullet in my own head and save you the trouble.*

"Originally, you were never meant to find out. You would remain separate from the other. But after the hospital, the *first* time, we didn't have many options." Spade stared into space as his mind changed track. "What the hell was he thinking?" he said more to himself, shaking his head.

Apparently, Vail understood. "I've asked myself that a million times."

I kicked Spade's chair again. "What the hell was *who* thinking?"

He looked up sharply, annoyed. "Will you stop that?"

I raised an eyebrow.

Spade let out an exasperated sigh. "What I meant is... what was Ember thinking, taking you to the hospital?"

"It's a mystery," Vail agreed, "but not the most pressing one."

"Which is?" Spade asked.

"Why the other one did not come back? Did he tell her not to?"

My jaw dropped. "The *other* one?"

"Eva Fox is her name."

Dropped further still. "Her name? As in my name?"

"Eva Fox is the name I've known you by," Vail said. "And John Ember had an alias also. We knew him as Thomas Colton, from a distance."

"Eva Fox," I repeated.

"We named you Eva after the Three Faces of Eve."

"You thought it was very clever," Spade added.

"Did I now?" An awkward silence followed and neither of them answered. "Okay, tell me about her, or me, or whoever. Essentially, she's another side of my mind, right?"

"Your subconscious, to be exact," Vail expounded. "This entity, Eva Fox, was only to be activated under specific circumstances for the 19. Fox knew that she existed as a subset of your mind, she knew everything about you, but you knew nothing of her. The subconscious sees all, albeit through a slightly different-colored lens."

Strawberry fields forever. It sure as hell was not a rose-colored lens.

"You went about your days as before, as Leyla Stone. Nothing changed. You went to work at the Sedition as usual, but every so often, in the night while you were sleeping, we would call Eva Fox to the 19."

"And how is this possible?"

Crickets again.

Spade and Vail exchanged meaningful glances, which I found extremely maddening. I fought the impulse to kick Spade's chair again.

Vail gave another meaningful nod and Spade began. "There is a plant called *brugmansia,* commonly known as—"

"Angel Trumpet," I finished impatiently. "It's a hallucinogen. They were all over South America." The grant I'd pulled in South America a few years back had begun in Colombia, but the trail had led me clear through Bolivia, hot on the trail of Butch and Sundance, and down to the lakes region of Chile. I'd encountered the plant all along the way, and though tempted, never experimented with it. The shrub's gorgeous yellow flowers resembled trumpets hanging upside down.

"Yes, it can be used as a hallucinogen," Spade said patiently. "But it's packed with several other powerful toxins, one of which is a form of scopolamine. Scopolamine is an extremely potent drug that leaves victims unaware of what they are doing but entirely conscious. Unaware... meaning they remember nothing after the fact."

I suddenly remembered that the cartels had used the same plant, which they called Colombian Devil's Breath, to get people to steal for them. One man even moved all of his valuable possessions out of his own apartment and into the hands of his robbers without remembering any of it. At the time, I'd been after the *real* mastermind of yet another bombing, and white-collar crime hardly registered. It's bad when the cartels take the back seat in the world of crimes against humanity.

"So, what? I ingest some scopolamine from this plant and become Eva Fox?"

"Not exactly. We needed to keep your intelligence intact. The Angel Trumpet takes your intelligence."

"Don't all drugs take your intelligence?" I couldn't think of a single time I'd made a particularly good decision under the influence, other than pool tournaments.

"No. For example, when you ingest hallucinogenic mushrooms, your intelligence is intact — different, but intact. You're generally aware you've taken the fungi, and that what is happening is a result of that, but there are some drugs that fully strip your intelligence to the point where you aren't aware you've taken a drug at all. This is the Angel Trumpet."

"It's like salvia," I said, as another memory bobbed to the surface.

Cam was in that one too. After Ben died, I self-medicated for about three months or so, and Cam was more than happy to indulge my tastes, as well as other benefits that came with it. I left him when I came out of mourning, broke his heart. I still felt a little bad about it. Now, I saw him nearly every day at work. We'd ironically been recruited together and ended up in the same striker class.

Not ironic, my mind insisted. *He was a test. The Heads put him there on purpose.*

I tried to avoid him as much as possible, as he constantly reminded me of Ben.

Spade nodded. "Anyway, Nico found a way in hypnotherapy to create a stable environment for the scopolamine to take place. In the end, you came out being fully aware in the subconscious, while the conscious slept."

"How the hell did you get me to take the drug?" I imagined them taking turns slipping it into my water at the Sedition. Was it also in this water sitting in front of me? I eyed the glass suspiciously again.

"Your vitamins," Spade answered sheepishly. "Eva Fox switched them out when necessary. In an emergency, Ember himself would go to your house."

"I'll be damned." Ember knew where I lived. Of course, he was a damn Head. "Have I been getting the red pill or the blue pill?" I muttered to myself sarcastically.

"Both."

I narrowed my eyes at him. "So, I take my vitamin cocktail, go to bed, and then what?"

"You know that odd state where you're conscious but dreaming? And that feeling when you're drifting off to sleep, and you jerk yourself awake?"

"Yes." I normally experienced at least one of them every night, though again, not lately.

"The first is the hypnagogic state of consciousness. Hypnagogia is the experience of the transitional state from wakefulness to sleep. It's the phase of threshold consciousness. Lucid dreaming, hallucinations, and sleep paralysis all occur here. Conversely, the transitional state from sleep to wakefulness is the hypnopompic experience."

Spade paused to refill his water glass, ruling out my roofie theory. I looked over at Vail, who for once refused to meet my gaze with his intense eye contact. This part of the conversation clearly made him uncomfortable.

"The latter is called a hypnic jerk, an involuntary twitch that occurs during the hypnagogic state. Our theory on the hypnic jerk is that it prevents you from dropping into REM sleep too fast. If you were to do that, you might slip into a state of unconsciousness, and not wake again. The hypnic jerk helps to regulate the sleep cycle. We mixed the scopolamine with a powerful sedative, designed to quickly drop the consciousness into deep sleep before the scopolamine kicked in. The sedative inhibited the hypnic jerk. It put out the conscious."

I regretted the morphine. Now in full swing, my brain and body were nearly too stoned to follow, and I just wanted to go back to sleep. Why hadn't I thought to steal some opioid antagonists as well?

"However, the other side of the mind, the subconscious, became frozen in the hypnagogic state. When the scopolamine kicked in, you would wake in the subconscious, your alter ego. Your conscious self went dormant and the subconscious rose."

"This is already extremely confusing, but there's more to it, isn't there?"

He sighed. "There was another component in place to safeguard you, in case you were compromised or captured, so that not just anyone could pull Eva Fox out of you. Understand, the hypnagogic state is an extremely narrow window. We created a catalyst, one that had to occur at just the right moment, just after the sedative kicked in but before the scopolamine took effect."

"What was the catalyst?"

Another awkward pause as Spade and Vail exchanged yet another set of meaningful glances. Christ, it was like we were three-way speed dating or something.

"Let me guess: this is what you don't know how to do," I deduced, remembering their little argument at the very beginning of this ludicrous conversation nearly twenty-four hours ago. A lot could change in a day. I ran my hands through my hair and somehow resisted pulling it out.

Vail answered. "Ember did, the crew did and I assumed Spade knew, and he assumed I knew, but Ember left us a little prematurely, and disadvantaged because of it."

"Great."

"Missing the catalyst to the catalyst, so to speak," Vail reflected, like some beatnik poet.

Spade continued on as though this were only a minor glitch. "Then you woke in the subconscious mind as Eva Fox and went to the 19 or wherever Ember sent you. After a few hours of work, you went home and back to sleep, aware that you would remember nothing later."

Aware that I would be unaware.... What a mind job!

I sighed, crossed my arms and sat back in my chair. "All of that, for nothing."

They both looked at me quizzically.

"Ember's dead, we're all on the run, and Eva Fox is nowhere to be found."

Spade shook his head. "Not for nothing. Eva Fox is still in there. We just have to get her to come out."

"And just how are you going to do that?" Even if they had the catalyst, I didn't know if I would cooperate.

"Ember must have left something behind. We'll find it," Spade said half-heartedly.

"What if we don't?" I asked, playing devil's advocate.

"We'll find it, Stone," Spade reiterated. "We have to."

Ah, here was the real reason Ember assigned Vail to protect my life with his. "Why?"

"She knows something."

"And what's that?"

Vail leaned in close. "What Eva Fox knows is very important. That is to say, in essence, what *you* know is very important. That night before the attack, Fox was out on detail, her shadow work. She believed she was very close to finding the true source behind Gemination. Yeah, we know they're the army for the Faction, but we want the specific *they* of Gemination. One of the Faction was revealed, the one responsible for Gemination."

"How do you not know that? You were one of the Faction."

"No," he said forcefully. "I am not one of the Faction—never before, never again. I was hired muscle, only receiving orders from their lackeys. I never met the people that gave them."

"One of the hamsters, huh?" I meant this as an insult, but unfortunately, he didn't take it as one.

"Quite right, a hamster, nothing more," he agreed. "As I said before, Ember found out about the raid on the 19 right before it happened. That's why I'm here. He also managed to get Eva Fox as far away as possible, which is fortunate, except that it also means she took whatever she found with her." He tapped his index to his temple. "We don't know who the Gemination Head is, but we think you do. I feel certain that whatever Eva Fox found out that night would give us the source target, and if we find the source, we can take it out by the root."

Finally, the *Truth* in why I was here. Spade and Vail didn't need me; they needed what I had, something locked away in the deep recesses of my mind. Whatever psychological warfare project Spade and Ember had drummed up failed. Would they cut it out of me with some new horror? What would happen to me when they got what they were after? Clean up the mess and start over again? Was I that disposable?

"I don't know anything," I said stubbornly. *And I wouldn't tell you if I did.*

"Eva Fox does," Vail repeated.

"Then you need Eva Fox," I growled.

"You are Eva Fox," Vail almost pleaded.

"Not anymore." For a moment, the atmosphere grew very tense, the air stilled. Vail and I locked eye to eye, and time began to slow, to alter itself. For a moment, I thought a fight was imminent and balled my hands into fists in my lap.

Spade broke the tension with a gentle touch on my arm, and I automatically uncurled my fists. "Leyla Stone." He again somehow forced me to look him in the eye, like we were polar ends of a magnet. "Eva Fox is not your enemy and neither are we." He pulled his chair a little closer, kept hold of my arm. "Listen, Stone, all this—" He gestured around. "—us on the run and all... it might not be too late."

"Too late for what?" I asked cautiously.

"To go back," he said optimistically. "What I'm hoping is that what Eva Fox found out will save the Sedition, as in stop the Sedition from making a grave error. The Heads don't know that what lies behind Gemination is the Faction. If we can find information, evidence, a name, anything that will turn the Sedition on its true enemy, Gemination and the Faction, we can stop an alliance from happening. I'm sure of it. We can still fix this, make it a grant like any other. We can go back home, back to the Sedition."

Vail scoffed. "Do you really believe that?"

"I have to," Spade spoke softly. "*We* have to," he said to me. "We have to try, Stone. We can't give up on them yet. What do you say? One last grant to stop the world?"

I shut the room out and dropped into my own mind, saw Ember and his nice white uniform splattered with blood. Ember had died for this, and I would have died for Ember, so by default, I had to go along with it.

I looked up and met Spade's eyes sincerely. "What do you want me to do?"

"For now, until we figure out a new modus operandi, stay alive—that's the main thing. Can you do that?"

Stay alive.

If Ember couldn't stay alive, how could I? A pang of guilt tugged at my heartstrings. Intellectually, I knew his death wasn't my fault, but the bottom line was that I didn't save him. That simple fact alone might gnaw away at me for the rest of my life, regardless of the circumstances that surrounded it.

The morphine cloud rose again, and this time I let it carry me away.

CHAPTER 35

I'm having a flashback that feels as real as a lucid dream. For a minute, I think I'm there.

> *I'm at the bar, sitting at the back table, loading the gun. Vail sits in the booth to my right and his electric, blue eyes freeze the breath inside my chest. Then the pale faces that belong to what I call the carbons walk through the door. I glance back to the booth, but Vail is gone, and in his place sits a very familiar person: me. She's smiling back at me, then flicks her eyes back to the Geminates, and I follow her trail to find Vail and several others, all faces I don't recognize, who surely must be part of the 19. They're wearing suits, but bearing no weapons.*

Then I realize this is neither a flashback nor a lucid dream; it's a daydream, and a weird one at that. My eyes are open, my body is on autopilot, but I'm gone. I remember this is how I got through formal education: autopilot.

A voice called me back to the table. I'd been hovering around in the ether, not sure for how long. I blinked a few times, and Vail's face lazily swam into view, patiently waiting for me to come back to reality, and from the expression on his face, it seemed as though he'd done this hundreds of times. Common personality trait of the mentally ill, I guessed.

"How did Eva Fox get in and out of her... my... house without being spotted and followed?" I asked abruptly, giving no explanation for my sudden absence.

Spade looked at me skeptically. "I don't know," he said slowly. "We hardly knew anything about Eva Fox. It was better that way. Her only instructions were: if you are summoned, come and do not be found out."

Vail chimed in. "Maybe she has a hidden door or something."

I suddenly envisioned superheroes and secret lairs. "Okay, well, I think I'd know about it if it was in my house."

"Don't be so sure." He rose and planted himself in the doorway between the kitchen and the living room.

I rolled my eyes. "Has the Sedition been to my house, Spade?"

"No, not yet, but it will happen soon."

Satisfied, I switched directions. "Did they follow you?"

"Of course, though they don't think I'm aware of it. Foolish to try to outsmart a striker, but that's their weakness. They've forgotten what it was to be strikers. Now Head of the strikers, their ego tells them that they are infallible, above and beyond the striker mind."

I sighed. "What the hell happened to the Heads?"

"The original seven were brilliant. As with any organization, I suspect the Sedition's truth started to deviate when new blood came in, and from what I saw today, the wrong people became the Sedition Heads—

people with agendas—but to tell you the truth, they're not the ones we have to worry about. It's the others." He raised an eyebrow at Vail, still leaning in the doorframe.

"The others?" I inquired.

"Guests," Spade said to me, while keeping his eyes on Vail. His voice grew strange, ultra-articulate. "There was a guest on the Sedition council today, one I think you would have found rather familiar."

Vail said nothing as they stared at each other.

I would have been more curious, but my mind was fixated on Ember's drive, the one I'd unwisely left behind. I let the silence go on for a few minutes, and then broke it. "I need to go to my house."

The silence continued.

"Spade, I need to go home," I repeated.

He slowly came out of his reverie and turned to me as Vail walked back into the living room.

What the hell was that all about? Wait and see.

He shook his head. "What part of *stay alive* don't you understand? The Sedition will be waiting for you, and they want you dead as much as Gemination does."

"You said yourself they don't remember their striker days, and I *am* a striker." Spade's speech about going back to the Sedition had given me hope, and the drive had to be the key to it all. "I can get in without them knowing. I've done it before."

A few weeks ago wasn't the first time I'd considered going on the run. After the Indigo grant, as the only survivor, I'd hid out in the caretaker's cottage for a day while contemplating my path. It was the physical intel the Sedition needed that made me go back. I'd planned to use it as leverage in the negotiations for my life, but Ember had taken it to where I didn't even need to do that.

You've got what we need, don't you? He'd asked, wiping the last of grime off my face. *You can give it to me. You can trust me.*

And so I had, but had I been wrong to trust him?

Spade looked at me doubtfully.

"Listen," Spade, "everything I have of any value is inside that house, information-wise, I mean. I just need a few things, in and out. It's important."

"Fine. I only relent because I know you will do this regardless of what I say. Just know that they will move as soon as they detect you, and be assured, they will detect you quickly."

"I'm aware of that." *Battle won.* "Who tailed you, by the way?"

"I'm not sure, but if Olly Skelton did his job, and Jase Avery is as smart as I give him credit for, it will be his team."

I smiled. Avery, a bull of a man, headed our sister team. The other name, however, I didn't know. "Who is Olly Skelton?"

"Oliver Skelton is a Sedition Head, and Ember's only ally."

I joined Vail in the living room for a moment to survey the street below. The world looked as normal as ever, a drug deal and a prostitute working every corner as far as the eye could see — glorious. He gave me a sidelong glance as though he knew about the drive.

"Be careful, Stone."

I scoffed. "What does that even mean? If I was careful, if *any* of us were careful, we wouldn't be here.

We'd be sitting in some suburban house with a white picket fence, 2.5 kids, a dog, a cat, and a lawn mower."

He turned to face me. "Is that what you think being careful looks like?"

I thought for a moment. "No, that's what being 'sheeple' looks like."

"Waiting patiently for the wolf to come get you." He took a step toward me, and I pulled myself up to my full height. "When you go to your suburban home with your picket fence, don't wait for the wolf."

"I'll do my best."

I turned around, and Spade met me with a set of car keys. "There's a little blue Volvo in the parking garage. Take that."

"Where did you get it?"

"Doesn't matter. It's clean."

I left them standing by the bay window in the living room, the tension between them mounting. That was a story that needed explaining, but not today.

CHAPTER 36

Jase Avery watched the little blue Volvo pull out of the parking garage and turn back towards the city. However, he'd parked too far away to see who sat behind the wheel. "Who is that?"

The earpiece crackled and Jackson Corbin's voice came on. "None other than Leyla Stone," he answered, the relief in his voice audible.

"Should we follow?" Maren Vancent, athletic and bronzed from her recent trip to Brazil, sat in his passenger's seat.

Avery thought for a moment and looked up at the building, trying to discern where Spade might be—in a window, watching surely. What would he expect? Someone to keep an eye on her, of course. What the hell she was up to, he had no idea.

"No, Vance, we'll stay here. Corbin, Elkan, follow her, but I'll give you an extra man. Pick Bish up on your way."

Crispin Bishop sat in the back seat, still livid that Stone had fooled him that night after the cemetery on Cherry Hill. Well, perhaps fooled wasn't the right word, but she had still made him look bad, regardless of the circumstance.

"On our way," came the response.

"Bish?" Avery raised an eyebrow. The black man hadn't moved a muscle since they'd left the Sedition. He could be mistaken for sleeping, even, if it weren't for the smoldering eyes.

"I'm on it," Bishop said gruffly, as the car pulled up. He got out of the car and slammed the door.

Maren Vancent winced and pulled her long brown hair up into a high ponytail. "He's still mad, hasn't said much in the last few days. My usually animated, Chatty Cathy partner has gone the way of a stoic Charlie Chaplin."

"Well, it doesn't matter anymore," Avery stated. "Not like he's going to be called up for a review by the Heads or anything. Those days are over."

The finality of his last statement hit him like a ton of bricks. The game had really changed. They weren't going back — any of them.

"God help us," he added.

"I think God is sitting this one out," Vancent said, a wan smile on her face.

CHAPTER 37

They watched in silence. The blue Volvo seven stories below Spade and Vail emerged from underneath the building. After it turned the block, a gray sedan pulled out to follow her, first stopping to pick up a man in another car en route.

"And so it begins," Spade announced epically.

"He was there today?" Vail asked, though not so much in question as confirmation.

Spade nodded almost imperceptibly. "First time I've seen him."

"First time in a long time anyone has seen him. How certain are you that it was *him*?"

Spade smiled weakly. "As certain as one can be in a world of doubles."

"What did he want?" The two cars disappeared from sight, headed north. "Or appear to want?" he clarified.

"Her. They positively identified Stone at the hospital, and he's made a deal with the Sedition. Mutual benefit."

"What name is he going by these days?"

"Trenholm, Ansel Trenholm, living at 123 Fake Street."

"He must be feeling quite confident to make a public appearance. That doesn't bode well."

No, it doesn't bode well, Spade thought, *but you're playing a dangerous game, which doesn't bode well either.* "She doesn't know, does she?" he asked, again in confirmation.

Vail clenched his jaw. "No."

"Why not?"

"I want her to decide for herself."

The silence resumed. An awkward space existed between the two men, as they were not so friendly. John Ember had been the only thread keeping them together, and since he was dead, that thread had worn thin. Nonetheless, they would have to put their differences aside for the benefit of the whole.

This time Vail spoke first. "Did you tell her about the bullet we pulled out of her arm?"

"No, she didn't ask."

"At some point, she'll ask. She'll wonder how she took a direct hit like that and ended up with so little damage, and healed so quickly without bot assistance."

"Perhaps," Spade conceded with no real concern.

"And what will you tell her when she asks?"

"This is the first time she's been shot. She doesn't know any different. She'll just count herself lucky. She always has. Here's further validation."

"I hope you know what you're doing."

"Me too." Spade pulled his cell phone out of his breast pocket and dialed. The other end picked up on the first ring. "She's on her way," he relayed, and listened for a moment. "I'm timing it. I will tell you when she's inside."

CHAPTER 38

I pulled the Volvo off into the forest about a mile from the house, and walked the rest of the way through the woods. My house sat out in the country on close to two hundred acres. A hell of a commute to work, but I preferred it to the alternative — no neighbors, no noise, and certainly no interruptions.

The closest building, an old gas station, sat about five miles south, and judging by the faded gas prices on the weathered sign, the place had long been abandoned, probably since before I was born. $1.19/gallon... the sign belonged in a museum. Gas now topped an all-time high of over ten dollars a gallon.

Madness.

The house itself had belonged to an adultering, crooked congressman. I'd purchased the estate easily in an auction. Many seemed to think the place was cursed, but then my life was too, so it fit.

I paused at the edge of the wood on the perimeter of the property, and honed my senses for another set of eyes: human, bot, or otherwise. Either no one was watching the house, or they had me fooled. Taking a massive leap of faith, I stepped into the open field and hustled to the steps, half expecting a bullet to bring me to my knees. I slipped inside the front door, locked it, and disabled the security system on a timer, which would cut all the cameras on the property for the next thirty minutes. When the Sedition came, I didn't want them to see anything past me coming up the front steps. I didn't plan to stay that long, but there had been a lot of plans lately that hadn't quite panned out.

I ran up the stairs to the third floor, and into the sitting room that adjoined my bedroom. I kicked open a panel in the wall and pulled out a small black backpack, which contained all necessary and relevant information to my history as an emissary at the Sedition. From the beginning, I readied myself for a time when I might have to disappear, and now it was paying off. All I needed was the drive. I pulled a pocketknife out of the backpack and sliced open one of the folds of the canopy bed I slept in occasionally. The drive easily slipped out into my hand and I held it in front of me for a moment, trying to think like Ember.

Show no one, tell no one, trust no one.

The first two I obeyed, the third, not so much. I tucked the drive into my bra and turned to get going, but then changed my mind and went into the bathroom to collect a few personal effects. Certainly, I could have a few creature comforts, a toothbrush, for example. I paused at the sight of myself in the mirror, a black eye blossoming where I'd smacked my face on the windshield. *Damn Vail.* On top of that, I was completely disheveled, half wild looking.

I rummaged through the drawers looking for some concealer and came across the vitamins. *The damn vitamins.* A green plastic day-of-the week container stared at me ominously from its drawer. As I moved my hand pick up the container, I noticed a small but visible tremor running through it. What the hell was that all about? I clenched my fist and hit it on the counter hard, forcing it to stop.

I snatched the container off the counter and opened the one marked "F" for Friday, and inspected the contents: turmeric, holy basil, some glucosamine, and a multi-vitamin. None looked suspicious. I shrugged and threw them in the backpack for a closer inspection at a later date. Halfway out the bathroom, I hesitated.

Look again.

I bent down underneath the sink and opened the cabinet where I kept the larger jars of vitamins, and dumped the contents of the bottles into my hand, not caring that most of it spilled onto the floor. The turmeric capsules had apparently bust open inside the jar, and turmeric dust rained down in the bathroom.

Great, my hands will be orange for a week.

Only, they weren't. The dust on my hands wasn't orange. In fact, it wasn't powdered herb at all. Barely visible, a thin layer of white coated my hands, and it felt like sand — very fine sand. I leapt back up to the sink and turned on the faucet, half expecting it to actually be some kind of acid that would burn my flesh off, but stopped when I realized where it came from: the Zen garden. I knew this, but how? And why?

I stared into the mirror, unable to break away. What the hell was this new game? If the "me" in the mirror started talking, I wouldn't be the least bit surprised. It might actually be helpful.

"Are you watching?" I asked the mirror, and then held up my hands for her to see. "What is this?"

No answer. *Go look.*

I flew back down the stairs, back through the kitchen, and paused before stepping out the backdoor. The sun had already begun to set, the darkest day of the year fast approaching. I surveyed the outside world, but still, either no one was around or they were better than me. I didn't bank on the latter. I took the path down to the Zen garden, which, oddly enough, was here when I moved in. A big square of sand with a few rocks sat under a shelter to protect it from the rain, an odd choice for the congressman who was a "meat and potatoes for dinner" kind of guy, but perhaps one of his wives built it... or girlfriends, maybe a hippie-trippie, new-age mistress.

I had to admit, though, the technique helped. I went to the Zen Garden when my mind became stuck, when it had run into what seemed to be an impenetrable wall. Sometimes, when meditation wasn't effective and my hands needed something to do, to pass the time as my mind spun in an attempt to solve a grant, I came here. Insight often accompanied this state.

I scanned the sand and found the exact same pattern I drew last, everything exactly as I had left it... except for the small rock in the upper northeast corner. I picked up the rock and held it in my hand for a little while. *Dig.* Right under the surface, a small coin appeared. I held it up to the deepening red of the sunset, and recognized the symbol as belonging to a Spanish galleon, commonly known as a pirate doubloon. Had Eva Fox actually left me clues? I unleashed my unlimited semiosis to find out.

CHAPTER 39

He rolled to his side and spat out a bloody glob. This was getting old. How long had it been now? He'd never get out of the damn infirmary at this pace. The bots had kept him alive, but now he was on his own stem cells. He'd forgotten how long it took the body to heal on its own.

"Greetings, old friend," a voice came from the door.

He'd been too busy spitting to notice he had a visitor. "Well, well, well." Ember rose and half sauntered, half limped across the cold, tile floor. "What are you doing down here with us grunts?" He grimaced.

"You visited last, figured I owed you."

"That you do." He eased himself into a rolling office chair. His old friend did the same, and they faced each other, silent for a few moments. "And where's my associate?" Ember finally asked. "Haven't seen him in a while."

"Busy trying to find your girl."

"She won't go easy."

"I don't doubt it, but she might like me."

"She might," Ember conceded. "Though I don't wish her on anybody."

"I can handle her."

Ember shook her head. "That's your ego talking. Nobody can handle her."

"You did."

"And look how that turned out." He ticked off his fingers. "One, two, three, four, five bullets."

"It was worth it to keep her alive."

Ember changed the subject. "How long had it been before our last meeting?"

"Nearly seven years, I reckon."

"Ah, the good ole' days."

"Indeed, some fun, huh?"

Ember shrugged. "In some ways."

"For a while, anyway, until you went rogue."

"I didn't go rogue," Ember stated patiently. "I grew into myself."

His old friend raised an eyebrow. "And what was wrong with your old self?"

"He didn't have empathy."

"And why was that a problem?"

"You'll see," Ember said disarmingly, the eternal crimson smile wide on his face.

CHAPTER 40

Pieces of eight, pirates... Ben's favorite. I ran back into the house, this time hardly paying any attention to the environment. I went for the library in the west wing, grabbed the rolling ladder, and pulled it down to the "S" section for Robert Louis Stevenson. I climbed up and found *Treasure Island*. As I reached up to grab it, I wavered for a moment, my imagination spinning wildly at this point. I grasped the binding and the book came out easily, which did not cause the bookcase to swing out and reveal a hidden staircase.

"Well, of course not," I said aloud. "That would be ridiculous." Though, in secret, I was a bit disappointed.

I flipped the book open and it landed on a loose page. I held it up in the fading light. A page ripped out of a bible and in the middle a black circle, *the black spot*. The black spot meant death to the recipient, but bestowed ill luck upon the giver, when put on the page of a bible.

I took the book and shook it upside down, thinking perhaps there were more pages, more clues. The bible page fluttered past me, down the ladder, but instead of landing on the ground, it landed in the palm of a hand directly under me, black spot side up.

A fist closed around it, crushing the paper, and then let it fall to the ground.

Fuck.

A moment later, I lay on my back on top of one of the library's research tables, pinned by three geminates. These fuckers were seriously fast and strong. One had both my legs, and the other two each had a shoulder. I knew better than to fight them.

Never waste strength on struggle. Bide your time patiently. Wait for the opportune moment.

"Well, hello again," I said cheerily.

Upon closer inspection, they weren't identical at all. It was just the pale, waxy skin and black eyes that made them look so similar, but the one at my feet was certainly taller and broader than the other two, and the one on my left an impossible shade paler than the one on the right. I let them hold me down and focused on how I was going to get the pen out from under me, which they'd unwittingly placed me on, so that I could jab it into all of their eyes.

"Why are you all male? It's rather sexist."

The door slammed shut. "Because males are easier to control," an eloquent voice answered, and a pair of high heels came click-clacking toward me.

Speak of the devil.

"The first ones we made were like stallions and mares. We've got geldings now, but geldings with a wicked temper."

"So, you're not one, then?" I guessed.

She appeared above my head holding my backpack. "Depends on who you ask," she answered cryptically. She was thin and tall, even taller than the one at the other end. Asian featured, she had sleek black hair and dark almond eyes, but no accent. Half-Japanese, I suspected, but there had to be an Anglo in there for that kind of height.

"And what's your name?"

"Again, depends on who you ask." She reached down my shirt and pulled the flash drive out of my bra. "Thanks for retrieving this for us."

"And what exactly is that?"

She smiled thinly. "That is no longer your concern." She pulled an ampule and syringe out of her pocket and drew the contents out. "We'll see you on the other side."

Lethal injection? Really?

If ever there was an opportune moment, this was it. I screamed as loud as I could and used the element of surprise to reach the pen under my back. I buried one end in the left one's eye and pulled it back directly into the eye of the right one. I then launched myself forward at the geminate at my feet, but he deflected me. I scrambled up the ladder and searched my immediate vicinity for something sharp.

Damn, nothing but books.

Below me, the woman laughed. "Where do you think you're going?"

I didn't answer.

The two geminates lay twitching on the floor on either side of the table.

She hadn't moved an inch, and just smirked. "That's why I brought three of them. I knew you'd most likely take at least one of them." She walked over to the bottom of the ladder, where the surviving geminate stood like a guard dog.

Never give the enemy a moment to recover.

I swept my arm behind a row of books and rained down a fury of compressed trees. It was a particularly heavy shelf, with a big set of encyclopedias. At the same time, I jumped down, eye on the syringe in the woman's hand. I landed directly on top of her and slammed her head into the marble floor, splattering the smooth surface with ruby spinart. I grabbed the syringe out of her hand and buried it in the back of her neck.

See you on the other side, bitch.

I pulled it out and wheeled around for the third eye, but a hand pulled the syringe out of my hand, and his other grabbed my throat, pinned me against the bookshelf, and started to squeeze. This didn't look good. I had maybe a minute before I passed out since I'd had no preparation and didn't have a full breath in me. I started pulling books from behind me, bashing his head with as many as I could. I'd no clue how this would actually help, but I didn't know what else to do.

Mercifully, he did the work for me. He chucked me across the room, and I landed next to one of the disabled geminates.

Perfect. I pulled the gun from his belt and open fired on the geminate at the bookcase. I emptied the entire clip and the last shot finally hit his eye.

I breathed a sigh of relief, then took in my surroundings to make sure there were no reinforcements. The house sat as silent as the grave. I glanced down at the geminate, and there sat a red dot centered directly on my chest.

Laser sighting. Gun.

CHAPTER 41

I dove to the side and backed up against the wall anticipating shots, but there were none, and no red dot followed me. I scanned the room and found the red dot sitting on the wall next to the fireplace, completely stationary. I crawled slowly over to it. It didn't move. I passed my hand quickly in front of it, and it didn't move. I left my hand in front of it for a while, and didn't get shot.

Not laser sighting, but a light — a light coming from beyond the bookcase.

I'd shot up the bookcase pretty good trying to hit the geminate in the eye. One of the bullets had gone clear through, and a red light now shined out of it.

What the hell? Is this where Eva Fox had been leading me?

I cautiously crept up to the bookcase and cleared out the books, appropriately in the metaphysical section, and peered through the bullet hole, but it wasn't big enough to see anything beyond red. I glanced down at the geminate at my feet, who hadn't moved at all, but I didn't take too much comfort in this as I half expected them to all come back to life. At least they'd be partially blind.

The crumpled paper sat amid the books I'd hurled at the Geminate. I took a few deep breaths to clear my head and the adrenaline, took a seat next to the Geminate so I could keep an eye on him, and opened it once again. Yes, *the* black spot, on a bible page... few would recognize which bible the page came from, but I was one of them. Good ole' King James, and though not religious in the slightest, I had seen that book every Sunday growing up, and it had bored me to tears.

Few books in the library were actually mine. Most belonged to the former owner. When the house had been auctioned off, the congressman's personal book collection, along with other effects, had gone with it. There were several religious texts, mostly Christian. Funny how often the most "devout" were actually the most corrupt — pure attrition. I pulled the ladder over and climbed up to the religious reading section. A lone, empty space stared out at me from the middle of the senator's bible collection. The only empty space I saw, for that matter, as I scanned the room. Not a coincidence. I reached through the slot the bible had once occupied, and only hit the back of the bookcase. I slid down the ladder and then began to search for it alphabetically. No luck with the B's, K's, J's, or V's, and I slumped against the bookcase, dismayed. I had precious little time left, maybe none at all, but I couldn't leave. This was more important. I found myself saying this in my mind. They were not my words. They were Ember's.

I closed my eyes and went back over the clues, or what I thought were clues: sand, Zen garden, coin, *Treasure Island*, black spot, bible page, bible.

Damn it, Eva Fox, I can't bloody well go through every book in the stacks. I took a deep breath. *Perhaps the book isn't in the bookcase at all.*

I'd found sand under the sink, a coin in the Zen garden, a bible page inside a different book — all items out of place, none belonging. Well, where would be the most unlikely place to find a bible? Hell. A trip across the River Styx was out of the question, but the equivalent of hell in a house? The basement, though I had no basement. I often found that strange, a big house like this having no basement. Where else? *Fire.* Very unlikely place to find a book.

I crossed the room to the fireplace, knelt on the hearth, and made a shocking discovery: ash. The fireplace had been used. A few weeks ago, I had cleaned this fireplace out, and had not used it since. Come to think of it, I had cleaned this fireplace the evening before accompanying Ember to the hospital. I'd had a roaring fire going in the library while I worked on creating our hospital passes, and I could have sworn I'd taken out the ashes after, but....

I had just been a science experiment, which apparently had created more than one person inside me, so how the hell did I know anything? My memory couldn't be trusted.

Sifting through the ash, I made another shocking discovery. The ash was not wood ash, but paper ash, and there were some pages that weren't quite burned. I scooped these into the ash bucket, took them over to the library table, clicked on the lamp, pulled a magnifying glass out of a drawer, and began to examine them. They were from a bible, all right. My alter ego self had burned a bible. I was pretty sure hell reserved a special place for people that did that. Luckily, I didn't believe in hell. I did, however, believe that burning a book, any kind of book, was a sin.

The only legible scrap came from Isaiah 51:6: *Lift up your eyes and look around.* I began to doubt myself. Perhaps I was making all this up. Maybe Eva Fox did strange things to keep herself entertained. I needed to go, as the maximum time mark had passed by quite a bit, and pushing my luck any further was a recipe for disaster. Yet again, I couldn't make myself leave.

I went back to the fireplace and reached up inside the chimney for the damper. It was closed — not at all unusual, as the flue was apt to be closed after use, especially with the chill of approaching winter in the air. But I felt a draft, meaning it wasn't quite closed. Something was lodged between the damper and the rock. I took a deep breath and pushed it open. Something heavy clunked against my hand and then dropped into the pile of ash: *The King James Bible*, partially burned. I smiled. Surely, I must deserve a cookie for this. I briefly leafed through what remained of the bible, and then pulled a flashlight out of my backpack, put my head right in the ashes, and shined the light up the chimney. Nothing unusual.

Other direction.

All the fireplaces in this mansion had fancy ash pits. After clearing the bible remains and ash away from the hearth, I pulled up the grate and peered inside. As expected, lots of ash. I put my hand down into the pit to feel around, hoping I would not come across some kind of creature. At some point, my hand crossed over a bump in the floor of the pit. I went back over it, feeling with my fingertips as if I were reading braille. The bump was actually a button.

I pushed it.

A great rumbling started from behind me in the library, and I spun around expecting to see the wall caving in, the house self-destructing. Instead, a portion of the bookcase had *actually* swung out to reveal a hidden staircase.

"No fucking way," I said aloud. I stood frozen for a moment.

Just what kind of reality have I dropped into? This is my house, is it not?

CHAPTER 42

The emissary in me, still trying to abide by Sedition protocol, spoke up. I had to decide whether to keep following the insane trail of clues or cut my losses and come back another day. I couldn't go by my curiosity alone, though I could hardly stop it. If I figured out how the hell to close the damn thing and cover my tracks well enough, I could come back, but likely I'd never make it out of the house. My time limit was blown. *Never stay more than seven minutes...* the first half of that Novem. I had done twice that—easy. I wouldn't make it down the driveway at this point, as the Sedition surely headed up it.

The sound of the front door opening made my decision for me.

Oh, what the hell.

I hastily swept the remains of the book into the ash bucket, dumped them into the ash pit, and replaced the grate. I then grabbed my backpack and sprinted across the room, hurtling over bodies, snatching the drive out of the Kanji's hand, and shoved a larger book over the bullet hole to hide it—not the best job, but it would do for now. There was too much carnage in the room to notice anything else.

I slipped behind the bookcase and dropped onto a spiral staircase that coiled down under the house. The bookcase slammed shut behind me, perhaps triggered by some censor on the staircase, and left me encased in the red light. I stood there for moment, breathing, listening. Muffled footsteps came running in my direction, and I heard another set go up the stairs. The bookcase closing only sounded as though I'd slammed a door, but they knew I'd be smarter than to slam the door on my way out, and would think it a diversion.

I rummaged through the backpack until I found the flashlight, and clicked it on. My hand came across a gun, which I also pulled out, just in case, and I wound down the spiral stairs.

The congressman was full of surprises. So, the house has a basement, after all. I should have known.

I reached the bottom of the stairs and shone the flashlight in all directions. It was not a basement at all, only a very small room, and at the base of the stairs sat a motorcycle.

"What the hell is this? The fucking bat cave?" I asked aloud, stunned, to put it mildly—secret lair, indeed, though not much of one.

I felt around all sides of the room, but none of the walls seemed the least bit unusual. Then I inspected the motorcycle, which didn't have a key, rendering it pretty much useless. But why else would there be a motorcycle in a secret room under a house? It was clearly meant for transportation. I slung the backpack over my shoulder and swung my right leg over the seat of the bike. Such a strange feeling, as I hadn't been on a bike in a long time. My right hand unconsciously curled around the throttle, a movement so familiar.

The past came flooding in and I pushed it away. A curious sensation followed, and the slightest vibration spread out under my body. It took me a moment to realize that the engine had turned over and the bike had kicked on. The motorcycle was completely silent. I pulled my hand back quickly, as though the bike was alive, and the vibration stopped. This was getting weirder by the minute.

Is this actually real?

I placed my hand back on the throttle, and the bike again silently roared to life. I clicked on the headlight to get a broader look at my surroundings, but instead of projecting onto the wall, the headlight illuminated a long, narrow passage. I was sure there had been a wall there before, had physically felt it with my hands, but with what had been done to me, how could I trust my perception? Spade had said my mind was stable, but I couldn't quite buy it. Maybe this was all a grandiose hallucination and I was really stumbling around in my bathroom upstairs. Or perhaps, I wasn't in my house at all, but in a padded room at the Sedition.

I decided that, real or perceived, I would continue on.

The logical, albeit insane, answer was that the wall and the bike were connected, the wall sliding open simultaneously when I placed my hand on the throttle. I hadn't seen it because it was dark, and hadn't heard it because the action was soundless, just like the motorcycle.

Barely wide enough for the bike, the passage left no room for error, but I didn't need any. I put the kickstand up, pulled the clutch in with my left hand, and shifted down to first gear. Then I let out the clutch and turned up the throttle, entering Mr. Toad's Wild Ride. At first, I drove slowly, cautiously, but before long I was flying. *Old habits die hard.*

After a few minutes, another faint red light appeared in the distance, looming ahead like a beacon. I decided it must be an exit, the other end. Perhaps it was a tunnel that served as an escape route. I wondered where it would put me out.

As I grew closer, the passage widened significantly, and clearly did not lead outside. The light came from a beacon situated over a large metal door, a door with no doorknob.

I stopped the bike in front of the door, shifted down to neutral, and put the kickstand down. The bike immediately shut off as I took my hand off the throttle. This time I registered surprise for only a moment, as I stared, transfixed by the door, its gray metal completely smooth. It looked to be an automatic pocket door, but with no knob or keypad. Surely a camera spied on me from somewhere, but I couldn't see or sense one.

"Hello?" I asked tentatively.

No response. I imagined Eva Fox on the other side, grinning sardonically, watching me on a screen relayed from the camera I couldn't see. She would meet me at the door and brain me with a wrench. Then I'd wake up in a dark cell, never to emerge again, while she took my place in the world. By the time Vail and Spade figured it out, I'd be long dead, wasted away to nothing, but since Eva Fox was the one they wanted, they wouldn't care. Spade would say, *'It was Eva Fox in the dungeon with the wrench,'* and they would both laugh.

All of this was impossible, of course, considering Eva Fox actually resided inside my head. They'd have to get her out with a meat cleaver.

"Look, this is attached to my house, which means I own this damn place, so open the god-damned door."

Still nothing.

I placed my palms against the door and pushed — very solid, no doubt about that. No amount of kicking, slamming, or probably even explosives, for that matter, would take it down. I thought for a moment, and examined the motorcycle. It operated on fingerprint recognition, and the door probably worked the same way. Simple, really.

Never complicate the grant.

I doubted Eva Fox followed Sedition rules, judging by how hard she'd made it to get to this point. I thought of the invisible biometrics scanner on the wall at the Sedition.

No key. No doorknob. A throttle operates a bike, a doorknob opens a door. Both result in moving forward. My heart picked up an irregular beat as adrenaline began to rage through my system. I pulled a revolver out of my jacket as I pushed my left palm into where I thought a doorknob might be.

The door slid soundlessly open to the right, revealing a concrete room with a bank of monitors filling most of the wall in front of me, a security system of the highest caliber.

Before I had time take in the details, a voice called out to me, a voice I'd know anywhere. "Hello, Leyla."

THE END

ACKNOWLEDGEMENTS

To the Plains of Jar in Laos, where all of this began, and to the world at large for being my personal office, whether my desk was a massage table, a bathtub, a boulder, a hay bale, or an airplane tray table. In particular, the deep, dark months of Washington State, the writer's dream environment.

To all the people that have unwittingly added to the story, via a short conversation, remark, gesture, mannerism, or facial expression: you may not have seen me, but I saw you.

Thanks to Evolved Publishing—Dave, Kimberly, and Richard—for giving Leyla Stone a chance.

Thanks to Jesse, who saw the story evolve over many years and told me it was great even when it was full of plot holes and clichés; my biological and cosmic families—von Stein, Cheatham, Willimon, Pleiadean; my fellow LMT's and first readers—Heidi, Jess, and Oliver; the sanctuary of Ojo Caliente for many quiet, winter months of writing; the love (band) of my life, Murder by Death, for unfailing inspiration whenever I was in need of a dark moment; the unyieldingly, candid lyrics of Dolores O'Riordan; Bob Kidera and the SouthWest Writers; lifelong friend and fellow author, Megan H. Shepherd, for always encouraging and supporting my un-traditional approach to life; and to Leila Gilliam von Stein V—the vessel I inhabit.

ABOUT THE AUTHOR

Melsa M. Manton grew up roaming the mountains of Western North Carolina. An early education of Aliens, Predator, Terminator, and Stephen King led to a love of science fiction and she began writing as soon as her fine motor skills allowed.

She studied International Affairs in Washington D.C. with the intention of diving into the political realm, but ended up diving into the ocean instead. An avid scuba diver, she spent seven summers sailing and teaching diving worldwide. For the next ten years, the wanderlust took her all over the world, from Russia to Tasmania, with many places in between, and eventually set her on a path of holistic medicine. She runs Blue Desert Hale, a health and wellness center, in the mountains of New Mexico.

Her life path has morphed considerably over the years, but there is one thing she has done consistently through it all. To write is to live.

Melsa's personal motto: **DREAM BIG OR DIE.**

For more, please visit Melsa online at:
Website: www.MelsaManton.com
Twitter: @MelsaMManton
Facebook: www.facebook.com/melsa.manton.108
Instagram: www.instagram.com/melsammanton/

WHAT'S NEXT?

Be sure to watch for the second book in this "Gemination" series to release within a few weeks of this book.

SEE NO MORE

What do you do when you come face to face with your own psyche, and it's not one you recognize?

The Sedition is crumbling and the Faction is growing stronger, but there's a chance that Stone can stop it and restore equilibrium and order. Good, old-fashioned demolition-as-distraction becomes the strategy in hopes of goading the Faction into making a mistake, into revealing their éminence grise.

As defectives from both sides join Stone and nanotechnology renders privacy obsolete, the uncertain future sparks the volatile component of her psyche and threatens what remains of her sanity. And the Faction is hunting her for more than just retaliation—they want her mind.